Greenwash

Greenwash

A global conspiracy,
A local crime,

An environmental disaster.

GILLIAN LONG

Millaa House Publishing
2023

Greenwash

First Published, 2023
ISBN: 9780645576078
Millaa House Publishing
PO Box 89
Millaa Millaa
Queensland 4886

Author's note

Far North Queensland, Australia, shows evidence of relatively recent volcanic eruptions and earthquakes, which implies the likelihood of more to come. Any seismic activity in an area of geological instability can have significant consequences. One such area lies hidden in the deep ocean, approximately 70 kilometres east southeast of Cairns, where a section of eroded continental shelf, about 5 kilometres square, waits for the right kind of seismic shove to slide two kilometres into the murky depths of the Queensland trough. An underwater landslide of such magnitude could trigger a tsunami, swamping Queensland's east coast. It's effects could reach as far away as Brisbane, Solomon Islands, and Papua New Guinea.

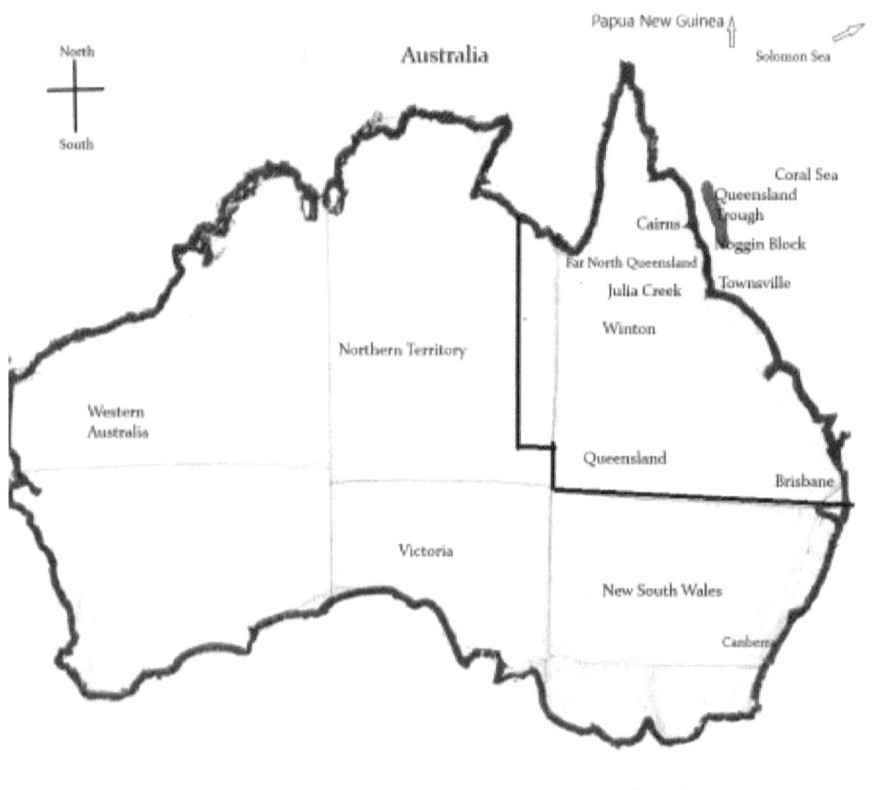

Greed is the cemetery
where accountability lies buried.

Conspiracy to a Crime

L ord Roger Barwon hurried along Pall Mall, dead leaves and litter scurrying ahead driven on by a bitter wind. The sky darkened and a few drops of rain splashed onto the road, sending up a musty smell of damp tarmac laced with the sourness of cat's piss, although of course it could be spilled diesel.

Barwon opened his umbrella and muttered. 'Bloody weather might have held off a moment or two longer!'

He made a dash for his club, turning into Waterloo Place, and leaping up the steps to the mat under the portico. A new message pinged into his pocket, and he took out his phone.

'Damn!' The Maltese national was waiting. Typical. And after Richards had texted, he would be late. Like herding cats. Barwon remembered Richards, or Tricky Dicky, had a penchant for being late for hall when they were at Oxford together. How many years ago?

He pulled a long face, put his phone back in his pocket, and took a moment to fold his umbrella, shaking off excess water before he brushed back his luxuriant silver hair. An enormous poster on the building across the way, stated *We want our country back*. Barwon sighed. Britain was going to pot, and it was the Tories fault. They had become infiltrated by the middle classes for whom politics was all about money and power, with little consideration for tradition.

A drop of rain trickled down his forehead, and he took out his handkerchief to mop his brow and neck. The last thing he could cope with today were water droplets spotting his immaculate Henry Poole suit, especially when one needed to make an impression on the Maltese national.

The Maltese national still went by the very Russian name, Viktor Prokhorov. Although, golden passport aside, the man remained in constant communication with the Tsar of his homeland, taking as his due the arrival of regular gifts of Beluga caviar. Genuine Caspian Sea stuff, not the Chinese-farmed version.

Barwon found Prokhorov waiting in the guest area, sitting on the edge of his chair, hands on knees, as if preparing to get up.

He didn't, not even when Barwon held out his own manicured hand.

'Viktor, so good to see you, my friend.'

Viktor ignored the outstretched hand and growled something incomprehensible. When he finally rose, he thrust his stubby hands into his lime-coloured Ralph Lauren peacoat, dragging down the line of the jacket to make it look like something he'd bought at Oxfam's.

The man was obsessed with germs, but he might have worn a suit, although small mercies, he had put on a tie. Barwon supposed it was a concession, although the entire ensemble smelled of stale tobacco smoke. Why on earth would the man worry about germs when he would probably die of emphysema?

Barwon wrinkled his nose, turning away to see who else might be in today. He rather enjoyed entertaining in his club. It gave him the upper hand. Or that was the case on most occasions. Now he was at a distinct disadvantage, having to hang around waiting for Tricky Dickie while Prokhorov glowered.

'Awful weather.' Barwon said, but Viktor didn't respond. Small talk was a one-sided affair with the Maltese national, and he didn't know why he bothered.

When Richards finally arrived, he was unapologetic although full of that annoying boyish enthusiasm it seemed he had never lost. Barwon's lips stretched and curved over his expensive teeth, although his gaze remained cool as he introduced the two men before leading them into luncheon.

Over Sole Meuniere and a rather good bottle of Loire Valley Sancerre, they discussed the inclusion of Australia in *Grecotec's* activities, making gas the 'green energy' of worldwide desperation to reduce carbon pollution.

Grecotec's campaign had taken off at a surprisingly rapid pace, and Barwon had been invited to speak at the Washington conference. He smiled. Globally, sovereign administrations drowning in a sea of neoliberal economics and environmental condemnation, clutched at the lowest hanging fruit to save themselves, while the Russian Tsar, sitting on the largest gas reserves in the world, smiled.

Tristan Richards pushed his half-eaten plate of food away and leaned forward to insist the antipodean venture must appear separate from *Grecotec's* activity. 'I have just the right men to act as directors for a subsidiary holding company to cover the Australian venture. *Paramount Holdings* is a shelf company registered in the Caymans, and will take full responsibility, so long as the money is there.' He grinned and leaned back in his chair. 'By the way, I promised my friends, Viktor would invite them for a short sail on his yacht before the Washington Gas conference in June. You'll be there Viktor? I thought a short sortie about the Caribbean might give us a chance to get to know each other.'

Viktor grunted, helped himself to the leftover mashed potatoes on Tristan's plate and mashed them into his Meuniere sauce.

Barwon shuddered and looked away. Viktor's manners were the one thing he found difficult to reconcile. Another thought struck him. Richards had been a fond proponent of Game Theory at university and had tried to prove it at every opportunity. It was how he had acquired his nickname. He pressed his lips together and glanced back at Viktor, but the man was still shovelling potato into his mouth. There and then, Barwon vowed this would not be a zero-sum game. The Australian venture would not be traceable back to him. He wasn't about to become the Australian's dupe, nor would he end up choking on Novichok.

Part One

Earth's Warning

The earthquake occurred at 09:35 at a depth of 10 kilometres. It was small in magnitude and shallow, in a spot that until recently had laid undisturbed for millennia. Yet the enormous pressure from human activity along an old fault caused a strike-slip displacement. It set up a reaction, creating new pressure points along interconnecting geological fracture lines that radiated out beneath the Great Barrier Reef as far as the Australian continental shelf. The fissures reached the Queensland trough, a two thousand metres deep underwater trench. The area of the quake was sparsely populated, and few people felt the earth tremble, let alone recognised the potential consequences.

Moments earlier, Dr Jack Fallon had arrived to take up his new job and was waiting for the lift to arrive in the airless steel and concrete basement carpark of the MGEE building in Townsville. He ran his finger around his collar, easing the starchy material from his neck. Fuel fumes and hot tire vapour threatened asphyxiation, while the lift indicator light remained stubbornly pointing at level 6. He turned away to search for stairs.

A distant rumble, like that of a heavy truck, seemed to move towards him and the ground beneath his feet shivered. Jack was familiar with earthquakes and didn't hesitate, bolting past his hire car, up the ramp, and out into the open street to where the anti-mining activist group was still blocking the access road to the building.

Earlier, the activists had tried to prevent Jack's arrival. He had ignored them then, and he refused to acknowledge them now. Instead, he opened his phone to search for the automated geo-seismic monitoring site, finding a 3.6 magnitude quake had registered two minutes ago, up near the Clarke River Basin a hundred and thirty kilometres northwest of where he stood. Too small and too far away to be of any great danger.

In all probability, if he hadn't been underground, he wouldn't have felt it. He closed his phone and ran his hand over his mouth. So, the quakes were still happening. Had they increased since he and Professor Prentice had been monitoring them? He should contact his old university supervisor, now he was back in Queensland.

The activist group, who called themselves *The Prophets*, hadn't seemed to notice the earth moving, but his appearance from out of the bowels of the building animated them. They marched towards him, waggling banners that seemed to depict some kind of anthropomorphic wounded earth, red blood flowing from a gash in its mantel.

Jack inhaled, setting his jaw in preparation for the inevitable confrontation, and pushed past them and up a broad flight of stairs to the main entrance of the building. Cries of 'murderer' followed him, filling his mind with old imagery of the chanting kids in the schoolyard. He blinked away the memory, tightening his lips to still the pulse in his jaw, and negotiated a revolving door that hustled him into the air-conditioned tranquillity of a lofty marble and glass foyer. A smiling blonde sat behind an organically free-form desk, positioned in front of a wall covered with large brass and jet lettering spelling out the company's name: *MuzloGaz Exploration and Extraction*.

Ten minutes later, Jack was on the sixth floor, seated in his new boss's corner office overlooking the ocean. Chad Myers outlined his expectations in a Texan drawl, reminding Jack of Ed's dad, Henry Morrison. It was Henry Morrison's reference that lay on the desk in front of Chad.

Chad, unlike Henry Morrison, took care of his image, wearing a branded shirt, with open collar showing a gold chain gleaming on hairless skin, and perfect white teeth against a Bahaman expensive suntan. The hair on his head was the colour of old copper pipes, and his eyes were an indeterminate grey, impenetrable but calculating as they examined Jack with a look that told him to step carefully.

Jack had thought he'd be doing exploratory work, but it seemed his job was a whole lot bigger than he'd expected. No wonder they had despaired at having to hire him. The company had been looking for a senior Geotechnical Engineer with at least fifteen years of experience. Jack had eight years in the Pilbara, but the pandemic had made the industry a job seeker's paradise and here he was, with a position back in his home state, on twice the money. Although, truth be told, he suspected the job offer was more to do with Henry Morrison's name than any of Jack's endeavours.

Chad Myers pointed at a large wall map behind his desk. 'Your area is the top of the channel country, from Julia Creek to Camooweal, south to Winton and Boulia to the Northern Territory border.'

'That's a big area.'

Chad eyed him for a moment before he said, 'An' hotter than a billy goat in a pepper patch. On your way out, you can stop off at Roy Malone's area in the Charters Towers region and get a feel for how he does things.'

Sitting on the desk, facing Jack, was a framed photo—Chad with his arm around a scantily clad woman, standing onboard a massive white yacht. They were drinking champagne. Behind them spume-capped azure waters ran up palm-tree lined beaches.

Chad picked it up. 'I see you admiring the yacht. Not mine regrettably. It belongs to a business acquaintance. A British aristocrat, Lord Roger Barwon. Do you know him?'

Jack smiled at the American's lame attempt to normalise knowing people in the British aristocracy.

'Actually, the yacht belongs to his partner, a man by the name of Viktor Prokhorov. We had some business to conduct after the Washington gas conference and took a quick trip around the Caribbean. Running with the big dogs, you comprende. We'll probably meet up again at the conference in Korea next year.'

'Prokhorov. Isn't he the Russian petrochemical oligarch?'

Chad shrugged. 'Tristan Richards introduced us, and Lord Barwon said Viktor was Maltese, or at least that's where the head office is located.'

'Must be a different bloke.' Jack put on a suitably impressed expression as he examined the photo, and in truth the yacht looked like a pretty nice lifestyle.

Chad stood up. 'I'll introduce you to your gear. Mary has it in her office.'

Jack followed him next door. A middle-aged woman with grey streaked hair and Dame Edna style glasses sat behind a desk covered with boxes.

When they walked in, she was on the phone and placed her hand over the mouthpiece. 'It's Roy. He's worried... wants to discuss the yield.'

Chad waved her away. 'I'll talk to him later. Tell him to try another acidizing treatment with a bit more pressure.'

Jack's gaze swivelled towards Chad. It was the company's big marketing point that they didn't use chemicals for gas extraction other than harmless stuff like that used in household products.

Chad didn't appear to notice the flash of concern in Jack's expression as he said, 'Mary Busby, meet Jack Fallon.' Then he turned back to Jack. 'I'll leave you with Mary. She'll look after you.'

Mary replaced the phone and said, 'Glad you arrived safely. The Prophets downstairs didn't give you too much trouble, I hope. They're a harmless bunch really, just a bit strange, although they make accessing the building tricky.' She grinned before she opened a drawer. 'I have some paperwork for you, and your equipment is in all these boxes.' Her hand swept across the cluttered desk.

Everything else flew from his mind as he picked up box after box. Even out in the remotest parts of Boulia Shire he'd be connected and have GIS capability. Everything a surveyor, geologist and engineer could want, and more was in those boxes, brand new and just waiting for him to put it all together.

Mary said, 'You'll have a team here organising the equipment to set up the first site, but you'll need to run it all past the landowner, keep them sweet. Needless to say, water and sand are important considerations. We can truck them in, but it's expensive. Better to find a local supply. Some of the drilling and survey crew will be with you initially, but most are contractors, whom you'll need to book in advance.

Jack's brow crinkled. 'I was expecting an induction and some site visits.'

Mary's voice went up an octave. 'You just had your induction with Chad.' She softened her tone. 'You can stop at Roy's area near Charters Towers on your way out west. See how he does things. You've done this stuff before, haven't you?' She stared at him above the half-moon in her glass lens.

He fingered one of the boxes hoping she wouldn't pursue that line further. He'd never taken charge of this kind of operation before although he'd done all the related grunt work.

Mary sighed and continued. 'The construction team are ready to leave any time after next week, so you'll need to establish your main site pretty quickly. Or let Chad know you're having difficulties. They were hoping to go up to Coen and establish a site for Murray, but he's having trouble, so all hopes are pinned on the west.'

'No pressure then.'

Mary laughed.

Jack spent the rest of that day and the next talking to the legal people, the research team and construction engineers, finding out about his management responsibilities. How hard could it be?

Two days later, he pulled up in front of Roy Malone's office, a demountable in a compound of similar buildings north-of Charters Towers and west of the Burdekin River. Roy managed an area from Bowen to Greenvale. He was a gruff old bloke, originally from somewhere in the north of England, grizzled and old school. He struck Jack as being one of those people suspicious of new theories or different ways of doing things. Take the paperwork cluttering his desk. It was all online and interactive, but Roy seemed to prefer hard copies.

Jack straightened his back. 'Roy, can I ask your advice on something?'

Roy pushed aside the profiles. 'You may?'

Taking a deep breath, Jack asked, 'Does the company share baseline data publicly?'

Roy pushed his glasses up the bridge of his nose. 'What d'you mean?'

'I have a friend, actually he supervised my thesis when I was at Uni, and we stayed in touch. When I told him I was starting work here he asked.'

'What does he want it for?'

Jack shrugged. 'Students experience, I guess.'

'Pack it in! What are you—another frigging wasak?'

'Pardon?' Jack took a step back at Roy's reaction, although he had no idea what a wasak was.

Roy moderated his tone to one of patronising concern. 'Laddie, you'll need to play it down a little. Already Chad reckons you are no team player. You go trying stuff like that, you'll confirm his theory.' Roy paused, sucking air between his teeth. 'It's inexperience, I suppose.'

Jack was thirty-four, with a double degree in geotechnical engineering and geophysics. Twelve years ago, he had won the dean's prize for his honours thesis. Three and a half years later, he was awarded his PhD for a seismic study into the stability of the north-eastern continental shelf, before gaining mining engineering experience through an eight-year slog in the Pilbara. He didn't think that amounted to a lack of experience, although admittedly he had never been in charge of an entire area before.

'Is that how you see me, Roy?' He knew people thought he was younger than he was, and it was a distinct disadvantage in this field, but there was little he could do about their impressions.

Roy scrutinised Jack for a minute. 'I'll give you my philosophy on life for free. You're either a researcher, sharing with all for nothing, or a miner looking to make a profit. Pick a team and stick with it. None of this foot in two camps malarkey. Pick one. Give it all your trust, loyalty, and maintain the hard graft. Most important, keep your nose out of others' troughs. It's when we try to keep everyone happy that doubt and dissent creeps in. I don't know what your experience was in Western Australia, but here we get enough trouble from do-gooders' and Greenies who know nowt. That group, what's their name—the Prophets, got a hold of the pigs-tail through just such nonsense. Now, they're camped outside headquarters so a man can't get near the place.'

'I ran into them.'

'There you go. If we give them what you're proposing, we'll never hear the end of it. If it helps you sleep at night, there are plenty of American studies they can access, showing what we do is safe. He laughed. 'In fact, we're the ones saving Australia. Haven't you heard about the gas-led economic recovery? How the hell can you look after the planet without an economy? You answer me that.'

Jack didn't respond. It was pointless arguing with the man. He brought the conversation to a close. 'Thanks for the advice.'

Roy grinned. 'Come on, I'll buy you a beer.'

The next day, as Jack drove west towards Julia Creek, he thought about what Roy had said. Most he could dismiss, but the one thing that stuck was the bit about having to pick a team. At university, his mate Pete Macalister used to say something similar. But outside of sports, what the hell did pick a team mean, anyway? He reckoned it was code for don't think for yourself, just go along to get along. It was bullshit. He didn't consider himself a hypocrite, and he reckoned gas could be extracted safely. So long as you applied all the necessary precautions, the data wouldn't be a worry. Admittedly, much of the data at the university was being analysed for the output of greenhouse gases, but that was different and, like so many others, he pinned his hopes on technological advances for sequestrating carbon.

He stopped in Julia Creek and checked into the hotel. The town sat atop the Great Artesian Basin, 650 kilometres west of Townsville, in the heart of outback North Queensland. The place was typical of Queensland country hotels; a wooden structure standing two storeys high with open verandas, capped by corrugated roofing iron.

Inside, banners told Jack to *Frack-off* out of the community and *Lock the Gate* against the MGEE bastards. The banners leaned against old posters advertising dinosaur trails and pristine outback tours. Stale grog seeped from towelling mats, adding to air already saturated with the odour of sweat and the local's rage at miners. How had he thought he could high-step into this community? He knew the type of people, grew up with them. Hell. He supposed he was one of them. He would need to tread carefully, or they would run him out of town.

The Unwitting Accessory

Jack sat on his haunches in an ancient watercourse surveying the landscape, not for gas deposits, but in admiration of its beauty. Above his head, a cloudless sky domed over a vast expanse of flat savannah. His gaze took in the rocky ground, the sand-coloured grass, the pink bluff, and the scattered shrubs. The bluff had been cut out by a river, which a millennia ago had moved a kilometre north to where it ran today. A single tree cast a puddle of shade over his head.

He stood up and stretched. This was the perfect spot. He retraced his steps to his car. He'd do a few more checks and measurements before he called in the survey team, but first he needed to talk to Barnett. This was his land, and he should be on-side before Jack went any further.

When Jack telephoned, Barnett invited him to the house for lunch. So, on the following Sunday, he headed out to Barnett Station. A recent tropical low had moved through this region, soaking life-giving waters into the parched soil, and already a light green wash coloured the red earth, making the earth appear to vibrate against the indigo sky.

The homestead, with square colonial lines, corrugated-iron roof, and white-pillared verandas was so quintessentially Australian, Jack wondered if he'd seen it featured in a movie or a magazine. He parked in a cleared area between the house and machinery sheds and stepped out the car. Immediately, the heat sucked moisture from his skin.

He opened a gate in the white paling fence separating the house yard from the farm and walked along a path scattered with petals dropped from a rose arbour. Alongside the house, an orchard displayed grapevines, olives, citrus, pomegranates, and other trees he couldn't make out.

Two dogs spilled off the veranda to greet him. A young red Kelpie, tongue lolling through a mouth opened in greeting, bounded ahead. An old

Kelpie-cross-sheepdog followed it, more tentative on unsure legs, her body shaking in sync with her wagging tail.

Jim Barnett stepped off the veranda and sent out a sharp whistle. The dogs stopped, waiting, and watching until it became too much for the young dog, who broke ranks dancing back and forth in indecision between Jim and Jack.

Jim whistled again and both dogs sat. 'Hello son, sorry about that, I'm trying to train the young mutt but he's not there yet. Not like this old girl.' He touched the old dog's head, and she looked up at him adoringly. 'She's retired now but helps to keep the young ones in line.'

'You've a beautiful place here.'

'Yup, she's a good 'un. It's Isabella's doing, of course. Wasn't like this before she moved in. More like shearers' quarters but good enough for me. No place to bring a wife though, but she turned it into something special. I've always been more interested in the land than where I lay my head, but this is Isabella's castle.' He grimaced. 'We're in the path of the monsoons, so there's generally good water, at least in summer. There have been years when the river's run dry, but they're rare or used to be.'

'Climate change?'

'I guess that's what it is although I'm still confused by the arguments. Either the climate's changing or it isn't. These bloody scientists and politicians can't ever give a straight answer on the subject.'

Jack remained silent. People might want absolutes, but in science it wasn't that simple.

'Come along in, then. Isabella is looking forward to meeting you. She's always hankering after company, complaining we don't entertain enough.'

A woman, tall and elegant, came out from the house as he and Barnett climbed the veranda stairs. Clearly, she was once a great beauty and still held herself with its inherited confidence. Grey-streaked dark hair fell in a wave over a creamy olive cheek, hiding the evidence of years of outback sun on her neck. Yet her posture retained its loveliness, with the crinkling around her eyes a witness to her happiness despite the harsh climate.

Ignoring Jack's outstretched hand, she pulled him into her embrace, kissing him on one cheek then the other, the scent of roses filling his senses.

'There is only Italian hospitality in this house. Outside on the farm is the domain of the Calvinists, but in here is my realm and we do not shake hands. We embrace our friends.'

'And poison our enemies.' A man of about Jack's age, or perhaps a little younger, walked out. He was dark, and tall, and so similar to Isabella, Jack reasoned this must be the son.

'Fergus Barnett.' He thrust out his hand. 'Don't worry about Mum. She tries to make me kiss everyone, but she hasn't yet succeeded. I still manage to shake hands.'

His grin was all encompassing, and Jack found himself drawn into the circle of the man's charm, even though he had the easy-going attitude only someone of privilege and wealth could own unconsciously. That same mannerism was not reflected in his father. Jim Barnett had battled for what he had—a self-made man who doted on his wife and offspring and took a back seat at home the likes of which he would not tolerate in the public domain.

Isabella Barnett ignored her son and stood head cocked to examine Jack. 'Such a fine young man. Look at those eyes, like reflections of the sky.' She arched one dark-winged brow at her husband.

Jack felt heat rising up his neck and glanced across the paddocks, but at that moment a commotion inside the house took the focus off him. Two boys, much younger than Fergus, rushed out a side door. They were identical with the sandy colouring and the grey eyes of their father. They skidded to a halt and hovered, waiting for an introduction.

'My twins, Paul and Rico, home for Easter,' Isabella said, gazing fondly at the two boys. 'They're in their final year at school and then they can come home again.'

'We'll be at Ag college next year.' Both boys chorused and then laughed self-consciously at their spontaneous duet.

'A drink before lunch?' Isabella took Jack's arm to walk inside with the others traipsing after her. 'It is so sad you have come for lunch on Sunday.' She blew air from pursed lips so the fringe on her forehead lifted with disdain. 'On any other day, you would be treated to fine Italian cuisine, but Sunday is Calvin's day, and we must eat roast beef and Yorkshire puddings. So hot! For the afternoon we must lie in the shade to recover.'

Jack smiled at her cracks at what he assumed was Barnett's protestant background.

Inside, the house was cool and shadowed after the brilliant light outside. Colourful rugs and chintz-covered armchairs and sofas were scattered around a large airy living room. Snowy curtains, animated by hidden breezes, billowed against long French styled windows. A dark leather recliner, squatting in front of the television, seemed the sole protest against the room's light femininity.

Jack shivered.

'You're cold caro mio?'

'Not really, just the contrast. It's nice actually, just a bit of a shift from outside.'

'It's water evaporation, such a wonderful invention. These Aussie's are so clever.'

'I think the ancient Egyptians actually invented it.' Fergus said.

Ignoring her son, Isabella said, 'Where are you from Jack?'

'I grew up in a place called Evelyn, near Millaa Millaa on the Atherton Tablelands.'

'You're from the high country. No wonder you like the cold then, so beautiful, green, and misty but too much rain for me. How can my olives and grapes grow in all that mist? What do you farm Jack?'

'Mum, he's a mining engineer...Beer Jack?'

'Thanks.' He took the beer from Fergus's hand. 'I grew up on a farm.'

'Then your parents. What do they do at Evelyn, Jack?'

Isabella still clutched his arm, her fingers gnarled with what looked like the onset of rheumatoid arthritis.

Jack sipped the beer to give himself space to think of an answer. His life's story was complicated. 'My father is the farmer...' The blood rose up his neck as he recalled a vision of their once prosperous farm.

Barnett was interested immediately. 'You didn't say. Dairy is it?'

'No, beef or at least it was. The herd's reduced now. My father's too old to manage by himself and since I've been gone, well...' Jack racked his brain for a diversion.

'And your Mama?' Isabella's inquisitive black eyes studied him carefully as if she could see around the nebulous nature of his response.

'Don't know.' Even to his own ears, he sounded evasive.

Her smile faltered. 'How is it you do not know?'

He straightened his shoulders and looked her in the eye. Screw it. There was nothing to hide, and it was not a secret. 'I haven't seen my mother since I was a kid.'

'But...What happened to her?'

'Bella love, I can smell the Yorkshire puddings and I reckon they're burning.'

'Ah.' Isabella cried and scurried from the sitting room.

But Jack knew she would be back, picking at the scab that hid his history. He should get it out into the open because it would come out, anyway.

Jim said, 'Come on back out to the veranda. It's a bit warmer and we have a while before lunch is ready.' Once they were back outside he said, 'sorry about Isabella. She wants to know everything about a man and there's just no getting away from it.' He drained his beer and turned to his son. 'Paul, get us another beer. Rico, go help him.'

The three men stood in companionable calm, gazing out over the vast landscape. Jack took a long slug of his beer, realising that everyone would want to know everything about him. That was the way of country folk, even when they didn't ask directly, someone would know something, and pretty soon everyone would know everything there was to know about him, along with stuff that he didn't even know himself.

An anguished cry emanating from deep within the house broke the silence. 'You little brat! I'll kill you. Get out!'

Jack cast a glance at Jim, who maintained an indifferent gaze across the paddocks.

'My sister.' Fergus said by way of illumination.

The sound of breaking crockery; a young masculine laugh, followed by a slammed door.

Isabella's voice. 'You boys, outside now!'

A minute later, Rico walked out grinning, followed by Paul, whose face was sombre.

'Where are the beers?'

The twins spun on their heels in unison and traipsed back into the house.

Jim shook his head. 'Bloody kids. Sorry, it's not always this much Bedlam.'

'Oh yes it is.' Fergus laughed. 'We're used to it and have stopped noticing. It's the Italian blood.'

Isabella came out with a drink in her hand. 'It is not Italian, this behaviour.' Her face reflected fury. 'It is Scottish temper. That red hair!'

'Her hair's not red, Mum, she keeps telling you.' Fergus pantomimed a hand flicking hair out of the way.

Rico returned with the beers. 'Gran said it's strawberry.'

'What colour is a strawberry, then?' Isabella glared at Rico.

'It's grief.' Paul, obviously the more sensitive twin, said.

'A strawberry is grief!' Isabella rounded on her son.

'No Mum.' Paul frowned. 'Anyway, Rico's been winding her up again.'

Paul was clearly protective of the sister that Jack presumed they were discussing.

Jim unscrewed another beer. 'Christ. Well, she'll have to get over it soon or I'll build a hut for her to live in on the other side of the bluff.'

Isabella frowned. 'James, do not blaspheme, and you will do no such thing. If you spend some time talking with her and try to entice her from that room, she will recover, but you won't even try. You know she will only listen to you.' Isabella rolled her eyes at Jack. 'Always Papa's girl.'

Jack kept his gaze neutral, thinking she sounded like a spoiled brat.

Fergus explained. 'My sister has had her heart broken. She found her fiancé in bed with her friend.' A smile formed. 'She now hates all men, including her brothers.' The smile widened. 'But mate, I have to tell you, her friend is so hot and well, it would take a better man than most to resist.'

Jim scowled, and Fergus subsided into silence, drank the last of his beer and gazed out over the garden to the land beyond.

There was a line of trees about five hundred metres away that Jack assumed followed a watercourse, but otherwise the view stretched toward the horizon, where endless savannah met a pale sky.

When they finished their drinks, Isabella said, ' Come. Lunch is ready. James, you must make her come out, at least to eat. Perhaps this handsome young man will take her mind off things.'

While Jim went off in one direction and Isabella went back to the kitchen, Jack followed Fergus and the twins through to another room containing a large square table. A carafe of red wine took centre place along with a rustic-looking loaf of bread, olives in oil, and a bowl of black grapes. On the sideboard, a haunch of roast beef rested next to covered vegetable dishes and a gravy boat, all reflecting in a bevelled wall mirror. To his untrained eye, the ensemble appeared antique. The furniture was similarly old, carved wood, heavy in the spacious dining room.

Fergus pointed to a chair. 'This do you, mate?'

'Thanks.' Jack pulled out the chair just as Jim walked in holding a girl, or rather a young woman, by her wrist. Her feet were bare, legs encased in baggy jeans with a long-sleeved khaki tee shirt several sizes too big, pulled over the top. The tee shirt had old stains that washing hadn't removed and some slogan obscured by wear. The strawberry hair was in a ponytail, pulled back tightly from a delicate oval face. Jack thought her hair was more the colour of ripe wheat lit by the rays of a setting sun. She had her mother's creamy skin and extraordinary dark-winged eyebrows above stormy eyes, and a sulky full-lipped mouth.

She waited, awkward and defiant, as Jim introduced her to Jack.

'Sophia, this is Jack Fallon. He's an engineer with the gas mining company I was talking about; wants to survey our place for gas. That's right, isn't it Jack?'

Jack gripped the back of his chair. 'We've actually met before.'

'You don't say.' Jim glanced from Jack to Sophia, but Sophia's face remained blank.

Isabella walked in holding a serving dish. 'You know my daughter? From where?'

'It was a long time ago at university in Townsville, or rather at a friend's graduation party.' He looked at Sophia. 'Do you remember Pete Macalister?'

An ominous ripple sucked the sound from the room. Venom flared across her face before acid spilled from her mouth. 'This man is a friend of my ex-fiancé, and you invite him to lunch and expect me to eat with him.'

A scalding wave of heat slapped him in the face. 'Ah. Sorry, I didn't know. I haven't seen Pete for years. We lost touch when I went to Western Australia.' Crap, how far could he get his foot into his mouth?

Jim pushed her into a seat and stalked across to the sideboard to carve the beef. 'It's a small world. Get used to it my girl.'

Everyone else took their places around the table in silence, while Sophia stared at the table and Isabella passed the vegetables and gravy. Then Fergus told a story about some race-day meet he had attended, and talk swirled around the table, but Jack remained acutely aware of her. Not so much a spoiled brat, but more reminiscent of a wounded beast.

Barnett carried a platter to the table. 'Help yourself, Jack.'

Isabella said, 'Now, Jack, you were telling us about your mama. Why have you not seen her for years?'

'Leave the fellow alone, Bella. His family is his own business.'

'He is in my house, so I must know who he is. One cannot know a man without knowing his family.'

Jack glanced at Jim. 'It's okay, Mr Barnett.' He turned to Isabella. 'My mother vanished when I was about eleven. I don't know anything else. I don't know why she left or where she is now.' He felt his voice catch and took a gulp of wine to combat the unexpected emotion.

'That is too sad. Such a young boy.' Isabella reached over to plonk a pile of meat on his plate and then pushed the gravy boat towards him. For a minute, everyone was occupied with filling their plates.

Then Isabella said, 'But how can a person vanish...'

'Bella enough, let the man eat.'

Jack gratefully lifted a forkful of beef to his mouth and caught Sofia watching him. She averted her eyes and pushed vegetables around her plate. He noticed she had refused the meat on offer. Dark rings underscored her eyes, and hollows in her cheeks made her beautiful face seem gaunt. A surge of empathy welled up in him for her sense of loss.

'Soph, what's this?' Rico held out his arm, showing a spray of tiny red spots.

Her glance brushed across him. 'Leprosy, and I gave it to you for riffling through my diary, you little brat.'

'Sophia!'

'Well, tell Rico to stay out of my room.'

'Mum, I don't have leprosy do I?' Rico's eyes were round with worry, as if he believed his sister. 'What is leprosy, anyway?'

Jack choked back a laugh. He couldn't blame Sophia for being cranky with Rico if he went through her diary, especially with any secret angst she might have drooled onto its pages.

Isabella rolled her eyes. But the interchange had broken the tension.

Jim turned to Jack. 'So, Jack, tell me about this survey. What can we expect, and for how long?'

Jack put his knife and fork down on his plate. 'At this stage, I'd like to begin drilling about three kays southeast of here. On the other side of the bluff.' His head nodded in the direction. 'I think it shows the most likely signs, but it means setting up a camp. If I can get your agreement, Mr Barnett, I'll make that our base camp.'

'Show me on the map after lunch. We can talk about details then, but if you have to choose a spot, that's not a bad one from my perspective. Over the bluff is pretty parched, most rains fall this side, so the grazing is not often so good over there.'

'James, no business-talk. More roast beef, Jack?'

'No thanks. This is really delicious, Mrs Barnett.'

'Crawler.'

'Sophia!' Isabella glared at her daughter.

'Pardon?' Jack was thrown by her rudeness.

'Oh, forget it.'

Jim sighed. 'You'll apologise, young lady. You're behaving like a spoiled teenager.'

'Sorry.' She ducked her head as if she really was apologetic, but a moment later her chin came up. 'But it's true. He's buttering you up, so you will give him your blessing to ruin this land, just like they've done in central Queensland. Now, his company is going to rape and pillage the land in the north.'

'That's enough, or you'll go to your room.' Jim slammed his hand down on the table.

'Well, I would like to be in my room, but you dragged me out to listen to this drivel. It's well known that MGEE has fracked chemicals like Propanol and Butoxyethanol into the water tables in South Australia, W.A. and New South Wales. The same company is responsible for the earthquakes around Ohio and Texas in the US for God's sake, and you're going to let them loose here, making people sick from their own drinking water. They'll poison the aquifer, you'll see, but by then the land will be well and truly fucked.'

'Sophia!'

'Oh, I'm going.' She thrust back her chair and stood up. 'You wait and see, although by then it'll be too late. He'll have ruined everything and will move on to ruin the next thing.' Tears filled her eyes, and she turned and stomped from the room.

Isabella bit her lip. 'I'm so sorry, Jack. She has not been herself since she came home.'

'It's okay, Mrs Barnett.' Jack ran his palm over his mouth. Everything she said was true although MGEE had been made to clean up their act since then, but he was impressed by how much she knew.

After lunch, Jack sat down with Fergus and Jim, and they poured over a map. Jack placed his finger on the spot he planned to sink the first well.

Jim looked thoughtful. 'I don't have much use for that bit of land son, so if you cause havoc like my Sophia claims you will, I won't mind too much. But you'll pay for it.'

Jack paused, then decided Jim's statement was rhetorical and said, 'I'd like to discuss what I'll be doing on that section.'

'Okay, but I'm warning you, you'll pay through the nose if you bugger it up.' Jim held out his hand, 'My solicitors have been all over the contracts with your firm, so we'll call it a deal, but I take no responsibility for my daughter's comments or if she leads some environmental tree-hugging crusade against you.'

Jack scrutinised Jim's face with some alarm. 'Is that likely?'

Jim laughed. 'I don't think it's her style, although I'd put nothing beyond my daughter.'

An hour later, Jack drove away from Barnett Station, his thoughts on what Sophia had said. The memory of meeting her at Pete's graduation party years ago, was still vivid. She had been out of his league then and still was. He needed to focus on the present. In a few days, he would be heading back to the head office in Townsville and would call in on Pete. Since going to work in Western Australia almost straight after Uni, he hadn't seen him since that party.

But he should also head home, check on his dad, and while he was there, call in on the Morrisons. It would be good to see Ed again. FaceTime chats were okay, but he missed hanging out with him. Besides, he should thank Mr Morrison for putting in a good word. It was probably the old man's reference that had scored him the job.

The Idealism of Youth

E *ight years earlier.*
    Jack packed up his meagre belongings in the university residence and visited his supervisor. Professor Vernon Prentice wasn't in his office, so he left a note, thanking him for all his support and saying goodbye. Then he headed off to his mate Pete's house. He would stay one night for the party and then head home.

Pete's family home was nestled in the lee of a hill overlooking the Coral Sea. The house was large, and pretentious with the wealth of privilege that came with having a father who was a prominent barrister. One reason Pete was holding the graduation party, other than completing his final law exams, was to invite his new boss, Tad Hinckler, to the house to impress him. That was his dad's idea. Jack thought it was a pretty lame one, but Pete had said, that was how people made money, networking with the right crowd.

Jack arrived at the party already in full swing, people sitting around on the lawn or by the pool bar, drinking. After saying hello to Mrs Macalister in the kitchen, he wandered out to the garden. Pete was an avid collector of friends, and every law graduate and lecturer was there, along with a good number of undergrads and many of Mr Macalister's legal crowd, from pretty secretaries to balding judges. He was the odd man out, and he reckoned he and Pete were only friends because they had played rugby on the same team.

Jack was trying out the memory trick of making associations to remember names, but he was terrible at it. Then he saw Pete's sister, Larny, come out of the house with a friend. Larny had just finished second-year medicine. She had been playing tennis, judging from the gear she wore. While Larny was a looker, the friend who had followed her from the house left Jack's mouth dry.

Pete introduced her as Sophia and slid his arm around her shoulders. 'Sophia's studying medicine with Larny. She lives out west and is staying on in the big smoke for a week or two over the hols. Ah, here's my new boss. I'll introduce you but make a good impression, won't you mate? This is important to me.'

Jack reluctantly turned his gaze from Sophia and looked at where Pete had indicated. Tad Hinckler was a handsome, fair-haired, clean-shaven man, in his late forties, once a lawyer he was now a self-made billionaire. Everything from the Akubra hat to his boots, blue jeans, and belt, were all made by R. M. Williams. His green shirt was part of his environmental uniform.

For Jack, the outfit said everything about the man. He was rumoured to have the ear of the Australian government, some said more than just their ear. Most significantly, he was leading the lobby to overturn the 1970s ban on oil and gas exploration under the Great Barrier Reef. At one point, Jack really thought he might succeed. Why Pete would want to work for him was anyone's guess.

When he had asked, Pete said the usual. 'Mate, you have to pick a team.'

Jack didn't think Pete had chosen a very good team. As it turned out, Jack didn't have to try very hard to impress Hinckler, who was more interested in Sophia. So, he nursed his beer and listened, drifting in and out of the conversation while sneaking glances at Sophia.

Out of the blue, Hinckler turned to him and said, 'So what's your thing, Jack?'

'Pardon?'

'You know, Pete here has environmental law...what about you?'

'Mining, I guess.'

'He's too modest.' Pete grinned and ran off Jack's qualifications with an air of proprietorial pride that surprised Jack.

Hinckler scrutinised Jack's face as if he had suddenly realised he was human. Then he'd fished inside his jacket pocket and brought out a card. 'We could use your qualifications. Call me if you're interested.'

Jack didn't take the card, a point that earned a frown from Pete.

Sophia snatched the card and laughed. 'Look at you lot sizing each other up like gladiators in a Roman arena.' She put on a deep voice. 'On one side, we have the defenders of mother nature, and on the other, the pillagers of the earth.'

Hinckler grinned. 'It's not always that simple.'

Jack glanced from Sophia to Hinckler and then to Pete. He couldn't believe she had cast him as the pillager, particularly when faced with people like Tad Hinckler.

'Excuse me.' He said. 'I think I need another beer.'

Hinckler fell into step as Jack walked towards the kitchen. 'Did you hear the state government is considering opening up the reef to oil exploration?'

'It'll never happen.'

'It might now. Most of the reef's dead, north of here anyway, with all the bleaching. We're talking to them at the moment. I could use a man with your qualifications.'

'No thanks.'

'Just think about it, will you? The pay and conditions are better than you'll get as a graduate mining engineer.' He tucked his card into Jack's shirt pocket and sauntered back towards Pete and Sophia.

The next day, Jack caught a bus north, alighting at Innisfail to hike the last 60 kilometres to his home in the mountains. The sun was low on the horizon when he arrived, so he cut across the paddocks rather than taking the long way around by road. As he approached the house, dogs barked.

He heard his father's voice. 'Shut the fuck up.'

If anything, the lowering light made the dark shack fold in on itself, slumping in defeat behind its own event horizon, sucked into its own black despair against which Jack stiffened his shoulders.

'Oh, it's you what's making them dogs go apeshit. I thought it was pigs. Lucky I didn't take a pot shot... sneaking out of the scrub like that.'

'Hello Dad'.

Barry Fallon slumped in a canvass chair on the veranda, a hunting rifle across his knees. A gun cleaning kit lay open on the floor at his bare feet, beside an empty glass. He belched loudly and scratched his bare chest. 'Don't think I've got dinner waiting on you this late. You should have been home yesterday. You said you finished yesterday, so where you bin all this fukken time? Never can rely on anything you say, just like your whoring mother.'

'I left a message on the answer machine I would stay over at Pete's place.'

'Yeah, yeah, get me another rum then.' He leaned down to pick up his glass.

Jack took the tumbler from his father's outstretched hand, deciding a fight was not worth the consequences. At least the old man was still coherent. He must have begun drinking late in the day.

'Better make it a big one, three, maybe four fingers. It's my last for the night. Me an' the boys got a big mob of pigs to round up in the valley tomorrow. Need to have me wits to shoot straight. Hey, want to get out and see how real men do things, instead of staying home like a big girl's blouse?'

Jack stopped mid-step. He didn't correct his dad's outdated insults. It was pointless, but he was stunned by the invitation. He had never been asked to go along pig hunting, not since he'd disgraced himself when he was twelve. Barry had taken him out hunting then, just the two of them, but Jack refused to shoot the pig and his father never forgave him.

It was a mother pig with a little one trotting behind her with its tail up, completely oblivious to imminent death stalking them. A memory of his own mother blurred his vision, and he froze, finger still curled on the trigger as he slumped against the trunk. The gun went off, and the bullet whizzed between him and Barry. The noise warned the pigs, and they disappeared into the forest.

His father went wild, cuffing him and calling him every name under the sun, and until now, he'd never been asked to go pig hunting again. Not that the absence had bothered him.

'I might give it a miss, thanks Dad. I've too much to catch up with around the farm.'

'Suit yourself.'

'I'll need the Ute, so maybe I can drop you off and pick you up later.'

'Nah, you take it. Noddy's coming in the morning, wants one of the pups. The rest of the boys will be here also. We'll be doing this patch tomorrow, I reckon.'

Jack headed inside to his bedroom and switched on the light. The bare bulb brightened slowly, sending out rays of stark contrast to the shadowy corners. Moths immediately battered their bodies against the grimy glass window. He put his backpack on the floor, looking around his bedroom with resignation. The place smelled of mould, white ants, and dirt. He should not have come home, but what choice did he have? He couldn't abandon his father.

Barry's voice interrupted his reflection. 'Where the fuck's my rum, you lazy piece of shit?'

The next morning, the sound of crashing and cursing drew Jack from sleep. He rolled onto his back and listened to the familiar sounds of Barry's morning ablutions, set to a background monotony of Chowchillas calling in the forest. The sounds of tires on gravel interrupted the birdsong, and then the dogs began barking.

His bedroom door crashed open. 'Out of bed lazy bones, you're not in the city now.' Barry stood, nearly as tall as the doorway, his chest almost as wide. His skin was leathered and yellowing like old parchment, his hair thick, grey, and short. Bushy eyebrows arched above piercing blue eyes. Red meaty fists were thrust against his hips, as he held his arms akimbo.

Jack sighed and got up. Five minutes later, he was at the kennel watching his father cradle a puppy like it was precious porcelain before he handed it to Noddy.

Noddy was a weasel of a human being, but he was Barry's best mate. Jack had never liked any of his dad's friends much, but Noddy was the worst. He'd been around for as long as Jack could remember, more so in the early days when his dad had been building the boarding kennels, with big plans to go into business with Noddy. It had never happened, not after his mum, Molly, had taken off.

Noddy glanced at Jack. 'Which one would you pick?'

Jack shrugged. 'Don't know Noddy. Not my thing.'

'But do you reckon, male or female? I need it for my new job.'

Jack could see the man was bursting with news, but he didn't want to get into friendly conversation. He merely shrugged.

'Yeah.' Noddy stood up. He was a wiry man with thinning, grey hair tied in a rat's tail by an old bit of leather strap. The puppy squirmed in his arms. 'I'll be needing a good guard dog for the place at Bramston Beach. Got a job caretaking. Some mining outfit. That's your thing, isn't it?'

Two Utes arrived, putting an end to the conversation, and Barry took the puppy from Noddy, putting it back with its mother, and taking a moment to fondle her ears. Then both Barry and Noddy ambled off to greet their fellow pig hunters and prepare for a day of hunting.

When they had gone, Jack drove to Ed's place. Henry Morrison was home with his wife, but Ed was still out.

Mrs Morrison hugged him. 'Congratulations Dr Fallon.' She pushed back the blonde wave from her face and kissed his cheek. It was the first time anyone had congratulated him on the completion of his PhD. Overwhelming gratitude reminded him of how much he'd missed Ed and his family.

She said, 'We're expecting Ed back any minute.'

Of course, it was a Saturday. Ed would be at Rugby practice.

Dr Morrison jiggled his eyebrows as he clasped Jack's hand in both of his. He was a burly man with a round face and a bulbous nose. Shorter than his wife, he only reached Jack's shoulder. Yet, what he lacked in statue, he made up for with his booming Texan drawl, spoken without the slang Chad favoured.

'It's good to see you back, son, and congratulations. Ed's been keeping us up to date on your progress. I hear you did very well, but I expected nothing less.'

'Thanks.' He followed them through the house and outside to the pool deck.

'Beer?' Morrison asked.

Jack shook his head. 'I'm driving.'

'Coke then?'

'No. I'm right, thanks.'

'So...' Morrison rose onto his toes. 'I spoke to a mate of mine in the Pilbara. He's expecting your call. I'll text you his number.'

Morrison laughed at Jack's surprise. 'You didn't think I would remember, did you? I never make a promise I don't keep.' He brushed away Jack's thanks. 'By the way, have you noticed the increase in earth tremors?'

Jack nodded. 'Yes. My supervisor at Uni and I were monitoring them.'

'Look, until Ed gets here, come and have a look at something for me.' Morrison walked inside and Jack followed him to his study, a deeply masculine domain that smelled of cigars and leather. An enormous geological survey map of Australia covered one wall.

Morrison said, 'Here we are. He pointed to an area around Gibson's Reef with several pins in a cluster. 'What do you make of that?'

Jack shook his head. They're minor tremors.'

'Mostly under 2.5 and shallow. Not likely to do any damage, you think?'

Jack grimaced. 'Odd all the same.'

'This is the area I would expect to see them, although even here they are growing in frequency.' Morrison pointed at the red pins placed at intervals along the North Queensland Orogen from Princess Charlotte Bay in the North-East Cape, down past the Palmerville Fault and through Almaden, then to an area West of Ingham along the Clark River Fault. From there, the pins followed a line west to Charters Towers and off into the Eromanga Basin in Central West Queensland. Most of the pins were clustered around the Clark River Basin.

Jack nodded. 'There was also a 2.6 yesterday morning along the Ravenshoe fault line.'

'That's interesting.' Morrison opened his laptop. 'You're right. Near enough to your dad's place. Any more of this and we may yet see diamonds spewing forth from the deep.' Morrison chuckled self-consciously. It was an old joke they'd shared when Jack was a kid and Morrison would try to get Ed involved in stories about Gaia's jewelled riches, embarrassing Ed, but sparking Jack's imagination with his tales.

Just at that moment, Ed walked in. His thick blond hair was still wet from the shower. A graze oozed along his muscular forearm. He was more like his mother, both in his good looks and outgoing affability, although his sturdy muscular frame was like his father's but taller.

'I might have guessed this would be where I'd find you.' He pulled Jack into a bear hug. 'It's good to see you home again, mate.'

Ed had joined the police force, disappointing his father, who had wanted him to follow in his old man's footsteps. But Ed had hated the idea of more school, as he'd called university. He was the physical kind, footie captain and all-round good guy who had married his childhood sweetheart, Tess Robertson, the school principal's daughter, who was now a chartered accountant. They lived with Ed's parents while they saved to buy their own home.

He and Tess had been the only kids at high school who had befriended Jack after his mother's abrupt disappearance and rumours swirled in the community about his family. It was a mutual friendship where Jack helped Ed with his schoolwork and Ed kept the bullies off Jack's skinny hide. Dr Morrison had poured his thwarted ambition for his son into Jack, and Ed had never minded, said it kept his dad off his case.

'Come on, let's get out of Dad's clutches. Tess wants us to meet in town for lunch. She has a friend she wants to introduce you to.'

Morrison said, 'No point match-making Ed. Jack's off to Western Australia.'

An Unfortunate Event

Jack arose early and set off to Townsville, a seven-hour trip from Julia Creek, driving into the rising sun. Within minutes he was travelling at 110km/h along the Flinders Highway, a bitumen ribbon running west to east across uninterrupted plains stretching away to the pale horizon. He squinted against the glare. It was time to report to Chad, but travelling at dawn increased the chances of kangaroos or wild pigs on the road.

Animals weren't his only worry. Mining road-trains and cattle trucks were frequent users of this road. Mining and farming were the lifeblood of the outback, along with tourism. With the pandemic border closures, tourism mostly comprised grey nomads, a peculiarly Australian phenomenon. The modern day wanderer, retired with independent means, time on their hands, and a motorhome with which to explore the vast expanse of Australia.

Motorhomes slowed him down, but it was the road-trains he had to watch. They travelled at speed, and some were 50 metres long. Yet, despite the increased concentration and glare, driving through the vast outback was where he most felt at home, where he had time to think and plan his next move. At the moment, setting up the new site at Barnett Station was his primary area of contemplation.

By the time he reached Charters Towers, a town less than two hours west of Townsville, his stomach was gnawing on his spine. He pulled up outside a greasy spoon on the edge of the town. The fly-blown poster in the window boasted the best pies and hamburgers this side of the Great Dividing Range.

As he locked the car, the ground beneath his feet wobbled. It was a weird and disorientating feeling, so brief he wondered if he had imagined it. But he knew earthquakes, and this was a minor tremor.

Inside the café, a pimply youth sat behind an orange laminated counter that would have taken pride of place in the 1970s. Jack nodded at the teenager and made his order before sitting at the only table to wait.

'Did I imagine the ground shaking a few minutes ago?'

The teenager shook his head. 'Happens all the time. Mining tremors they reckon.'

'Who reckons?'

The boy shrugged. 'My dad mostly.'

'Has it always been like that?'

'My dad reckons not. There's something funny going on, but I don't know, hey. Do you want your burger to eat here, or take-a-way?'

Jack ate in the café thinking about what the teenager had said, recalling a conversation he'd had with Henry Morrison years ago. It must have been when he had gone home after finishing his PhD. That was when Henry Morrison told Jack he had a mate who would give him the job in the Pilbara. Overwhelming gratitude reminded him of how much he'd missed Ed and his family.

Hell, Jack realised that was eight years ago. He ran his hands across the back of his neck, vowing to see them as soon as he had some time off. He owed Henry Morrison a lot and felt a sudden sense of shame at having neglected them, but in the meantime, the increasing seismic activity needed looking into.

He got up from the table, placed his empty plate on the counter, and asked the teenager for a bottle of water. Then he left the café. Perhaps he'd call in on Roy. It was only a half-hour detour along the Gregory Highway, and he could stay the night at the camp. He would talk to Roy about whether it was the fracking activity causing the tremors, or a natural phenomenon.

Although, if it was the fracking activity, Roy was likely doing something he wasn't supposed to be doing, like disposal of wastewater under pressure along fault lines, and the last thing Jack wanted was his professional reputation sullied by working for an unprincipled firm. Judging by the terse exchange at his induction meeting, he was beginning to suspect there were things Chad Myers hadn't wanted him questioning.

An hour later, Jack stood at a large wall map in Roy's office, pointing to the Barnett property where he had planned to drill. He explained what he'd found before, asking Roy's advice on his next move. Then he gingerly broached the subject of the tremors. The last thing he wanted was Roy thinking this was some kind of interrogation, even though Jack knew that was exactly what it was.

'By the way, I stopped at Charters Towers for lunch and a young bloke behind the counter said there was increasing seismic activity in the region. Have you noticed anything?'

Roy gave Jack a sour look. 'Don't fucking come at me with that.' He returned to his chair behind his desk. 'The whole of Charters Towers has been banging on about it for years. It's bullshit.'

'Didn't mean to imply anything. Simply curious.' Jack sat down opposite. 'But do you reckon it's bullshit? Years ago, a friend, an oil man—you may know him—Henry Morrison, said he'd noticed an increase.'

'I've heard his name, but what would he know about this region? He spends his time jetting around the world, much of it in Africa and America, I heard.'

'He lives just north of here, in the Atherton Tablelands. I think he was interested, that's all, given the region has been stable for so long.'

Roy sighed. 'The Queensland government stopped funding seismic monitoring and research some time ago, but before that, they detected over 110 earthquakes per year on average.'

'So, you're saying it's business as usual?'

'Guess so.' Roy shifted his gaze. 'You wanted a bed for the night. I'll get someone to take you to the guest quarter now and I'll see you at the mess for dinner.'

Jack followed Roy's foreman across the camp to a guest donga. The man's name was Ossie, a short and cheerful bandy-legged character of about fifty, whose skin reflected the resentment of a hard tropical life. He spoke with an accent, German or Dutch, Jack guessed.

'How is the yield here?'

Ossie grinned. 'It's fucked mate. Tried everything but barely a trickle...only good for sinking carbon.

'Geo sequestration? Is that what's going on here?'

Ossie pulled down the corners of his mouth. 'Tried, but it set off tremors. Too close to old fault lines. We need to move closer to the new fields.'

'Where?'

'North.'

'North, where?' Jack frowned. Murray's area covered the only places north other than the environmentally protected Wet Tropic ranges or the coastal belt. Unless it was further north. 'You mean Papua New Guinea?'

Ossie scrutinised Jack's face as if he needed to re-evaluate who he was. 'Forget it. Here's your room. You can get a feed over there.' He pointed at another group of demountable buildings and walked away, leaving Jack staring after him.

That night in the mess, Jack asked Roy if they were sequestrating carbon in the old wellbores.

'Don't listen to Ossie. He shoots his mouth off. We did try pumping carbon into the wells to raise the reservoir pressure and displace the remaining gas so it would flow into the production wells. It didn't work. We're about to pull out of the region, but that's still confidential. I'm ready to retire, but we don't want to scare any horses with fears of redundancy, okay?'

'So, you're not moving to PNG?' Jack grinned.

'What?' Roy's eyebrows met over his nose.

'Ossie said something about moving North.'

'I told you... Don't listen to Ossie. He's a reyt wazzock.'

Jack gazed at Roy for a long moment, wondering if it was worth asking him what a reyt wazzock was, before deciding it wasn't important. Instead, he said, 'Do you think pumping compressed carbon may have other consequences?

Roy shook his head. 'We've checked the carbon dioxide is not leaking from any gaps in the caprock.'

Jack placed his hand over his mouth and slid it across his chin, feeling the day-old growth prickling his palm. If carbon dioxide found a gap, it could migrate along the fault to the surface, leaking into the atmosphere. That was a significant risk to life around any leakage, never mind adding to the blanketing gasses heating the planet.

'You don't think that's risky?'

Roy interrupted. 'It's kept the methane safe for millennia. Why would carbon dioxide be any greater problem?'

'What about the destabilisation of the faults' increasing tremors in the region?'

'We don't know that's happening.'

'Perhaps we should collect some data...'

'That's not my job. N'ither yours.' Roy's accent was becoming more pronounced and less intelligible, while his face turned a dull shade of red.

Rather than taking this as a sign to back-off, Jack ploughed on. 'Do you remember I told you about my old supervisor at uni? He might have some students interested in collecting data if you're curious.'

Roy exploded. 'For fuck's sake Jack! Worry about your own neck of the woods and stop poking your nose where it doesn't belong.' He slammed his empty beer glass on the table. 'I'm off to bed.'

Jack watched Roy stalk out of the mess, his shoulders hunched. Now that was an interesting reaction.

The next morning, after breakfast, Jack said goodbye and thanked Roy for his hospitality. Roy mumbled something unintelligible and strode away, while Jack watched after him. There was definitely something going on here that Roy wasn't comfortable discussing. Jack's antennae were up, shrieking for answers. He shrugged and got into his four by four. Townsville was only a couple of hour's drive and his meeting with Chad was at midday, so he had plenty of time.

He started the engine but left it idling, deciding he would drop in to see Vernon Prentice at the university. If he took the Hervey Range road at Basalt, he would pass right by the university and it would cut an hour off the travel time, although he wasn't sure about the condition of the road. He placed a call and left a message on Vernon's answering service. It would be good to see him again.

Jack put the car into gear and took off slowly to keep down the dust. Even so, it billowed up behind the car. After he left the camp, he sped up along the dirt road leading to the Gregory Development Road. The day was heating rapidly, and Jack turned up the fan on the air conditioner. Then he switched on the ABC news channel. More floods down south. Pity there was no rain here, at least it would lay the dust.

The mining truck came up behind him fast, but with the dust, he didn't see it in his rear-view mirror until the last moment. As it barrelled towards him, he looked around to find a safe place to move off the road, but the shoulder on either side dropped away steeply. He pressed down on the accelerator and the needle crept over the 100 k mark. He was doing way above the 80 k speed limit, but the truck was still on his tail. The road ahead curved, and he took it too fast, the vehicle slipping sideways before he righted it and sped on.

The truck remained on his case, tailgating him. Surely the bastard must be able to see he couldn't move off the road. Then it nudged closer. Jack accelerated, but the truck remained too close. At the first opportunity, Jack pulled over to the side of the road, going too fast and fighting the steering to maintain his trajectory. The truck sped up, clipping the back of his car as it passed. The car spun around and hit the lip of the rocky incline. It flipped and rolled several times before smashing into a thicket of iron bark trees.

Two days later, Jack awoke in a sea of pain, his arm immobile in what he was to discover was a cast. A doctor fiddled with tubes leading from him to a stand next to the bed.

His voice croaked. 'Can I have some water?'

The doctor turned. 'You're awake.' She walked over to his side and took his wrist. 'I'm Samantha. Do you know who you are?'

He nodded.

She held a metal straw to his mouth. 'Can you remember what happened?'

Jack sucked up water, lubricating his dried throat before he said. 'Yeah, a truck totalled my car.'

She frowned. 'Tell me your name.'

'Jack Fallon.' He gazed at her with appreciation. Long dark hair pulled back in a ponytail. Large brown eyes fringed with dark lashes. Straight nose, a square-ish face with a wide, full-lipped mouth. Tall and slender in flats and scrubs.

She appraised him as she checked his pulse. 'You were pretty banged up when they brought you in, concussed, and your shoulder dislocated. It's set in a temporary cast to keep it immobile. Your seat belt held, although I'm surprised it didn't break any ribs. We're still checking on your organ functions. There was some blood in your urine, but so far all seems to be recovering well from the bruising. Your face will go down in a day or two, but the area around your eyes will turn all the colours of the rainbow, but at least it will match your chest and shoulder.' She smiled. 'Once the swelling in your shoulder subsides, we can see if there is any other damage to nerves or ligaments. Otherwise, the cast should be off in a week or so. How much pain are you in?'

He shook his head. 'Not too bad.' He lied, although he reckoned it might be off the scale.

She gazed at him for a moment. 'You are a terrible liar.' She smiled. 'Are you allergic to anything?'

'No.'

'If the pain gets worse, press the buzzer, and I'll ramp up the drip.'

She left him then, and he watched her moving away like a relaxed leopard, every sinew and muscle taut and rippling through the thin fabric of her dowdy scrubs. He closed his eyes, tried to ignore the pain, and after a while fell into a deep sleep, perhaps because of what was coursing into his veins.

The next morning, Jack awoke feeling a lot better and in much less pain. A police constable arrived to take a statement. He placed a packet of Jack's things on the table and his bag at the foot of his bed.

'Your things from the vehicle. Lucky the phone and laptop don't appear irreparably damaged, not as far as I could tell, anyway.' He pulled up a chair, sat down, and took out a notebook and a pencil. 'Can you tell me what happened? Take your time.'

Jack explained how the truck was travelling too fast and had pushed him off the road.

The police officer frowned. 'The witness, who called the ambulance, said you swerved for a kangaroo.'

'That's bullshit.'

'It's a notorious stretch, mate.' The officer closed his notebook. 'We'll look into it.' The copper didn't sound convincing.

That afternoon Chad arrived with an air of bonhomie, balloons, and grapes. 'You look sad enough to bring a tear to a glass eye.' He stopped. 'Hate to tell you, but there's a distinct look of the racoon around the eyes?' He chortled.

Jack grimaced. 'That airbag packs a good punch.'

'Well, you survived. Car's got a hitch in its gitalong, though.'

'Sorry about that, but it was one of our trucks that ran me off the road.'

Chad's eyebrows crawled up his forehead. 'You sure you're not overdrawing on the ol' memory bank? I heard it was a kangaroo. One of the men saw it. Saw you swerve and go off the road.'

'Was he driving a truck?'

'I think he was heading off for a bit of R-and-R. Flew out to Europe somewhere. Lucky he found you and called an ambulance, otherwise you'd be buzzard bait right now.' Chad patted the bed next to Jack's legs. 'Wash off your war paint, pardner. I hear trauma often interferes with recall. You look all done in. I'll let you rest now, but call me if you need anything.' He paused and examined Jack's face before saying, 'And for the lord's sake, don't go digging up more snakes than you can kill.'

Chad sounded more homespun than usual, like he was enjoying acting, the caring boss, but why were they all lying about a kangaroo? Could he have imagined the truck? Did trauma do that? No! It was real. He could still see it in the rear-view mirror. He didn't suppose he would get a straight answer on Roy's activities, either. Nevertheless, he gave it a try.

'When I spoke to Roy before the accident, he said he was retiring.'

'That so?'

'Ah hell, I thought it was official.'

'First I've heard.'

'The point is, he said, the area's finished.'

'Never.'

'He's been using the old wellbores as carbon sinks.'

Chad looked down at his feet for what seemed like an exceptionally long time before he said, 'I'm sorry you got so beat up, but you had no business being on that road in the first place. It's not your area and taking side-trips on company time... Well, look where that gets you. Next time, whistle before you walk into a stranger's camp.' He paused, and said, 'all the same, take a couple of weeks' vacation to heal. Go home for a while. Your doctor said, you'll need lots of rest to recover.'

'Are you saying none of this is true?'

'Jack, don't get caught in your own loop. We are a reputable company. Don't do anything without permits. Roy's area is still producing commercial quantities even though the yield is down. You've had a bad concussion, and it's not surprising you're out to hang the wrong horse thief.'

Jack scrutinised Chad's face to find tell-tale traces of lying, but he could see nothing. Surely, no one could lie like that with such a straight face. Maybe he had imagined all of it. He'd ask Roy the next time he saw him.

After Chad left, Jack called Vernon to apologise for missing the appointment he'd made when he left Roy's camp.

Vernon answered at the first ring. 'Jack, what happened? I had a message saying you were coming to see me, but when you didn't show, I was worried.'

Jack explained he was in the hospital after a car accident.

'Not too bad, I hope.'

'No. I'm okay.'

'That's lucky. I must admit I was a bit mystified when you didn't show. Are you up for visitors? I'm only next door. It won't take me long to walk over.'

After the call, Jack lay back on his pillows, exhausted. When he awoke, Vernon was sitting at his bedside. 'Sorry. Have you been here long?'

'A couple of hours, but I used the time to catch up on some reading.' Vernon held up his phone. 'The doctor reckons you just need rest and time to heal. I've arranged with Sheila for you to come home for a while. I hope that's all right with you, but I understand you don't have anywhere else at the moment, and your home on the Tablelands is four hours' drive away. The doc says you're in no fit state to drive that far, but we are around the corner. That's if you would like to get out of this joint for a while.'

Jack felt a lump form in his throat at Vernon's kindness. This was above and beyond. But what other choice did he have? He could stay in a motel, or he could phone Ed and ask him to come down and pick him up, but Vernon's offer had a double appeal. He could discuss his fears about the increasing seismic activity in the region.

Two days later, Jack left the hospital after promising to buy Doc Samantha a coffee on her next day off. He was stunned when she had wrung that promise from him. She was an attractive woman, and he couldn't understand why she might wish to see him again, given she must have seen every bit of his battered hide already. He didn't argue, just hoped his luck was changing. Run over by a truck one day, beautiful woman wanting a date on the next. What could possibly go wrong?

Chad Myers

Chad Myers looked up at the mezzanine running three sides around the room. Soaring ceilings, columns of marble, wooden wainscoting, ginormous Australian landscapes. This was clubland Aussie-style. The speaker behind the lectern was rattlin on bout gay flag-waving, loyalty, patriotism, and wire-brushing the Commos.

Nobody did patriotism like a Texan and Chad agreed with most of the sentiment, although he didn't understand what mining had to do with sandpapering the country's largest trading partner. Ah, the kicker; business must bolster the county's defence in whatever way they could. Dang. Wasn't that what they were doing, finding new energy fields? Or did the man just want coal mining to flourish? Couldn't tell, not unless you knew who had skin in the game. But that was a whole *nutter can of sauerkraut*, as his dad used to say. Jesus rest his miserable soul.

Australia was made of coal, just had to dig it out of the ground. Didn't need refining and storing like petroleum. Yet, if there was war, they'd need petroleum before coal. One day they might figure that bit out. One wack to the supply chain and a week or two later, no wheels, no wings, no boats. If business needed patriotism to support a war effort, the government needed a bit of strategic planning to ensure the country had enough arrows in the quiver, and he knew where the biggest pay load of arrows was waiting. He glanced at his boss in the chair next to his.

Graham Newman's head bobbed like one of those nodding-dog-car-ornaments as the Senator made his last point. Business must get off social media and pay more attention to employees, who would be the ones defending the country against the Reds. What the heck was he preaching? Chad didn't even have a social media account and most of the trouble he was in right now was over being nice to an employee, one he was god-darn sure wouldn't fight anything, or anyone, for his country. The man was definitely a darker shade of pink if not fully Red. Didn't have a loyal bone in his body.

He wondered if the Senator had ever managed anyone other than a policy officer, but Tristan Richards suggested he attend and what Tristan said was gospel as far as Chad was concerned. He was the man with a mainline to the Gs. Tristan wasn't here yet, but he and Graham were meeting him upstairs for coffee after lunch to fill him in on events. Not with the Senator of course. Arm's length and all that hog-spit, although one might assume the two men knew each other, even if they weren't in the same party, but politics wasn't Chad's game. He'd leave that to Tristan and Tad.

Tad sat on the other side of the room with the protégé. Chad couldn't remember his name, but the man had greased the corporate wheels, so they were as smooth as slickwater-gel. He'd done a heck of a job with the corporate structures and asset disbursement. Now there was a loyal son of a gun. Chad could smell it on a man. Never could trust those without that particular ambrosia.

They hadn't sat together for the luncheon. It was better if they each stayed in their own corners. A business triangle, Tristan called it. More like a musical one, with Barwon holding the nylon loop and banging the steel beater in time to the arm waving from Viktor and Vladimir.

Mercifully, only the triangle would attend the coffee conference upstairs. Chad wasn't sure he wanted Barwon and Viktor involved. After all, it was a small domestic matter, and he had already handled it, although he should have sacked Roy for that little fuck up, but at least Ossie wouldn't be returning to Australia for a while. Graham had sorted that with a plumb job in South Africa. Now they just needed to find a way to distract the bear.

The next morning, Chad flew back to Townsville. It was a small world alright. Who would have thought that Slickwater and Fallon had history? The man was a genius, and his suggestion had taken a weight off Chad's back. Now all he had to do was follow the Senator's advice and play nice with the employee for a while longer, while Tad and Slickwater did their thing, and then, as Viktor was fond of saying, *no man no more problems.*

Dawning Realisation

Sheila Prentice, Vernon's wife, was a severe-looking woman with steel-streaked dark hair, piercing grey eyes, and gaunt cheeks. She lectured psychology at the university, and by her own account, was considered a little eccentric.

The moment he met her, Jack recognised her eccentricity as a cover for a sharp intellect. Her gaze seemed to penetrate, laying bare his substratum as she placed her hand on his good shoulder, welcoming him into her home.

'I'm overwhelmed by your kindness.' Jack said, meaning every word.

'Don't mention it. I've heard a lot about you Jack, all good. Please treat our home as if it were your own, and don't mind Vernon and me. We argue all the time about everything.' She smiled to take the threat out of the statement. 'Trouble is, now we have Goggle. It takes all the fun out of it.'

She led the way to the back of the house. 'I've put you in the recreation room, so you won't have to climb the stairs.. No one uses it now our boys have left home. It has its own bathroom and leads outside to the swimming pool, through there.' She pointed through French doors where Jack could see a secluded area with a kidney-shaped swimming pool. 'You can just laze about and recover while we are at work.' She paused for a moment before saying, 'Vernon always had a special interest in your career. '

Jack nodded. 'It was Vernon who persuaded me to stay on at Uni to do my PhD.' He remembered it was after a public lecture. They were standing in the foyer when Vernon mentioned a spate of minor earthquakes at the northern end of the Tasman Orogen. He had raised his eyebrows at Jack, saying, sure you don't want to stay and find out why?

Jack had stayed, but he was more interested in what lay beneath the continental shelf off the eastern coast of Australia. The Newman state government of Queensland had approved shale mining at Abbot Point, and

Jack feared the end of the reef. The Australian government intervened and promptly created the world's largest marine park, banning drilling in it. Then a research team published a paper about their findings of a fractured monster 5.3^2 km on the cliff face of the continental shelf at the end of Noggin Passage off the Cairns coast. It was ready, with the right seismic shove, to slide up to two kilometres to the sea floor, causing a tsunami which would flood low-lying areas of the north-eastern Queensland coast.

Sheila pulled him back to the present. 'Get yourself settled and come through to the sitting room for a tipple. Dinner is in an hour. I am not a terrible cook, and it will be better than hospital food. She looked him up and down. You could use fattening a bit. Is there anything you can't eat?'

He shook his head.

When she'd gone, Jack sat on the bed, exhausted by the brief journey from the hospital. Maybe he could lie down for five minutes.

He awoke the next morning with the sun shining through the open curtains of the French doors. He showered and went to find Vernon and Sheila, embarrassed that he'd fallen asleep when she had obviously made dinner for him. Now, he could smell the coffee and followed the tantalising aroma to the kitchen, where he found Vernon cooking breakfast.

'Jack, how are you feeling today? Coffee's in that pot.' He pointed with his chin.

'Sorry, I fell asleep last night.'

'Good for you. Rest is what the doctor ordered, so don't be sorry, but you must be starving. Brunch coming up. We always eat late on a Saturday. Sheila likes to get in early to tend her roses. Silly idea growing roses in this joint, but she dotes on them as if they were pets or something.' He peered at Jack. 'Sit down before you fall down. I wonder if they should have let you out of that hospital. You are very pale.'

'I'm fine really, thanks Vernon. Much better after a night's uninterrupted sleep. I'll have some of that coffee, though.' Jack walked over to the coffeepot.

Vernon said, 'When you're up to it you can tell me why you called to make an appointment to see me.'

Jack sat at the kitchen table with his coffee. 'I just wanted to run something by you, but with all that's happened, well.'

'So, shoot. I'm listening.'

At that moment Sheila came in, stamping her feet on the doormat.

'Ah Sheila, look who's managed to struggle out of bed.'

'Jack dear, glad to see you up.'

Vernon flipped eggs onto plates and placed them on the table with several other bowls of food. 'Jack was just about to launch into why he wanted to see me.'

Sheila sat down. 'Do you mind if I listen in?'

Jack shook his head. 'I'm not sure it's about anything important. I just wanted to ask if Vernon had any data on the seismic activity in the region over the past few years.'

Vernon ground pepper over his eggs. 'I have been looking at that same issue. I wrote to Geoscience Australia to ask if they had raw data I could analyse, and I can tell you already, your suspicions are right.'

'You don't even know what his suspicions are yet, dear.' Sheila held out her hand to Vernon. 'Pass the mushrooms.'

'No, but I can guess they are the same as mine. Jack will have more insider information than I have.' He glanced at Jack. 'You said in your last email you had a job with a shale oil and gas company.'

Jack nodded. 'You're right. I did want data for the same reason.'

'Do you suspect something?'

Jack hesitated. 'I have no proof. Just wanted to satisfy myself.'

'What is it?'

'Not sure really, but no one is keen to answer my questions. Trouble is...' Jack wondered if he should confide in these good people. If his suspicions were right, they could be in danger. He was sure the truck driving him off the road was a warning, but that sounded paranoid, even to him. People didn't do things like that, not outside the movies.'

Sheila's brow crinkled as she looked from Jack to Vernon.

Vernon said, 'Just say it.'

'It's just a hunch.' He shrugged. 'If I can see the data and run some analysis, maybe it'll tell me something.'

'Ah, a fishing expedition. Right, I'll let you have my data and see what you can find.' Vernon attacked his eggs, while Jack weighed up whether he should ask Sheila about recall after a trauma. He was sure he hadn't made up the truck, but how could he know?

Eventually, he broached the subject. 'Sheila, you would know how trauma affects a person.'

'Certainly. My speciality.'

'If I recall a truck driving me off the road and a witness says I swerved for a kangaroo, how do I know if my memory is at fault, or the witness really saw something that I swear wasn't there?'

Sheila stopped, her fork halfway to her mouth. She put it down on her plate.

Vernon said, 'My God! Is that what happened, Jack?'

He shrugged. 'All I know is that I saw a truck bearing down on me. I sped up because there was nowhere to turn off the road. It kept coming until I hit a bend too fast and skidded, but I pulled out okay, then it rammed me, and I went off the road.'

'What did the police say?'

'They have a witness who swears I swerved for a kangaroo.'

'Can you contact the witness?'

'Apparently not. He's on holiday somewhere in Europe.'

Sheila said, 'There must be evidence left at the site or on the car's body.'

Vernon said, 'Where did the accident take place?'

Jack told him and Vernon said that's not so far. If you're up for it, why don't we go for a drive and take a look?'

That afternoon, when they arrived at the crash site, the damaged vehicle was gone, and the road looked as if it had recently been graded. A snapped tree truck was the only tell-tale sign that there had ever been an accident there. It proved nothing, of course. The insurance company would have collected the car, and the road may have been graded as part of a normal maintenance schedule. It had been pretty rough going when he had last travelled along it.

Sheila said, 'Maybe you could ask to see the car, wherever they've taken it.'

All weekend, Jack stewed on the scene they had viewed. Removing the car seemed pretty standard. Not that he would know but it wasn't beyond possibility. The accident had been five days ago. It was the road having been graded that worried him. Could he have imagined something like a truck running him off the road or was someone trying to cover their tracks by grading the road to remove evidence? Whichever way he looked at the situation, it was weird.

On the following Monday, Jack rang Mary at work to find out about the car, and where it had been taken. He claimed he had left some personal effects in it.

Mary said, 'Sorry Jack. I understand the car's been crushed. It was taken to the wreakers, but I am sure they would have checked it first. I will ring them and ask.'

'If you give me the wreakers name, I'll call in and see them.'

'No dear. I won't hear of it. You are supposed to be resting.'

After trying a different tack, Jack gave up. Mary wasn't about to tell him anything, but if the car had been crushed, it was pretty pointless, anyway.

He spent the next few days analysing data, finding the cluster around Gibson's Reef was growing. Gibson Reef was about 35 kilometres east of Bramston Beach, a small beach community an hour's drive south from Cairns, and 20 kilometres directly north of Innisfail. Neither he nor Vernon had an explanation for it. The two men sat at the kitchen table, pouring over data tables. 'That doesn't look like activity from Roy's region, although fracking earthquakes can occur up to 10 kilometres from the fracking site. This is a bit far for that.'

Vernon nodded. 'I agree.' He pointed to another section about 100 kilometres west, south-west. 'But this activity along the Ravenshoe and Palmerville fault lines is also increasing, which is more what I would expect to find. That's your colleague's region, isn't it?'

'That's Roy's region alright, but it's riddled with fault lines, which may also indicate natural causes, although those particular faults have been inactive for a long time. What worries me is the cluster impacting the reef.'

Vernon glanced at Jack. 'You're thinking of the Noggin Block.'

'Yeah. I guess it's a long shot.'

'You could come back to the uni and do some post-doctoral research.' Vernon smiled.

Jack sighed. 'Tempting as that sounds, I have a horrendous mortgage to pay off.'

A week later, Jack had his cast taken off, and all his medical reports came back clear. Samantha reminded him of his promise to take her for a coffee.

He suggested dinner instead. He was keen to impress her, now he was no longer her patient. The evening came and Vernon and Sheila dropped Jack in town, for he was currently without a vehicle. He could have taken a taxi, but the Prentices were attending some function at the sugar shaker, a round building that housed the Grand Chancellor hotel, so it was just as easy to ride into town with them.

As he exited the car, Vernon took a house key from his key ring and said, 'Just in case we're asleep when you get back.'

Jack walked to the address Samantha had given him and found her place on the third floor of a building overlooking the Strand, an esplanade that followed the city shoreline. When she opened the door he was bowled over at how good she looked, a low-cut black dress, high heels, and hair flowing like silk around her shoulders. As he leaned in to kiss her cheek, he was struck by her perfume, spicy, hot, and heady like her.

They strolled along the Strand to the restaurant, but as they approached the entrance they ran into Chad, flamboyantly kitted out in Hawaiian shirt, skinny jeans, and boots. He had his arm clamped around an attractive blonde woman, who didn't look older than eighteen, too young and vulnerable to be dating Chad.

'Jack! Good to see you up and about. And if I'm not mistaken, this is the lovely doctor who brought you back to health.'

Jack sighed. His evening was ruined. 'Hello Chad. Samantha, this is my boss, Chad Myers. He runs the company I work for.'

'Alas, the region of the company only, Samantha. Jack exaggerates.' Chad lowered his tone and leaned in with a pantomime whisper. 'He's prone to that you know.' He continued holding Samantha's hand, while his own date hovered at the edge of the group.

It was clear Chad wasn't going to introduce her, so Jack held out his hand. 'Hi, I'm Jack. Please, don't believe a word of it. I am not prone to exaggeration in the slightest.'

She took his hand and gave him an unsure smile but said nothing.

'Me thinks the man protests too much.' Chad leaned into his date as he misquoted Shakespeare, and she looked more bewildered than before. Then he turned back to Jack. 'Join us for dinner. I insist. Least I can do is buy the hero of the hour dinner. That is a good site you picked at the Barnett's place.

Survey results are showing promise.' He clapped Jack on the back, guiding him into the restaurant, and leaving him no way out.

Resigned, Jack made a face of apology towards Samantha.

She shrugged and smiled her thanks to Chad as he held her chair.

The waiter tended to Chad's date, while Jack hovered, wishing he'd just said no thanks. How had he let the man manoeuvre them into this? The last person on earth Jack wanted to have dinner with was Chad. He sighed and sat down next to Chad's date and opposite Samantha.

Chad said, 'So, Samantha, another week off work. Are you sure this is a medical assessment, not just a desire to keep him to yourself?' He grinned.

'He's no good to me. He won't be here.'

Jack said, 'I was planning to go home for a few days, if that's okay.'

Chad studied him for a moment. 'Are you okay to drive?'

'I have a clean bill of health.' Jack smiled at Samantha.

Chad took a fancy gold fountain pen out of his pocket and wrote an address of a car dealer on a napkin. 'There's a new four-by-four ready for you to pick up. If you like, you can take it tomorrow. Drive out west on Monday. Save you coming back into Townsville.' He winked at Samantha and laid the pen on the table. An engraving, *Paramount Holdings,* glittered along one side.

His goodwill floored Jack. It had not been what he expected.

Chad waved away his thanks and asked, 'Where are you staying at the moment?'

'At a friend's place.'

Chad raised his eyebrow at Samantha.

She smiled. 'Not me. It's his old professor's place.'

'Ah, do I know him or her?'

'Him. Professor Vernon Prentice.' Samantha said, giving Chad a long sideways look from beneath her lashes.

Jack glanced at Chad's date. He still didn't know her name. He changed the subject. 'Vernon and his wife kindly gave me a bed for a few days. He's a geophysicist, so I haven't been completely idle. We've been crunching data. It's been a useful exercise.'

The distraction worked almost better than Jack had intended. Chad's tone was sharp. 'What data? Nothing commercial in confidence, I hope.'

Jack laughed. 'Nothing like that. Vernon received some seismic records from Geoscience, and we've been going through that.' He stopped, realising he couldn't tell Chad why, or at least not his suspicions about Roy. Not yet anyway. He said, 'It's just something for which we both hold an interest.'

But Chad was no longer listening. He scrunched up his napkin and got up. 'Excuse me, I must make a call.'

Chad walked outside, and Jack picked up the pen to examine it. 'Who uses a fountain pen nowadays?' He unscrewed the barrel, and sure enough, there was an ink cartridge inside. 'Why bother?' He re-placed the barrel.

'I think it's cool.' Samantha took the pen from him and ran her finger along the engraving. 'This is gold and I reckon these stones along the clip are diamonds. I wonder if he'd miss it?'

The young date inhaled. 'You can't steal it.'

Samantha laughed. 'I won't need to. He'll give it to me if I ask.'

Jack glanced at the date. Poor woman. Those were the first words he'd heard her say all evening, but Samantha wasn't joking, and mean as it was, she was also probably right. He took the pen and put it back on the table. 'We'll just leave it where we found it, shall we?' He grinned at the date.

When Chad came back, he sat down and replaced his napkin on his lap, then slid the pen into his pocket. 'By the way, Mary has the Barnett contract documents back from the solicitors. It's all pretty straightforward, so she has booked the team for Monday. They are heading out to set up camp at the location you arranged. You can follow them out there. There is no need to come into the office.'

'That's really generous of you. Thanks, Chad.'

'Don't thank me. You've landed us a good contract and if the area is as promising as you told Roy it is, then it might be worth the price of a car or two. By the way, do you still have all the data you were analysing?'

Jack said, 'Yeah sure. Are you interested in it?'

'Not really, but you'll let us know if you find anything of interest, won't you?'

Jack nodded and changed the subject. 'Hey Chad, you don't know where they took the other car, do you?'

'I believed it went to the crushers. You did a good job of it. Try to keep this one in one piece, will you?'

Jack clenched his jaw. Generous or not, his boss just had a knack for rubbing him the wrong way, and the dinner was turning into a work-outing instead of a romantic evening for two.

It was only after dinner the evening improved. He walked Samantha home, and she invited him in. They went up in a lift to her large two-bedroom apartment.

'Nice.' Jack gazed around. 'Do you have the whole place to yourself?'

'I used to have a flatmate,' she said, 'but she moved back home. I'm looking for someone else to share with. Rents in this place are so expensive.'

'You're a doctor. You must earn heaps.'

Samantha scoffed. 'That's what everyone says, but the pay for junior doctors is not that great, not enough to live in any sort of real comfort.'

'This looks pretty good to me.'

Jack didn't have a real home, or not one he thought of as home. He saw the farm as his dad's home. When he had first started earning, he had taken Henry Morrison's advice and invested in a flashy penthouse in Cairns. It was an investment property for tax off-set purposes, and he'd never lived in it. Instead, it was rented out to wealthy tourists. Since leaving university, he'd lived in mining camps and motels, owning nothing more than what he could carry. Now, seeing Samantha's comfortable space, he wished he had his own home.

'You could share with me.' She wound her arms around his neck.

He buried his face in the space between her chin and shoulder. The smell of her perfume was still strong and alluring. 'You don't know how good that sounds.'

She moved her head and brushed her lips against his, at first a butterfly flicker and then with insistence. He slid his arms around her and pulled her close to his chest, feeling the firm mounds of her breasts as they pressed against him.

She drew back and took his hand. 'Come.'

He followed her through to the bedroom, where she kicked off her shoes.

The next morning, he let himself into the house, hoping Vernon and Sheila had gone to work already. The entrance hall was chaos.

Sheila's voice came from the kitchen. 'Who's there?' She rushed into the hall, followed closely by Vernon.

'It's only me. What the hell's happened here?'

Vernon said, 'Don't touch anything, Jack. The police will be back any minute.'

'What happened?'

'We were broken into.' Sheila touched his arm. 'I'm afraid your room is a wreck, and it looks like your laptop's been stolen. So has Vernon's. Luckily, I left mine at work.'

'Crikey, they made a mess. Did you lose much else?'

Sheila gazed around; her face creased into a maze of bewilderment. 'Just the laptops, I think, but with all this chaos, it's hard to tell.'

Vernon added, 'Easy to carry, I suppose, and we don't own much of real value. Sheila is not into jewellery. We have no art worth anything, and the rest of our stuff is bog standard fare.'

'Just as well,' Sheila interjected, and fresh tears welled in her eyes. 'It's the personal violation, isn't it?'

Vernon squeezed her hand and smiled. 'I guess the TV was too big to carry.'

After giving a statement to the police, Jack rang work to report the laptop stolen, then he picked up his new car and called into the office. Mary already had another laptop for him.

When she saw him, she folded her arms and drew her mouth into a thin line. 'I know none of this is exactly your fault, Jack, but it seems particularly careless, and Chad's patience is wearing thin. You had better take greater care of the new car and laptop. I suppose you still have your phone.' She paused. Chad was mostly concerned about the loss of commercial in confidence information, or other valuable company data. He asked me to find out if your password is secure and if you keep copies somewhere.'

'Of course. But there will be nothing on the laptop for the thieves to steal. I only save my data to the cloud.'

'I hope that's the company's cloud.'

Jack nodded. He saved all work data to the company's cloud, but personal stuff he saved to his own cloud. He didn't explain. So long as work stuff was available to the company, he didn't think the rest was Chad or Mary's business.

'Where is your phone?'

'I have it here.' He patted his top pocket.

She thrust a piece of paper at him. 'Sign here, and please, in future, take more care of company property.'

He left the office feeling like a recalcitrant child. Then drove back to Vernon's place, where he picked up his bag and took his leave, thanking them and promising to stay in touch.

The drive north to his home revived him, and by the time he turned west to head into the mountains, he was feeling lighter, even though the last stretch had him driving through thick fog.

Return to his Roots

B arry Fallon owned a six-hundred-acre farm across three titles in the high country of the Atherton Tablelands, once Djirbal land. The farm was left to Barry by his father, and his father's father before that. Jack's great grandfather, the son of an Irish timber getter, had bought and cleared the land of its primeval jungle, soon after the turn of the 20th century, and the grassy paddocks had subsequently supported large numbers of cattle.

Rain fell all year-round, releasing warm deluges in summer, and misty drizzle in winter. Sometimes the temperature dropped below freezing, and only occasionally exceeded the high twenties even in the hottest months, although that was changing as frequently the wind blew, not from the sea, but from the western interior. Still, the grass grew green and waist high on deep volcanic soil. Streams gathered in the upland, where remnant forest still covered the slopes. They tumbled down hills and over cliffs until they joined bigger rivers that plunged down mountains to the coastal fringe.

It was where Jack had spent all his formative years. Yet all he had ever wanted to do was escape. Now as he approached, that same desire engulfed him, but he felt an obligation to go home, at least to make sure his dad was alright. The last time Jack had been home was before he went to Western Australia.

Now, eight years on, it seemed nothing had changed, and Barry still did not own a mobile. Although to be fair, the mobile reception at the farm was patchy, at best. He had left a message on the answering machine to tell Barry he was coming home, but he doubted his dad would listen to it. It didn't really matter, as the house was never locked.

He drove up the long driveway, realising that it wasn't strictly true that nothing had changed. The place looked more unkempt than usual. Long grass brushed against the car chassis and caressed the doors on either side. It had never looked this neglected, and a sudden pang of guilt hit Jack square in the chest. He should have come home before now.

Jack could see Barry and his mates on the veranda, looking down at a row of dark lumps lined up on the grass outside. As he drove closer, he saw they were six dead boars. His arrival set the dogs off as if he was the vanguard of a home invasion.

Jack parked the car. The dogs, tied up in the house yard, was unusual. His dad had always given them food and water and put them to bed in their kennel before he did anything else. He loved his dogs; more than Jack ever thought he'd loved his son. Although it hadn't always been that way.

When Jack's mother, Molly, was still around, Barry had been a decent enough father, caring for his farm and family. It was only afterwards he took to drinking, but before that he'd been a patient man, and even though Jack was only ten or eleven, he was allowed to help when his dad and Noddy had built the kennels. In those days, his father had endless patience as he taught Jack how to hold a saw, hammer in a nail, and other handy stuff for which he had always been grateful.

At one stage, Barry and Noddy had planned to run a boarding kennel business together, so the buildings were designed accordingly. That was when Noddy had christened the kennels with a bottle of beer, calling them the Taj, although Jack doubted Noddy even knew what the real Taj Mahal was. Now the kennels, on the far side of the house, seemed to lean at a strange angle.

He walked towards the house and past the dead boars. Flies buzzed in a thick black phalanx, only scattering briefly as he passed. Even after all this time, the old dogs recognised him and started whining.

Barry said, 'Well, well. Just look what the cat dragged in. So, you're back then. I got your letters. Read em all too.' He looked around at his mates as if proud of himself. 'Not much of a writer myself, but.'

'Hello Dad.'

'You're just in time for a snifter. We're celebrating. Got all the bastards.' Barry pointed at the dead boars.

Jack inclined his head towards Noddy and the two other men, whom he recognised but had forgotten their names. One held a rum bottle in one hand and a glass in the other as if just about to pour himself a shot. Jack hoped they would leave, but it seemed they had just started celebrating.

Noddy said, 'How are you doing, Jacko boy? Although, not a boy anymore, hey?'

Another one of the men said, 'Grown tall. How was Western Australia?

Barry said, 'He's working for a Queensland mob now.'

The man holding the rum bottle said, 'Should have come out huntin' today. We could have used an extra man.'

His father scoffed and made a move to clip Jack's dark, unruly hair. 'Yah! He'll never hunt nothing, the big girl's blouse.'

Barry clapped his huge hand on Jack's shoulder, the one that had been dislocated, and Jack winced.

Barry's chin thrust out. 'What's got your goat?'

'Had a car accident.'

Barry turned to the man with the bottle. 'Well, a rum will cure that. Pour the lad one while you're there, mate.'

Jack didn't want a rum but took it all the same. 'What happened to the kennels?' He raised the glass to his mouth and the familiar smell of Barry's home distillation hit him like a punch.

'Something put a crack right through the concrete floor and one of the supporting columns.'

Jack lowered the glass. He couldn't drink the stuff. 'What something?' He gazed at his father, seeing the old parchment of his face, thinner and yellower than usual. He glanced at the rum in his hand and put the glass on the table.

Barry shrugged. 'Don't know. Sounded like a road-train coming right at the house, and everything went all shuddery like. But must have been a ghost, hey. I saw nothing. Dogs went ballistic, but.'

Jack pulled out his phone. There was no signal. 'Do you think it might have been an earthquake?'

His father shrugged. 'Whatever it was, I reckon I'll have to pull the lot down.'

Noddy chimed in. 'Na. I'll fix the structural damage. No problem.'

'How you going to do that when you're down working at the coast?' Barry said.

'I'll only take a day or two. Just leave it to me, mate. Good as new.'

Jack went into the gloomy house and flicked on the light switch. Nothing happened. 'Your light bulb's blown.'

'Nah son. That ghost road-train did something to the electric. Nothing works.'

'Have you called Ergon?' Ergon was the name of the electricity supply company in North Queensland.

Noddy smirked. 'Remember who did the electrical work on the Taj?' He pointed his thumbs at his own chest. 'Now the thing is, I'm unlicensed, and Ergon won't take kindly to that, but I'll fix it. Would have done it today, but we've been a bit busy.' He pointed to the pigs. 'I've got a few days off before I have to be back at work.'

Jack ignored him and said to Barry. 'Is there any food in the house?'

'Sorry son. Fridge isn't working, everything will be going off. We can make a BBQ and cook up a bit of pig. Dogs need feeding as well.'

Jack sighed. His father and his mates would start drinking now and maybe eat some wormy, fire-singed pig later on before falling drunk into swags. He didn't want to hang around. 'Why don't we go to the pub? We can get a feed and a bed there, Dad.'

'You go, my boy. Nice of you to call in an' see your old man, but it's not a good time.' He seemed to pull himself straight and said in an oddly formal voice. 'I'll telephone when the place is fixed up a bit, and you can come back for a visit.' He paused and rubbed his chin. Then raised his eyebrows. 'Nearly forgot. Your old school mate Ed was up this way a few weeks ago, said to tell you to call in. Why not spend the weekend with him? I'll be all right here with my mates, and Noddy will give us a hand to get things fixed up.' He turned to Noddy for confirmation, then said, 'Ah, one thing before you go. I was thinking of selling the rest of the cattle. Too much for me by myself. You won't mind, will you?'

Jack felt the same old twinge of guilt. 'Do whatever you reckon, Dad. They're your cattle.'

'Yours too, my boy. All of this is yours when I go.'

Jack felt a lump forming in his throat. 'Okay dad. Sell the cattle if you're sure. I'll head on over to see Ed. You have my mobile number. Call if you need anything. I'm only up for the weekend. Back to west Queensland on Monday, but I'll come back again soon.' Jack nodded to Barry's mates and walked away, remorse threatening to choke him, but he couldn't stay there. He just couldn't.

Barry called after him. 'Send me another letter to let me know how you're doing.'

Jack waved.

He drove to the top of the road where he could get a mobile signal and called Ed, who insisted he drive straight to Atherton. Dinner would be in an hour, and there was always a bed made up with his name on it. Jack experienced another surge of guilt at the relief he felt at avoiding his duty to his father, and at having neglected his best friend for so long. He drove to the Morrison's home.

By the time he arrived, cumulus clouds were building into giant gunmetal columns somewhere over the distant Coral Sea. The windsock on Henry Morrison's private runway told him the breeze was from the northeast, but there was no sign of the Pipistrel Panthera he flew, and the hanger in the distance had its doors closed.

He pulled up at the house as Tess was getting out of her car. She stood waiting for him, holding a leather satchel, or he supposed it was a briefcase, against her stomach. For a minute he was back at school, seeing the girl with brown plaits and thick fringe clutching her schoolbooks, while she waited for Ed to finished rugby practice. Now she was a stylishly dress young woman, in a fawn coloured skirt and jacket, a pink shirt and beige high heels. Her streaked blonde hair was swept away from her face in a style similar to Mrs Morrison's blonde wave.

'Tess. Look at you, all grown up and serious with your briefcase.' He stooped to kiss her cheek.

Tess was a chartered accountant working for a local firm. It had once been her mission in life to see Jack married to a nice girl and settled nearby. Although she had tried endlessly, she had not succeeded. Jack had gone on some good and some bad dates as a result. The last time he spoke to her, she said she had officially given that mission away as a lost cause.

'I missed you.' He grinned at her.

'I only saw you a few months ago, when you face timed Ed to tell him you were coming back to Queensland. Although you took your time coming to visit.'

'Still living with the parents, I see. I thought you would have built a house by now and have a couple of kids running around.'

She beamed.

'What?' He examined her pink blush.

She shook her head. 'Not until Ed's present.'

'You're pregnant.'

'Oh Jack, you spoilt the surprise. You will have to pretend when Ed tells you. We have bought a block of land too, and we're going to build a house. Can't get a builder at the moment. They are all too busy, but it's planned and approved, but don't let on I told you. Ed's busting to tell you himself.'

They found Ed sitting at the counter in the kitchen, still in his police uniform. It was clear he hadn't been long home from work.

Mrs Morrison was chopping vegetables and listening to Ed when she saw Jack and exclaimed. 'He's here.'

'Mate.' Ed got up. 'It's good to see you.'

Mrs Morrison wiped her hands on a tea towel and pushed her hair from her face. She hugged Jack. 'It's such a shame Henry missed you. He had to go off to Pretoria, but hopefully now you're working in Queensland, we'll see more of you.'

Ed gave Jack a beer and poured a tonic with ice and lemon for Tess. 'Want anything Mom?'

'No sweetheart. You all go out into the garden while I get dinner finished. I'll have a glass of wine later. I have that nice Californian red your dad brought home, last trip.'

Tess took a sip of her drink and said, 'I'll join you in a while. I just want to get out of my work clothes, and I'll help Mom with dinner. You should change yours too, Ed.'

'Yeah, I will. In a minute.'

Ed and Jack sat in the garden drinking beer, while Ed grilled Jack about what he'd been up to since he'd got back to Queensland. He heard Jack's account of his father in silence and promised to call in regularly to check on him.

Then Jack told Ed about the accident, explaining how his recall of events was so wildly different from an eyewitness account.

Ed nodded. 'That happens.'

'You're kidding me, mate. I know memory is a strange beast, but there is no way I imagined a truck chasing me down a dirt road and then bashing my car into a ditch.'

Ed pulled a wry face. 'It does seem a stretch. Why do you reckon they said that then? No reason for the copper to lie, so it must have been what the witness swore happened. But what's the motive?'

A thought struck Jack. 'Look, I might be paranoid, but a week after the accident, my laptop was stolen.' He paused and rubbed his palm across his mouth.

Ed laughed. 'Jesus, you have done well in the few weeks you've been back. What happened?'

'I don't know. Its nothing I guess. The connections are too tenuous, but after I got out the hospital I stayed with Vernon Prentice, my old university supervisor. His house was burgled and his and my laptops were stolen.'

'What do you mean, the connections are too tenuous?'

Jack sighed and told him about the earthquakes and Roy's reactions. 'I did wonder if the truck episode was just a warning, you know—mind your own goddamn business—type of thing. Then I told my boss I was analysing data on earthquakes with Vernon and suddenly both our laptops are stolen, and my boss wants to know where I store my data. I've never had an accident or a burglary in my entire life, and suddenly it happens when I start asking uncomfortable questions. It seems like too much of a coincidence.'

Ed said, 'I'm not saying you are wrong, mate, but Townsville is a bit of a lawless joint at times. Kids, you know, some of them are out of control.'

'That's what the police said when they took my statement about the burglary.' He sighed. 'Forget it. When I talk about the connections aloud, the whole thing sounds insane.'

Ed examined his friend for a moment, before saying, 'I can look into it, but if the witness is in Europe, we may have to wait for his return.'

They fell into a companionable silence, while they drank their beers, until Ed said, 'I ran into an old friend of yours a week ago. That environment lawyer bloke you went to uni with.'

'Pete Macalister?'

'That's him. We both had a bit of a wait for the Cairns court, and we started chatting.'

'That's bizarre. I was going to see Pete when I got back to Townsville, but with everything that happened, well, you know.'

'Yeah, I know. You're bloody hopeless at keeping in touch with your mates.'

'Give me a break, Ed. I kept in contact with you.'

'Only because I made you, but who else?'

'I wrote to my dad.'

'Okay. Who else?'

'Ah, fuck off. No one else was worth staying in touch.'

'Not even Mindy Henderson?'

'Shit.'

'She was heartbroken mate. You said you would ring her when you went to Western Australia, and you never did. She still brings it up when Tess sees her.'

'For fuck-sake Ed. That was eight years ago, and I only took her out a few times. Besides, the Pilbara was too far away to continue a relationship.'

'You should have told her yourself, instead of leaving me to do it.'

'That was my bad. Sorry.'

'Water under the bridge.'

'Why bring it up then?'

'Needed an apology.'

Jack laughed. 'Bastard.'

'Anyway, your mate Macalister has moved up from Townsville. Seems like he's done well for himself, gelled hair, flash sports car, expensive clothes, Rolex, manicured fingernails, the works.'

Jack smiled at the description. 'You nailed it. So, he hasn't changed then.' Jack paused. 'But you are right. I should have kept in touch.'

'You don't need to make excuses to me, mate. I already know what a slack friend you are. Macalister gave me his mobile number and his office address in Cairns, and I promised you would ring. He said he'd look forward to your call.'

'Thanks, I'll contact him tomorrow.'

'You may as well make a weekend of it. I'm on duty, so it'll be just Mom and Tess here. Of course, they'll welcome your company, but it'll probably be more fun visiting the night spots of Cairns. Dad won't be back from South

Africa for another week, but then they are going to go home for a holiday. Mom's talking of retiring to Texas.'

'They've been talking about going back to Texas since I first met you. They won't leave unless you go too.'

Ed chuckled. 'I guess we're all staying then. I have some news, but we need to wait until Tess gets here. Where the hell is she?' He got up. 'Another beer, mate?'

Deeper into the Mire

The next morning, Jack drove down the Kuranda Range to Cairns, a small city that squatted within the torrid zone north of the Tropic of Capricorn. It had been built on Yidinji country 150 years ago, when white people arrived hungry for the gold of the Atherton Tablelands. They had first established the seaport at Cairns before cutting an overland track through the jungle to reach the mountainous plateau. Then they went to war with the Indigenous people, pushing them to the fringes before clearing great swathes of land for sugarcane farming.

Fifty years ago, the small town boomed into a tourist mecca. The city and its suburbs ate up the old cane farms along a strip of low-lying alluvial plain, sandwiched between the jungle-clad mountains of the Wet Tropics and the Great Barrier Reef. Now it was a bustling city of about 150,000 inhabitants from all over the globe. Before the pandemic, that number increased during the southern hemisphere winter months as tourist arrived from all over the world, but now tourism was on life support.

Jack parked and walked along the esplanade, where he found Pete in a new high-rise building overlooking the ocean. Pete led him through to his own office on the fifth floor of the *Green Synergy* building. The view out the large plate-glass window included an oceanic panorama flanked on either side by forested mountain ranges running down to a white-capped aquamarine and sapphire sea. On the street below, busy citizens bustled back and forth between heat mirages floating above the hot asphalt. But up here in the air-conditioned splendour of the environmental consulting world, all the discomforts of living in a tropical paradise were ignored.

Jack's gaze left the view outside the window and swept the large airy office, one wall taken up with a map of North Queensland, dotted with pins and flags. It reminded him of Henry Morrison's study, although Pete's map appeared to mark out mining leases, whereas Morrison's map showed seismic activity. Besides, Pete's office was all glass and chrome, not the old-world comfort of Morrison's study.

'You're a lucky sod. Always were. You've done well, Pete.'

'Not so much with the luck. I know a lot of people and bring in a fair amount of work for the company. I expect to make partner within the next few years and move up a floor or two.' His eyes lifted skywards. 'Better view, although it's not hard to find good views if you are above ground level in Cairns. Most lawyer's offices are in low-set buildings, but our clients are mostly the big boys in mining and politics, so we don't deal with much street traffic. Anyway, enough about me. What are you up to nowadays? Your police officer friend told me you are with some gas company working out in Western Queensland? You should have taken that job Tad Hinckler offered when you had the chance.'

'That was a long time ago. Besides, I don't think he made any genuine offer, just wanted me to contact him.'

'That's how it works, my friend. Better than slogging it out in dusty outback furnaces.'

They fell silent. Jack was finding it hard work uncovering common ground with Pete in all this luxury. 'How is Hinckler?'

'Good. The same you know. Into every pie and politician, can always be found where the money is.'

Jack nodded. That was how he saw Hinckler, but it didn't seem to worry Pete. He wondered how he still felt about Sophia. 'By the way, I ran into your old flame. She's pretty pissed off with you.'

Pete shuddered. 'Sophia? Where did you see her?

'At her folks' place, out west.'

'She's a complete psycho mate. Terrifying.'

Jack laughed. 'Didn't she find you in bed with her friend?'

'Hell, yes, but she didn't need to go off like that, and I apologised. What else was I supposed to do?'

Maybe not sleep with her friend, but Jack kept that thought to himself.

Pete looked at his watch. 'Bugger, I'm late for a meeting. Look, you're not in a hurry, are you? Can you hang around? I'll get my assistant to get you a coffee and a newspaper. I won't be long. My meeting will be done by 12.

When I've finished, we can get out of here and catch up properly over a long lunch.'

Jack had nothing else to do, so he nodded. 'Sure. But I can wait in a café downstairs.'

'Not a chance. You are just as likely to disappear again, and I won't see you for another ten years.'

Jack raised his eyebrows at the implication but kept silent. It was a two-way street and Pete had not attempted to keep in touch, either.

Pete picked up his briefcase. Besides, I have something I want to discuss.'

'What's that?'

'Can it wait, mate? I really have to go.'

When Pete had left, Jack stood at the window until a woman in a figure-hugging outfit and high heels walked in with a tray. On it was a gold-trimmed cup and saucer, a matching coffee pot, jug and sugar bowl, and *The Cairns Post*.

'Shall I put it here? She asked, indicating a coffee table in front of a low sofa on the other side of the large office.

He nodded. 'Thanks.'

'I'm Noreen. My desk is just outside. Call me if you need anything.'

Jack walked towards the coffee as she closed the door. Even Pete's secretary fitted the image. He poured coffee into the cup, picked it up, leaving the saucer behind, and wandered over to the map to examine it. There was a pin in Barnett Station. He stepped closer. It didn't mark Sophia's family's house as he thought it might, but it was in the exact spot Jack was about to start drilling. The tag had the MGEE company name. Why the hell, would an environmental consultant mark that?

He took greater care in scrutinising the map, noting all his company's wells were marked, but so were several other mining ventures in the region. Maybe *Green Synergy* just tracked what was registered. He noticed an outlier stuck in a section of what he had thought was designated world heritage around the Ella Bay region. It had a pin and flag with *Paramount Holdings* written on it.

Where had he heard that name before? It couldn't be a mine unless it was historical. If memory served him correctly, there was some gold mining once done in that region. He stepped closer. The marked area was just north of Ella Bay and south of Bramston Beach, just outside the boundary of the national park. Bramston Beach was a tiny community about an hour's drive south of Cairns and half an hour north of Innisfail. He hadn't been there since he was a kid and struggled to remember it, but he was pretty sure there were no mining operations anywhere near there.

He had heard the state government was re-commercialising some closed mines because new technology enabled greater extraction from waste product. Re-opening old mines made some sense because managing closed mines was a nightmare, especially when there was the likelihood of seepage from heavy metals and other contaminants. But surely they would not permit re-opening a mine so close to the marine park, the reef and protected forest. It wasn't far from the Eubenangee Swamp National Park either, a significant and protected bird habitat.

He walked back to look out of the window while he drank his coffee. A glance at his watch told him it was 11:45. There were still 45 minutes until Pete came back. He gazed at the filing cabinet. There would be a file in there that would explain what was once mined at Bramston Beach. He shook his head. Tempting as it was to rifle through Pete's files, he could just ask. He walked over to the sofa and picked up the newspaper.

On the front page was a large picture of Tad Hinckler standing in front of a crowd of *End Coal Now!* protesters. They claimed Tad as their champion, their Voice to Power. Jack read the article in which Hinckler outlined why now, more than ever, the world needed clean green gas. The article quoted him talking about the phase-out of coal and how renewable energy could not meet energy demands.

The pandemic has created an energy and food crisis, exacerbating the effects of climate change on the poorest in Africa and heating the Indian subcontinent to unimaginable degrees. Australia and the Pacific nations are in the front line, but their contribution to the warming effects is minor by comparison with India, China, and America. Even so, Australia is a rich country and needs to do more to support climate mitigation strategies, but individuals and businesses have a role to play. We can't just leave it to governments. Already Australia is running short of gas and the costs are skyrocketing. More gas fields need to open up, and more dams need to be built to grow food in the outback. This will reduce energy prices in Australia. Northern Australia has an abundance of gas fields and Governments needs to support more exploration of this available green energy to make food production cheaper, and more bountiful.

Not everyone agrees. The leader of the local Green Alliance said calling gas 'green' was like...

Jack couldn't read any more and put the paper aside. Tad was spouting bull anyway and counter arguments, no matter how good they were, when given equal weight with the scientific perspective, became lazy journalism, only serving to confuse people.

How could the ordinary person in the street determine which assertions were truth and which were lies? Gas was not green, no matter how you defined it, nor was it renewable, not even when it was referred to as natural. Arsenic was natural, but one wouldn't propose people eat it. Why couldn't the journos define things clearly and tell people the actual choices they had instead of just reporting opposing ideological arguments, verbatim? Either they didn't do their research, or they were complicit in telling lies. Either way, there was a problem.

Or maybe they didn't consider it was their job to educate the masses. Yet, such confusion caused people to place their trust, not in the conventionally accepted scientific consensus, but in who they liked. They obviously liked Hinckler, but burning gas was as bad as burning coal, maybe worse if you included extraction methods.

He didn't like or trust Hinckler, and saw him as a fraud, but was he any better? Then another thought struck him. Why was Hinckler calling for more dams? The paper said, to grow food but dams in the right places would allow cheaper gas extraction. They drilled for water now, but that was costly. Was Hinkler arguing for more dams for extraction purposes or was he really concerned with growing food? He sighed. This was why he avoided politics. It was all smoke and mirrors and usually the truth lay embalmed beneath layers of obfuscation. It was more enlightening to see where the money trail led.

A surge of long-suppressed guilt fluttered against the barriers he had put up years ago. He got up to pace the office floor. Old justifications ran through his head, but he knew they were just that. What could he do...it was his job and at least he tried to do it as carefully as possible without polluting the environment. Hell, who was he kidding? But gas extraction wouldn't go away. If he didn't do it someone else would, someone like Roy who hadn't the scruples to do it cleanly and honestly.

The door opened, interrupting his cogitations. He expected Pete, but Tad walked in.

'Dr Fallon. Pete said you were in his office. Good to see you again. Must be ten years. You haven't changed. Maybe broadened out a bit, no longer the skinny kid from Uni, right? How are you?' He shook Jack's hand. 'Pete's held up, but I am taking you to lunch. He'll meet us there.'

Jack followed Tad out of the office and to the lift. He didn't want to have lunch with the bloke, but it would give him the opportunity to ask him a few questions, so he played along. Tad took him to a swanky new place on the wharf overlooking the marina.

From where Jack sat he could see his penthouse. He had never seen it in real life before, nor been inside it. Morrison had put him onto the deal, at that time just an architectural drawing with a glossy portfolio of promise. Jack hadn't a clue what he was doing, but he trusted Morrison, so all his savings from working in the Pilbara for a couple of years went into securing the top-floor apartment. It wasn't hard, and he figured if he was going to own a flat, it may as well be something fancy.

When the place was built, he'd handed it over to a property management group. The investment had paid off, and the money from holiday lets continued to pay off his mortgage. As his mortgage diminished, his rental increased in value. Cairns was growing, and the Marina had become the playground of the rich and sometimes famous.

Tad said, So what are you drinking, Jack?

'Just water, thanks.'

As Tad ordered, Jack's gaze took in the marina, home to a variety of vessels from dinghies to catamarans, trimarans, and trawlers. Most common were the yachts, expensive white keel boats, some with multiple decks. One very large yacht was anchored further out. It was the type of superyacht Jack had seen in the picture Chad had on his desk; millions of dollars-worth of floating steel, aluminium, and reinforced plastic.

After Tad had given their order to the waitress, Jack cautiously broached the subject of green gas.

To his surprise Hinckler laughed.

'I know what you are getting at mate, but we must move slowly. If we go all out, we lose. Gas is marginally better than coal and the coal lobby is terrifyingly powerful. Gas is a step in the right direction, and it will loosen coal's grip on the industry.'

'Won't a gas lobby just replace the coal lobby with a new stranglehold that shuts out real action on reducing greenhouse gases in the atmosphere?'

'Between you and me Jack, that train's already left. There is nothing we can do about the pollution already in the atmosphere. All we can do is mitigate its effects and technology will get us there.' He paused. 'Geologic sequestration is already proving promising with your firm MGEE has a license to test it in tertiary gas and oil production in Victoria.'

But not in Queensland. Jack gazed at him, face impassive. Here was confirmation of what Roy was doing, pressuring carbon into liquid form and forcing it into porous rock formations in the Clarke River basin to reduce the viscosity of the remaining product. It would certainly help meet the company's carbon reduction requirements and get out any reluctant gas remaining in the rock. No wonder Chad didn't want too many questions asked. If anyone knew, there would be an outcry over the groundwater in the region, especially along the Burdekin River catchment, which fed into the irrigation system of massive swathes of cropping lands. Never mind the illegality of doing it without a licence. He said nothing and waited, hoping to learn more.

Tad grinned. 'It's the technological answer to all our global heating prayers.'

Jack couldn't keep quiet any longer. 'I don't agree sequestration is the answer unless it's in solid form. It has consequences.'

'So, what would you suggest?'

'Trees. Biologic sequestration.'

Hinckler shook his head. 'That'll take too long and now we have new technology for striping carbon out of air.'

'You mean Direct Air Capture. That's a mere gnat fart by comparison with what's required, and the energy it takes is phenomenal. Trees and giant seaweed are cheaper and are available right now. If we make a serious attempt, paired with a reduction in carbon output, we might just avoid disaster. '

'And who is going to pay for that?'

'The Feds.'

'They are in too much debt already.'

Jack shook his head. That's crap and you know it. They issue the debt bonds and create the Australian dollar to buy them back. Debt and deficit, from the Australian government's perspective, are smoke and mirrors to obfuscate a lack of policy vision. But I'm not arguing about politics. Burying carbon in gas form, or even in liquid form, can have huge and dire ramifications for water quality if there is a breach or if there are issues with pressure in the reservoir that exceed sustainable levels. The process can, and has, triggered earthquakes particularly in stressed faults lines.'

He paused, realising that if this is what Roy had been doing for years, it could very well be the cause of the increase in quakes around the Clarke River Basin and along the fault lines.

'So, what's the solution? Nuclear?'

Jack shrugged. 'That's an option, and nuclear technology is improving in safety all the time, but it's expensive and its half-life has caused a storage problem. We've also seen the problems with natural disasters like the Japanese tsunami.' He shook his head. 'I think we need a serious plan that outlines the global steps for a transition. We can't continue with business as usual.'

Pete sat down. 'So says the man drilling for gas. Sorry, I'm late, but I can see you two are finding common ground already.'

Hinckler smiled and responded to Jack's business as usual remark. 'People said that about the pandemic, and yet it hasn't been any time at all since we've returned to normal. We even ignore the mounting deaths from the disease, so long as we aren't forced into another lockdown. It's in our natures to be selfish. Come and work for me Jack, and you can do the research and push your agenda for all its worth.'

Jack paused. Where had that non sequitur come from? He took a sip of the water that the waiter had placed in front of him as he contemplated the offer. It was tempting, although he had never trusted Hinckler, but why? Because of what he represented and who he called his friends. Yet Pete obviously trusted the man and was doing well. Besides, he didn't agree it was natural for humans to be selfish. That description didn't fit with a species that owed their survival and dominance to cooperation for the greater good.

Jack knew very little about *Green Synergy*, with the exception it evaluated environmental impacts, conducted research, provided consulting services, particularly in strategic planning and economic analysis, as well as providing legal representation to mining outfits like MGEE. But it's most public role was lobbying, and in that Tad was a master manipulator of public opinion, seen as Australia's answer to an environmental defender.

Somehow, it didn't add up. The firm represented mining interests and defended mining companies in court over environmental breaches. Jack was a miner. Perhaps his mistrust went with the territory. But it was something else, something to do with Hinckler's own self-interest. His attitude towards expediency was to get what he wanted, and to hell with the cost. Look at that grant he'd secured to mitigate damage to the reef. Hundreds of millions. It was all over the news when it was granted, but what had happened since? Nothing, as far as Jack knew. What was left of the reef had another massive bleaching event a few months ago.

The money could have gone to the university, but they were so strapped for cash they were unable to conduct further research. Yet despite all the government funding being thrown at *Green Synergy*, Hinckler wasn't collaborating or sharing with the research specialists.

Yet, wasn't he as bad, taking money for drilling for gas when he knew it contributed to global warming? The whole thing did his head in.

Hinckler was staring at him, and Jack realised he wanted an answer. 'I've only just started in this job.'

Pete interjected. 'So, it's not a no, then.'

Jack shook his head. 'Let me think about it, but thanks for the offer.'

It was only when he drove back to Julia Creek two days later that Jack remembered the question he wanted to ask about *Paramount Holdings* at Bramston Beach and why there were pins in the map of all the MGEE wells. It was probably not worth bothering about.

Stirring the Past

The spot on the Barnett property, where Jack had first squatted in the shade of that lonely tree in the old watercourse, was now unrecognisable. The tree was all that remained. The rest had been cleared, fenced, and filled with demountable buildings, vehicles, rigs, casings, storage tanks, pumps, mixers, sand, the usual clutter of drilling sites. A wastewater holding dam lay along the north side, and on the west was clean water for use on the site and in the drill, fed from a bore drilled into the aquifer to extract the water.

While the team had already done test drilling, they were about to start a full horizontal bore. Drilling was costly, and if he made a mistake, it would be another black mark for Chad to chalk up against him. But Jack had got to know the crew and respected their ability. They worked hard and efficiently, and although he checked everything; he was certain the steel casings would be properly installed. One of his greatest concerns was contaminating the groundwater. There was no going back from that. The last thing he wanted was to have gas leaks or even have water leaking into gas.

The foreman, Dave, guided the drill expertly, mud pumping until they reached below the water table and into what Jack hoped was the pay zone. By Saturday, water was flowing and then up came the gas. The wellbore was complete, and the rig was being packed for the next job. Jack was light with relief and pride at his first full drill and congratulated the team before he rang Chad.

'Good work Jack. I'll fly out Monday. Can you pick me up from the airport at ten?'

'There won't be many of the crew here, Chad. Most of them are heading out on Sunday for a bit of R and R before they begin the next drill.'

'Never mind, we need to talk about the next site, and I want to see the current site firsthand.'

On Saturday night, the Barnett's threw a party to celebrate, and the men were in high spirits as they piled into the troop carrier, leaving two roustabouts on watch. The whole district had turned out for the BBQ, many camped in Barnett's paddocks for the night. The distances were too great to drive for some, and others didn't want their drinking curtailed by having to drive home.

When Jack arrived with his men, they knew almost no one other than the Barnett's, but that didn't deter Dave, who made a beeline for a group of women near the fire pit. The others trailed behind him.

Jack went up to the house, where he found most of the family. After greetings and small talk were done, he walked out to the veranda. Fergus brought Jack a beer, and they stood in companionable silence, watching the crowd. Dust hung in the air, lit by campfires and strings of party lights. There was a faint waft of roses beneath the smell of smoke and overhead the sky was ablaze with stars.

Skies like this one had always given Jack a sense of purpose in his life, for it was a reminder of his minuscule place within the context of the physical universe that he found fascinating. If he hadn't become ensnared by the earth, he would have studied the universe.

Fergus said, 'Congratulations on the drill.'

'Thanks. One down, several more to go.'

'I didn't know there was to be more than one.'

'The next one will probably be south of here. I have a place pegged near Winton. The boss is coming out on Monday, so I'll find out more then. But I may be on site here for a while yet, at least until we establish the well head.'

They lapsed into silence again, and Fergus took a packet of cigarettes from his pocket. He knocked one out and offered it to Jack.

'No thanks, mate'.

Fergus cupped the lighter flame against the breeze and drew in smoke. He blew out a long stream before he said, 'Winton you say?'

'Probably. Not sure yet.'

'Our Sophia's going to Winton Hospital. Maybe you could visit her.'

'Oh.' Jack remained quiet for a moment before he said, 'What's wrong with her?'

'What?'

'Is she ill?'

'What? Sophia's not ill.'

'Sorry, I just thought...'

Fergus's frown cleared, and he threw back his head. 'That's funny. I'll have to tell her that one.'

A faint memory surfaced of Pete's graduation party when he mentioned she was studying medicine. 'Hell, I forgot. She's a doctor, isn't she?'

Just at that moment, she walked out of the house. 'Hello Fallon, poisoned the Great Artesian Basin yet?'

Jack couldn't help himself. 'Ran into your ex over the weekend.' As soon as the words had left his lips, he wished he could take them back.

'Bastard.' She threw the word over her shoulder and sauntered towards the group by the fire-pit.

He noticed Dave move closer; his head bent as if listening to something she said.

Fergus grinned. 'No points for diplomacy then.'

Jack scowled. 'What about her crack?'

'Touchy, but mate, you'd better be careful, or people will think you're an item, the way you speak to each other.' He paused before asking, 'Do you have a girl?'

Jack shook his head. He'd never been in a place where there were many available women and although he had had lots of dates, usually set up by Tess, they didn't count as *having a girl* whatever that meant. He thought of Samantha, but one date didn't make a girlfriend, even a friend, although they had a follow-up date for next Saturday. 'No.' He paused, supposing he should explain, but asked instead, 'what about you?'

'Ho, you're not propositioning me, are you?'

'Fuck off Fergus.'

'Just checking. You never can tell nowadays. Not that it's a problem, only I have a girl, so sorry mate.' He grinned. 'But seriously, wish me luck. I'm planning to ask her to marry me tonight.' He pulled a small square box from his pocket.

'Wow.' Jack hadn't noticed Fergus with anyone before, although he hadn't seen much of him since he'd been here drilling.

'Yep, Barb Miller. Herb Miller's daughter, next station over. Haven't you met her?'

'No.'

'Come on, we'll have to rectify that. Last I saw, Barb was in the kitchen with Mum. I'll introduce you now.'

Jack followed Fergus through the house to the kitchen, where he was introduced to a pretty blonde, with a compact body and hair swinging in a bob around her jaw. Her face was hot from the oven, and she wiped her forearm across her forehead and grinned at Jack.

'Heard all about you from Sophia.' She turned to Fergus. 'She didn't say he was such a handsome fellow.' She reached up and touched his face. 'Not as handsome as you, though.'

Fergus put his arm around her shoulders. He looked proud and Jack felt a shaft of envy. He'd never minded being alone but seeing the domestic happiness on Fergus's face was like a curtain opening on a similar scene from the distant past.

An image arose of his mum and dad holding each other in the kitchen. He remembered being embarrassed and had gone into his bedroom to get away from the obvious intimacy. That was before she'd disappeared without a word to anyone, not even her best friend. There were rumours she was seen at the airport and had left the country, although the police said there was no record of her leaving. The case had gone cold, and Jack had packed her memory away in a locked box buried in his subconscious. He certainly didn't want to think about her now, or ever for that matter. Even after all these years, the hole she had left was better left capped. He sometimes wondered if he would ever trust anyone enough to marry them.

Isabella said, 'Coming through.' She held a large metal tray with steaks and sausages.

'Let me take that for you.'

'Such a gentleman.' Isabella said, relinquishing the tray.

Jack was glad to have an excuse to get out of the kitchen and he walked outside to the BBQ where he placed the tray on the table next to Barnett.

'I see Isabella has you working already. Take note, Jack, this is how to cook a decent steak.'

When the meat was done, Jack helped Barnett carry it over to tables loaded with salads, bread, and other stuff, some of which he recognised, some he didn't. Jim called out for people to help themselves and handed Jack a plate. 'Cooks get first choice,' he said.

Jack gratefully loaded his plate with steak and salad. He was starving. He found a chair and sat down to eat.

Sophia plonked down next to him. 'Sorry I made that crack. Dave told me how conscientious you are...taking baseline measurements of air, water, soil, and aquifer water quality before you began drilling. Your men really like you.'

Jack chewed for a minute. Swallowed, contemplated apologising for his retort when she said, 'How was Pete?'

He glanced at her face. Was she still in love with the bastard? He shrugged. 'He was Pete, prosperous and full of it. Like he's always been.'

'Did he mention me?'

Jack shook his head.

'Liar.'

'Okay, he called you a psycho. Is that what you wanted to hear?'

'Doesn't surprise me. Why do you hate me, Jack?'

He stopped eating. 'What the hell are you talking about?'

'You treat me like I'm a poisonous snake that you need to stay well away from. Do you think I'm a psycho too? Actually, I wouldn't blame you. I know I haven't been at my best when you've been around, but I would like to be friends. Maybe you could show me around the site. Convince me it's environmentally safe. I would feel better if I knew it was.'

Jack put his plate on the ground by his feet. 'When?'

'Next week?'

Music drifted out from the house as someone turned on a streaming service to country rock.

'My boss is here next week.'

'Next weekend then. After that, I'll be in Winton.'

'Sorry, I have to go to Townsville.'

'What for? Ah, damn it. Didn't mean to pry. How about now?'

'It's dark.' There were lighting towers, but he didn't tell her that.

She looked up. 'There's a moon rising and lots of stars. I can see okay, and you can explain how it all works.'

'What about the party?'

'They won't miss us, look the dancing's started. Soon they'll be whooping and hollering.' She paused. 'Oh sorry, you might want to stay here and dance with someone.'

What he wanted to do was take her back to camp and have her all to himself, although he didn't think that was going to happen ever. Still, it would be awkward. He had a flash of guilt over Samantha, but they'd only ever gone on one date. Yet he knew she was expecting more. What was he thinking? Sophia wasn't interested, hadn't recovered from Pete's betrayal, but he didn't think any of it was a good idea.

He shook his head. 'Country rock is not my thing.'

'What is?'

'Don't know. Rock I guess.'

'Like whom?'

Jack drew a breath. Earlier today he'd been listening to Rival Sons through headphones, so that's who he said he liked. 'What about you?'

'I like classical music the most, then jazz, then alternative rock.'

'I don't mind jazz.' He remembered his mother had loved jazz. 'I don't know much about classical music, but I don't like this sentimental country stuff much.'

'Fergus loves it. That's why it's playing now. You know he's going to ask his girlfriend to marry him tonight?'

'I thought it was a secret.'

'Ha! Even Barb knows although she'll pretend it's a surprise. They'll do well together.'

They fell into silence watching the dancers, until she said, 'Well are you going to show me or not?'

Twenty minutes later, they drove into the mining compound and pulled up outside the demountable that acted as an office. One of the roustabouts came out. Jack got out of the car and spoke to him, then turned back to the car as Sophia got out. He walked around the car towards her. 'We can walk or drive around. Which would you prefer?'

'Let's walk. It's a lovely cool night and you lied. There are more lights here than on Brisbane's Storey Bridge.'

They walked across the flat gravelled ground, while Jack pointed to different buildings and machinery explaining their uses. 'We need all these trucks to bring in the equipment, heaters, hydration trucks, and pressure pumps. We'll erect the gas storage tanks also.

'So, what's a hydration truck when it's home?'

'The hydration truck mixes water, sand and chemicals and sends the mixture down the well'.

'I thought you said you didn't use chemicals?'

'We have to use some chemicals but they're not bad ones, just things like guar gum, which is the same stuff you eat in food. We mix it with water to help its viscosity because when it's thicker, it does a better job of carrying sand and dispersing it in the cracks. We don't want it to rush and settle at the base of the vertical shaft. Ah yes, there is also a bit of an anti-bacterial gel. Bacteria build-up can cause deadly gasses. The stuff we pump down the well ends up being a lot like that play-slime for kids. Anyway, the trucks carry the chemicals, sand, and the mixing machinery. We heat water from that well over there.' He pointed to a wellhead some distance away. 'So, at least we don't have to truck in water. It's pumped at high pressure down the well.'

'So why pump the stuff down the well. I don't get how that does anything and what's fracking?'

'If it's needed, we can place a manifold around the wellhead and then pump fracking fluid, the slimy stuff, into the well and it goes down with shit-loads of horsepower to get the right pressure.'

'What for?'

'The pressure cracks the rocks, and the silica gel-mix settles in the fissures to hold them open. It allows gas, trapped in shale, to escape.'

'It sounds lethal. How long does it all take?'

'The gas doesn't flow until we release the pressure by withdrawing the water that's been pumped down. Once all the preliminaries are done, a frac can take an hour and we may have to do several of them, sometimes as many as twenty.'

'And then what happens to the water?'

'It's stored in those tailing dams.'

'For how long?'

'As long as it needs to be.'

'I don't understand.'

'Well, it's polluted, so unless it's treated, it can't be released.'

'Polluted? I thought you didn't use bad chemicals.'

'We don't but the water comes up from ancient rock, bringing with it leached minerals and salts, lithium, radium, and that sort of thing. It's a problem.

'So, it just sits here forever?'

'No, we'll pump it back when we finish, but new technologies are using a process of membrane filtration to separate some commercially useful stuff like lithium. If we can render the water clean enough, it can be used for crops and environmental water. But after we cap the well, most of this stuff will go, except the storage tanks. The trucks will make periodic visits to collect the accumulated gas, which in the interim will be stored in those tanks. The tanks will remain at least until a pipeline is built and I'm not sure if they'll do that in the short term. I'll be gone in a couple of days and the only time you'll be bothered by me is when I do the rounds to check on things.'

She gazed at the well. 'Is that where you will frac.'

'We've already done that and there is no need for anything more. At the moment, the gas flow is good.'

'Is that unusual?'

'It's complicated.' He glanced at her, wondering if she was really interested or just making small talk, but he didn't want to explain. It would take all night.

'Alright, you can buy me a beer now, or a coffee, if that's all you have.'

Jack glanced around. 'The mess is closed.'

'Don't you have a place?'

'Yeah, but it's a bit basic.'

'That's okay. Do you have beer?'

'I think so.'

'Well, come on then.'

They walked back towards the accommodation area. Jack's donga was at the farthest end with a small veranda, a consideration not of rank but because he was there most of the time. Most of the others were either FIFOs or contractors, on-site for short periods at a time, or only for the job they needed to do.

He went inside to get the beers, hoping she would stay outside. His room was a mess, bed unmade, his clothes from the day in a heap on the bathroom floor.

'You're an untidy bugger,' she said, standing so close behind him, he could almost feel her breath.

He took two beers out of the fridge and said, 'We should go outside.'

She followed him out, and they sat on the steps. They drank in silence, his brooding, hers radiating a calm that he wished he could share. It seemed so peaceful. He sighed, releasing all the tension he hadn't realised he was holding on to and leaned back to gaze at the stars. The night sky was still, and despite the floodlights, the Milky Way shimmered in its depths.

She broke the silence. 'What happened to your mother, Jack?'

Does she ever stop with the questions? He sat up straight, downed his beer, and placed the empty bottle on the step. 'Come on, finish your beer and I'll take you home. They'll be sending out search parties before long.'

She laid her hand on his arm, leaned over, and brushed his shoulder with her cheek, like a cat. 'Sorry. I know I shouldn't pry.'

He got up and walked to the car.

That night, Jack's dreams were haunted by the past, Barry Fallon holding his young son's shoulder as they walked into the police station in the local village. In Jack's hand, he clutched a tiny golden bucket, a charm he'd found on the floor. He knew it belonged to his mother's bracelet.

Earlier, the eleven-year-old Jack had let himself into the silent house. He threw his school bag down and kicked off his boots before padding into the kitchen. Empty. Strange. He opened the fridge, and glanced over his shoulder, before sliding out the remains of his birthday cake. He carried the cake through to the sitting room and turned on the television.

Barry Fallon arrived an hour later. 'Where's your mother?'

Jack shrugged and returned his focus to the telly.

'When did you get home?'

'Usual time.' Jack said.

'Was your mother here?'

Jack shook his head, a little scared at his dad's tone.

'Was Noddy working on the kennels?'

Another head shake.

'Tch, lazy bastard.' Barry sucked his teeth. 'What the hell are all these crumbs? Go get the vacuum, then do your homework.'

Barry switched off the television and sat down on the sofa, a frown on his face.

Jack stopped. There was something glinting under the sofa.

Outside, the dogs whined, and Barry got up to tend to them. He saw Jack dawdling. 'Are your ears painted on? I said go and get the vacuum.' He walked out and Jack bent to retrieve the tiny golden bucket.

The Road to Damascus

The next morning Jack awoke, groggy and disoriented. He forced coffee into his system and drove to the airport at Julia Creek. There wasn't much to the airport other than baking bitumen, cyclone fencing, and a corrugated iron shed that acted at a terminal.

Right on time, the company plane touched down and after a few minutes Chad swung into the shed. He saw Jack standing near the desk and said, 'I can't stay long. I have to fly back this afternoon, but that's enough time to take a gander at the site.'

'Sure.' Jack felt the load lift from his shoulders. He had thought he'd be spending days with Chad, but he could handle a few hours. 'We can only get to the Barnett's site in that time.'

'I'll catch the Winton site next time when I am not so pushed, but I have a meeting with some international players. The boss is bringing them in for a meeting.'

Jack realised he was required to look impressed and made an attempt, although it felt more like a grimace. He gave up, took Chad's bag, and said, 'Car is this way.'

After they had toured the Barnett site and returned to Julia Creek, Chad said, 'Good progress. You deserve a few days R and R before you crack the next well.'

Jack took his opportunity. 'I was hoping to get up to Townsville for the weekend.'

'Okay. While you're up, we can discuss carbon mitigation strategies. The government's becoming a bit demanding on that front. Keep going like this, Jack and you'll become a valuable member of the team.'

There it was again. This thing about teams. His job was one of isolation, using his brain and his education to determine what might be under the ground and how best to extract it. Yet Chad expected him to be a team player. What the hell did he think being a team member meant? ·

Ed had once said it was all about fitting in and keeping your mouth shut. He gave an example of when there was an investigations into bad policing, it only took one or two corrupt cops to instil widespread fear. Good cops became afraid to speak out about corruption. Their silence was touted as loyalty and fidelity to the team and to breach that loyalty was to be ostracised. It was a powerfully coercive tool.

Jack decided he should probably keep those thoughts to himself. 'I'll drive into Townsville in a day or two, but I'll check on the Winton site before I leave.'

'Good man. So, got a date with that hot chick you took to dinner? Take an extra couple of days and come to the house for a BBQ on Sunday. Bring Samantha. That was her name, wasn't it?

'You've a good memory Chad.'

'She was something to remember.'

They fell silent for a while before Chad, as if he was speaking his thoughts aloud, said, 'Yes you've certainly done a good job here. I must admit we were a bit worried about hiring you, and Roy said you were a bit soft, but all I've seen is good work, despite my earlier misgivings about where you placed your loyalty.'

Jack placed his faith in math and science, seldom people. He saw Chad off with a sense of relief. The man set his teeth on edge. He'd known they were hesitant about hiring him, but it surprised him that Roy had white-anted him. He didn't think that was Roy's style, but he also knew that to Chad and some of the others, relationships were about unstinting loyalty. Yet, Jack hadn't met many people he would trust enough.

After he dropped Chad off he drove to the new site near Winton. The sun was the colour of corn-silk as it sank toward the western plains. Kangaroos scattered in front of him, and an emu raced along the road. His mobile rang and the automatic hands-free, picked up. It was Ed calling to say he'd followed up the witness statement for Jack's accident and it checked out.

Jack said, 'Hang on. I'll pull over.' He stopped on the hard shoulder, his mind reeling. The more time that had passed since the accident, the more he began to believe he'd imagined the whole thing. Was that possible? 'Did you speak to the witness?'

'No mate just spoke to the copper, and he emailed the statement.'

'What was the witness's name?'

'Olaf Oerlemans.'

The name meant nothing to Jack, except it sounded Dutch or German, maybe Scandinavian. 'Did you ask the copper about the car? There must have been some damage where the truck clipped me.'

Ed was silent for a moment. 'Sorry mate. He said there was nothing inconsistent with a single vehicle rollover.'

'Shit. Can you speak to the witness?'

'He's still overseas, apparently.'

'Ed, you do believe me?'

'Of course, but mate, there's no evidence of a crime, nothing I can do. You have to understand my position.'

Jack sighed. 'Yeah, thanks. I appreciate you trying.'

He hung up and pulled back onto the deserted road. As he drove he shredded memories, searching for clues, and motives. In no time at all, the lights of Winton appeared. He was approaching the home of Waltzing Matilda, dinosaur fossils, and Qantas.

As he drove through the town, he noticed a sign pointing to the hospital. Opposite the sign was a right turn into the new Damascus Development Road, which he took. The hospital sign reminded him of his promise to visit Sophia. 'Damn it.' He didn't want to think about her. When he had dropped her off at the party after the tour of the well site, he could barely speak to her.

She had opened her door and said, Are you angry with me, Jack?

He had shaken his head, terrified if he gave her an opening, she would be in there with her scalpel, hauling out long-suppressed fragments of his life he didn't want exposed to the light.

He didn't want it rushing back. Stupid childhood memories. Visions of his mother incarcerated in an immigration detention centre by error, or abducted by aliens, not so ridiculous for a kid to believe. Then he had read about psychotropic fugues and decided that's what had happened to her. She had merely gone out shopping and lost all memory of her past life, setting up a new existence somewhere. The school counsellor ruined that idea, explaining that fugue states were very unusual, and his mother would have been unlikely to suffer such long-term dissociation. After that, he never went near the counsellor again.

It was probably wise not to get too near Sophia, either. At the time he dropped her off at the party, he had made some lame excuse like he was tired, said goodnight, and had driven off. He shook his head. He didn't want to think about his mum or Sophia right now, but neither did he want to think about what Ed had said.

He turned his mind to the geology of the land in front of him. The early Cretaceous period had left behind different sedimentary rocks such as sandstone, siltstone and claystone in an area once filled by the Eromanga Sea into which rivers as big as the Amazon had once emptied. This was where dinosaurs had roamed through giant forests and swamps, and where gas now lurked in abundance within deep sediment folds. If he was lucky, he might even find commercially viable quantities of oil.

After checking the drill site, he drove back to town and checked into a motel. It was adequate and had air-conditioning, which was all he really wanted. He flicked on the TV to the 24-hour news channel. The Prophets had blocked the street leading to MGEE's office tower again. That would have Chad frothing at the mouth. The protesters had taken a leaf out of Extinction Rebellion's copybook and chained ankles to posts and glued hands to the bitumen. That had to be uncomfortable.

He turned off the TV and picked up his phone to flick through Twitter. It was like leafing through a magazine, a mindless pastime, until he saw an article about the collapse of the last remaining piece of the Larsen B Ice Shelf on the Antarctic Peninsula. He shut his phone and lay back on the bed.

The climate was changing faster than anyone had predicted, and he was part of it. He could no longer fool himself. He'd been wrong about a lot of things lately, like how his accident had occurred, but he knew that individual actions and collective street protests would do nothing to change the trajectory the earth was on. There was just too much money involved. Countries went to war over smaller issues. Only the collective goodwill of brave politicians could really make a difference. What was one man's action against a rising tide of business as usual? If he didn't do what he was doing, someone else would, and where would that leave him? Without a job, that was where, and the climate would continue its flight into destruction.

'Shit!' He sat up. He was fooling himself. He opened his phone again and rang Pete. 'Pete, mate, is that job still on offer?'

Samantha was furious when, a few days later, he told her he was moving to Cairns.

She sulked. 'I thought you were going to flat share with me.'

'We still can. You can move to Cairns.'

'You arsehole. You think your job is more important than mine?'

'No, course not, but I can't share a flat with you in Townsville if I'm living in Cairns. I'm just pointing out options. You can get a job easily at the Cairns Base hospital...Look, I didn't mean to demean your career. Being a doctor is a lot more important than my job. It's just that... hell... It was a stupid, thoughtless thing to say. I'm sorry.'

She relented then. They were getting ready to go to Chad's house party, and Jack hadn't yet told his boss he had another job offer. 'You won't mention this, will you? I haven't handed in my resignation yet, and Chad will be wild. I'd rather do it at work tomorrow, let the missiles ruin his office rather than his party.' He let out a sigh. 'It's all been a bit rushed you know. The decision, and the offer, happened quickly. I haven't had time to think.'

'Well, perhaps you will change your mind.' She wrapped her slim arms around him and pressed against his groin.' Just think what you'll be missing.'

He groaned. 'I can still come to Townsville, just as much as I could from out bush.'

'Then flat share.'

He gazed at her. 'I have a place in Cairns. I bought it as an investment years ago and still have a mortgage to pay off. I'll be living in it during the week, so renting another apartment in Townsville might be a stretch, especially as I can only come to Townsville for the weekends. You could come and live in my flat. You'd love it. It has a great view of the marina.'

She flounced away and picked up her handbag.

'It's not the same.'

'Okay. Why don't you advertise for a flatmate, then?'

'Oh, you'll never understand. Come on, let's get going. We'll be late.'

At the party, Samantha ignored Jack and flirted outrageously with Chad. Jack watched, wryly wondering why it didn't bother him. Samantha was clever, beautiful, sexy, and she found him attractive, but he didn't think there was a future to their relationship. Maybe she and Chad would have a better chance. A thought intruded, and he wondered if Samantha had always only wanted a flatmate. But why sleep with him? He shook his head and walked over to speak with Roy.

'Hey Roy. How are you doing?'

Roy looked uncomfortable and muttered. 'Not bad. Got a bit of indigestion. Excuse me.' He went off into the house and left Jack sitting alone. Seemed no one wanted to be seen talking with him, well they wouldn't have to for long.

The next morning, Jack handed Chad his report on the Barnett Station well's productivity and an update on the Winton site. There was not much to say since Chad had only visited a few days before, but Jack wanted to soften him up before he handed in his resignation.

When he did, Chad was not as angry as Jack imagined he would be. Nor did he seem surprised. 'You can work a month's notice and do a handover to Roy before you go.'

'To Roy...? I thought he was retiring.'

'Well, you thought wrong. You seem to get a lot wrong, Fallon.' He picked up the report. 'I presume this is accurate.'

Jack nodded. He couldn't expect the bloke to be happy. He summoned courage. The company should know what was going on in Roy's region and even if they didn't believe him, or if they already knew, at least he would have a clear conscience. 'I've been noticing an increase in seismic activity.'

Two white blotches shone in the dull red of Chad's cheeks. Jack paused knowing he was stepping into dangerous territory. He took a breath and continued. 'I checked out some data and there has been an exponential increase in activity at the northern region of the Thomson-Orogen fold, east of the Greenvale province along the Lynd Mylonite Zone.' He got up to point out the area on the wall map. 'There is a correlation coefficient of 0.9 with the sinking of each of the wells in Roy's region.'

'What are you blathering on about? That's Roy's area you're pointing at.'

'That's the point. This area has these intersecting fault lines I think might...'

Chad interrupted. 'You think this will be the place to drill?'

'Ah, no that was...'

'For fuck's sake, man, spit it out.'

'It's where there is an increasing cluster of seismic activity occurring and I reckon it could have something to do with Roy's fracking.'

'What?' Chad's face reddened further. 'What the fuck has Roy said? I think this discussion ends now; you hear. You'll start a panic. Tell me about your region, and what you're doing to get the quantities you're achieving. You must be doing something. How else are you managing to get the flow rates your well is producing?'

'Look Chad, the data shows a sixfold increase in the region and...

'Enough Jack! Everyone knows correlation is not causation. This is an old volcanic region, so what do you think? There are bound to be earthquakes and earthquake clusters from time to time. The plate's under pressure. The 2009 quake moved New Zealand's South Island 30 centimetres closer to Australia after that 7.8 magnitude earthquake in the Puysegur subduction zone, so there's bound to be a bit of give here and there for a while. The whole fucking fold is under stress from the Pacific Plate and that's nothing to do with our operations. Fuck the seismic activity. I want to know what you're doing.' His finger jabbed at the air.

Jack held his nerve. 'My concern is that the activity is spreading. There are more quakes around Gibson Reef. I know that is not Roy's area, but I am concerned that the activity in these fault lines may be affecting areas around the continental shelf. That's risky because there are large, eroded outcrops along that shelf, and it wouldn't take much to create a land slip.'

'Fallon. Stop. Your area's production figures! Talk to me about them.' Chad was shouting now. 'I don't want to hear anything else. Just get to the fucking figures... explain what you are doing.'

'Nothing Chad, I'm doing nothing out of the ordinary. I find the deposits, negotiate contracts, do the design and modelling work, coordinate the teams, write your reports, and make sure of the project's safety. I'm not a chemical engineer. I don't mix fracking fluid, nor do I carry out drilling work. I've got good production sites, it's nothing unusual. Gas from shale is notoriously short-lived, unless you're very lucky, and I don't know if mine will continue producing the way they've started. They could go the way that Roy's have gone sooner than you think.' An idea dawned on him. 'Before I go, I could do some exploration with Roy and see if there might be better spots to drill. I seem to have a knack for finding good deposits.' He held his breath, waiting for Chad's response.

Chad seemed to calm down. 'You'll only have a month. That's not much time, but maybe Tad can wait...' He leaned back in his chair; his mouth pursed in thought.

Chad's silence encouraged Jack, and he said, 'Roy's sites haven't been producing for years and are probably nearly depleted. He needs new sites, and I can help. That terrain is fairly rugged, but I grew up in that sort of country. I know it well.'

'Oh yeah, that's right, Samantha said you're some kind of hillbilly?'

Jack maintained his calm although he'd have liked to punch Chad in his fake-tanned face. He looked at the floor and breathed evenly.

'I'll talk to Roy, but now fuck off out of my office. I've got work and you're in my way.'

It was only later Jack remembered that Chad had said, *Tad would have to wait.* What did he mean? Jack didn't remember telling Chad he was going to be working for Tad, although he might have mentioned *Green Synergy*. He shook his head. Was his memory getting worse? He rang Samantha, but she said she had to work, so Jack went back to his motel.

At about 7.30 pm, he walked along the Strand, looking for somewhere to get a decent meal before he went back to Winton. It was Monday night, and most restaurant were closed, but he could see one in the distance, lit up behind a copse of trees. The aroma of brine and algae wafted from the sea front, mingling with the scent of flowering Melaleucas overhead. Waves lapped and gurgled against the concrete sea walls.

It was a pleasant evening, and he wished Samantha hadn't had to work. It would have been nice to have her company even if she was mad at him for going to live in Cairns. It crossed his mind that maybe she had said something to Chad about his resignation and going to work for Tad, but surely not. He had specifically asked her not to.

As he approached the restaurant, he saw two familiar figures walking up the steps to the entrance. It was Samantha, arm in arm with Chad. Her long slender legs tottered on those unmistakable heels, her curvaceous form squeezed in a figure-hugging dress he'd not seen before, red, and backless. Chad's hairy arm, protruding from a wild Hawaiian shirt, was clamped around her waist.

Rage surged into his throat, and he choked it back. He didn't own her; she could see whomsoever she pleased. Why was he angry? He didn't love her or hadn't really thought about love. Chad's party should have been fair warning, although she didn't have to lie and say she was working. So much for that relationship then. Perhaps she would get a flat mate after all, one who lived in Townsville, and already had a very swanky house. He turned and walked off in the other direction. He was no longer hungry.

Over the next few weeks, Jack finalised his hand over, said his goodbyes to the teams and went to see the Barnett's telling them he was leaving. They made him promise to come back for a visit and to stay in touch. He promised, but it was just what people did. He didn't expect to see them again, and he felt a slow kind of sadness creeping up on him.

Fergus said, 'Have you told Sophia?'

Jack shook his head. He hadn't seen Sophia since the night of the BBQ when he'd shown her around the site.

'You'd better say goodbye, mate, if not for your sake, at least for ours. Sophia doesn't tolerate people she likes disappearing from her life. She'll make my life miserable unless you go and see her. You'll do it, won't you, please Jack?'

'Okay. I've got to go back to Winton again, so I'll call her then.'

He drove away from the station, wondering why Fergus was so insistent. It was not like he and Sophia were friends. He hardly knew her.

Two days later, he rang Winton hospital and asked to speak to her.

The first question she asked was, 'Where are you?'

'At the motel.'

'Come for dinner tonight.'

'All right. Where?'

She gave him the address.

The sun was low on the horizon when he pulled into her driveway. She was standing at the screen door with her foot caught behind the calf of her other leg, feet bare and hair loose around her shoulders. She had on a white shirt and straight grey skirt that looked like a regular work outfit.

'I didn't know what you liked.' He held out a six-pack of beers in one hand and a bottle of white wine in the other.'

She took the wine. 'You have the beer.'

'I'm driving.'

'One won't hurt.'

He followed her inside. An opera played in the background. It was nice, but he had no idea what it was. The house was old colonial in style, high-ceilinged with a large screened concrete veranda. Inside, wooden floorboards creaked as he stepped on them. There was very little by way of furniture, no curtains, or carpets, or any of the comforts he would have expected she would want.

'Sorry, the house is a bit spartan. I'm at the hospital most of the time, so I don't mind much. This is the official doctor's residence, but I haven't had time to make it comfortable. I guess it was built at a time when doctors had stay at home wives to do that kind of thing, but I'm not here for long, anyway.'

'I thought you had moved here.'

'No, it's just a locum position until I figure out what I want to do. I was thinking of specialising in obstetrics, but I don't know. Fergus said you are leaving. You didn't stay with your company for very long. Is that a common trait?'

He bristled. 'What's that supposed to mean?'

'Sorry, that was horrible.' She ran her hand through her hair. ' Damn it Fallon, I can never say the right thing to you, can I?'

He relaxed. 'My guilt caught up with me.'

'What does that mean?'

'Can't keep on polluting mother earth's atmosphere with greenhouse gasses. When I was last in Cairns, Tad Hinckler offered me a job and I accepted.'

'That crook.'

'What?'

'Tad Hinckler is a crook.'

'Last time he offered me a job, you called him an environmental defender and me a vandal. *Pillager of the earth,* I think were your exact words.'

'Did I say that? When?'

'At Pete's graduation party.'

'You remember that?'

'I do. I was hurt.'

She laughed. 'Crikey, how many years ago was that? Since I first met you, I've been saying things to upset you.'

He followed her through the house to the kitchen, where she took two glasses from a cupboard, pouring wine into one. 'Do you want a glass of wine or beer? I warn you dinner isn't much, just a supermarket chook and salad. I think it's called a bachelor's handbag.'

Jack smiled at the term. 'That's fine, and I will have a beer, but I don't need a glass. Thanks.'

She put the remaining wine and the beers in the fridge and walked to the back door. 'Let's sit outside while the sun goes down.'

'What is this music?'

She paused; her head cocked to one side. 'The Marriage of Figaro. This track is *Dove sono I bei momenti* or where are those shining moments?' She translated for him.

They sat on the back steps and, as they sipped their drinks, they watched the sun sink in the west. Dust hung like mist over bare ground. Occasional tussocks of grass, sprouted patchily through some new green shoots from the recent rains. Beyond the yard fence, an Australian bustard stalked across the vacant ground searching for grasshoppers, its grey-brown feathers ruffling in the breeze, its neck held still as if posing for them.

Gradually night fell and one by one stars came out like pinpoints in the dark mantel. Jack finished his beer and placed the bottle on the step next to him. This was the most peaceful he'd felt in a long time.

She shivered. 'It's getting chilly. Let's go in and get some dinner.'

She served up two plates and told him where the cutlery was. As she carried the plates through to the dining room, she called for him to bring the wine and another glass.

She poured them both a glass of wine. He was going to object, then thought what the hell, one more drink wouldn't hurt.

She changed the music. 'This one's Madam Butterfly. I always think it's so poignant.'

The dinner was just as she had said, supermarket chook and salad, but he didn't mind. The atmosphere made it seem delicious.

'When are you leaving?' she asked.

'I go to Roy's area near Charters Towers tomorrow. I'm going to look over some seismic profiles with him, see if I can find more gas deposits, or that is what Chad wants me to do.'

'What do you want to do?'

'You get to the point quickly, don't you? He smiled. He wanted to confide in her, but he barely knew her, and cast around for a new subject. 'What about you?'

'What do I want or when am I leaving?'

He felt the heat in his neck. 'I don't know, I guess both.'

'I have another month here, and then I don't know. Maybe Brisbane.'

'Is that where you were before?'

'No. I was at Townsville hospital before.'

'Of course. You were there with Pete.'

She sighed. 'Don't remind me.'

'Sorry.'

'It's alright. I'm over him and his betrayal. In fact, I'm glad he showed his true colours before I married him. What about you, Jack? Do you have someone?'

He hesitated. 'No.'

She tilted her head. 'That sounds like you aren't sure.'

He smiled. 'You don't miss much, do you?'

'Well...'

'I did, or thought I had, but I was wrong.'

'Who was she, or he?'

He looked at her across the table. What the hell, they had to talk about something. It may as well be his appalling love life. 'She was my doctor.'

'That's not very ethical.'

He laughed. 'I had a car accident and met her while I was in Townsville hospital. We only dated a few times...'

'And what happened?'

'She found someone else.'

Sophia gazed at Jack for a long minute before she said, 'Her name is not Samantha, by any chance?'

'Don't tell me you know her.'

Sophia pressed her lips together. 'There are not many unmarried women doctors at the hospital. It wasn't a hard guess, and we shared a flat.' She paused as if weighing up something. Then she said, 'She was the person I found Pete in bed with.'

Jack drank his wine and poured another. 'I wish I had known.'

She looked at him with sympathy. 'At least you know you are better off without her. Who has she taken off with now?'

'Chad, my boss.'

Sophia laughed. 'Sorry, I shouldn't laugh but you don't like your boss, do you? Serve him right. She's a viper.' A thoughtful look crossed her face, and she said, 'finish your wine.'

She went to a cabinet, opened it, and pulled out an unopened bottle of very expensive looking single malt in a teardrop shaped bottle. '*Glenglassaugh 50-Year-Old Single Malt Scotch* Whisky,' she read off the label. 'This belonged to her. I stole it when I left. It was given to her by some rich dude she dated and it's worth thousands. She said, ten grand, but I am not sure I believe her. But fair game, I reckon. Payment for my fiancé.' She took off the top and poured some into his empty glass, then her own. She placed the bottle back on the table and said, 'Cheers.'

He picked up his own glass. 'Isn't it a sacrilege to pour whisky into a wine glass, especially one that's had wine in it?'

She shrugged, sculled hers and blinked, then said, 'Oh its rather fine. You should savour it.'

'I warn you, if I drink this, I will officially be over the limit and I will blame you.'

'You can crash on the sofa. Drink and we'll have another.'

Jack woke up next morning with a rig trying to drill its way out of his skull. Sophia was sprawled naked next to him. *Oh crap, what have I done now?* He slid off the bed, not wanting to wake her, picked up his clothes and tiptoed to the bathroom. When he came out, she was still asleep.

He walked towards the front door and stopped. He couldn't just walk out and pretend nothing had happened. He turned around and went back to the bedroom door. She was still out for the count, on her stomach, her arm hanging over the edge, her feet in the space he had vacated. A strand of hair, thick and dark blond with that hint of the strawberry her mum had said gave her a temper, lay across her mouth, lifting with every breath from her slack, partly opened mouth. He lifted it and laid it back across her shoulder.

She murmured and licked her lips, then scrunched into a ball on her side, knees to her stomach.

He glanced at his watch: 5:30 am. It was too early to wake her, so he went through to the kitchen and looked in the cupboards for coffee making and headache relieving ingredients. He found both, and five minutes later sat on the back doorstep, with the kitchen door open at his back, sipping his coffee and reading the news on his phone.

Headlines on the ABC app read, Massive Fish Kill off FNQ Coast.

A massive fish kill off the North Queensland coast between Cairns and Innisfail has been attributed to a recent earthquake off the coast north of Innisfail.

Thousands of belly-up fish were discovered yesterday morning by a marine biologist who lives in the area and was walking his dog along the beach at Flying Fish point. Dr Daniel Brigslow says the last time he saw something similar was off the coast of India, where a toxic algae bloom caused the death of thousands of fish. Dr Brigslow said, he's never seen anything like it along this coast, which is usually teaming with life in the clear protected waters of the Barrier Reef.

Yesterday Geo-science expert Professor Vernon Prentice speculated that the 3.1 earthquake off the coast of Innisfail two days ago, may have caused a methane leak creating low-oxygen conditions. Dr. Brigslow agreed with Professor Prentice that the kill might have been as a result of the earthquake, or it could be some other toxic run off from agricultural or mining chemicals. A Government spokesperson said, the cause of the massive kill would be investigated.

Jack stopped reading, looked at his watch again, and decided he would call Vernon later, but today he needed to get to Roy's area and have a look at what was really going on in his area. Was the fish kill a natural phenomenon or something else?

At that moment, Sophia walked into the kitchen. 'Oh, you are here. I thought you had buggered off without saying goodbye.'

Part Two

A New Start.

J ack had only been with *Green Synergy* for a few months, and life was looking good. He had finally taken possession of, and moved into, his very comfortable penthouse overlooking the marina, and work was a delightful morning stroll along the shoreline from his home.

Then a second fish die off hit the headlines. The deaths came on top of another reef bleaching, and the federal Government was under siege, not just from international bodies like the UNESCO World Heritage Centre, but closer to home. There was an election on the horizon and both environmentalists and the fishing industry were demanding answers. *Green Synergy* received a massive grant to investigate and stop whatever it was that was killing the fish.

Tad Hinckler, Jack's new boss, had given Jack the responsibility of coordinating the project, saying, 'You're the only Ph.D. on the payroll and we'll need to convince people we have the boffins to do the job. To date, Jack had found the work required a great deal of research and some project management, although no financial management responsibilities.

Determining the cause of the fish kill wasn't his area of expertise, but how hard could it be? This was project management 1-0-1, and he could do that in his sleep. He would find the various experts and leave them to do their jobs. All he had to do was recruit them, coordinate their activities, and report on their findings. He would need soil and farm run-off testing, water quality testing, and air testing around fault lines onshore. It might be toxic runoff from a swamp or something else entirely. He would keep an open mind despite Vernon's assertion it could be the result of seismic activity.

Vernon's initial theory that gasses, such as carbon dioxide or methane, might be leaking from a fault offshore was a distinct possibility and if that was the case he may also find leaks around other fault lines on shore. He'd already organised sampling of dead fish for post-mortems, or whatever marine biologists might call it, but most of all he was hankering to get the university involved with another look at the ocean floor, particularly along the continental shelf. If this was a seismic problem in relation to earthquakes, he wanted to know, although he wasn't banking on it.

A Trichodesmium, or sea scum algal bloom, had occurred a few weeks ago and pink scum was still washing up on Cairns northern beaches. Large quantities of the algae may also have caused the fish deaths, although it seemed unlikely as fish usually had enough sense to avoid algal blooms, if there was a way around them.

The disturbing mass of pink scum on popular tourist beaches had caused other problems. The Prophets were outraged and had moved to Cairns en-masse, plastering biblical tracts all over the city, stating that: *at the end-of-days the sea will become blood and every living thing in it will die.*

Local environmental groups were pointing at cane farmers, who had had enough of taking the blame and pointed the finger right back, claiming Greenies caused the problems with their campaigns for wilderness, which due to lack of proper land management allowed wild pigs and deer to erode the land. Outrage grew and once again Tad Hinckler was at the centre of it. Somehow, regardless of whose side they were on, everyone turned to Tad for answers.

Jack walked along the shoreline of Bramston Beach, where the fish had washed up. The stench was nauseating, but he held up his phone to capture the mess of dead fish on camera. On the horizon, a massive yacht sailed north. There had been quite a number of yachts turning up in Queensland as the rich fled from pandemic lockdowns, and the trickle that had begun back then hadn't stopped.

He walked back to his car; a company four by four with *Green Synergy's* logo on the door; a gas guzzling irony that hadn't escaped Jack. As he opened the door, a Ute drove by, with *Paramount Holdings* emblazoned on its passenger door.

Was that Noddy driving? He knew his dad's friend had a job down this way, and a memory surfaced of him taking one of Barry's puppies to act as a guard dog, but that was nine years ago. Surely he wasn't still here.

Then another thought struck him. The name *Paramount Holdings* was on the pin in the map on Pete's office wall, and the engraving on Chad's fountain pen. What was *Paramount Holdings* and how were all these disparate people linked to one company? He jumped into his car and took off after the Ute, keeping his distance. He didn't particularly want to talk to Noddy, but he was curious. He followed the Ute out of Bramston village along roads that gradually became tracks through rainforest. They were heading south towards the Seymour Range and Ella Bay National Park. He cast his mind back to the map on Pete's wall.

The Seymour Range is part of the Barnard province, a geological structure that runs from Cairns to Innisfail and out to the Australian continental shelf. The Range is just one of several uplift sections of the Barnard Province and lies east of the shear zone between the Barnard and the much larger Hodgkinson Province which had been the cause of the gold rush to the Atherton Tablelands in the early settler days when Cairns was merely a port of access to the hinterland.

The Hodgkinson Province underpins a large section of Far North Queensland, including the Wet Tropics World Heritage area. The shear zone between the two geological formations runs along a fault line from Innisfail to Cairns, forming the Russell and Mulgrave Rivers alluvial plain.

Jack crossed the Range at its lowest point near a boat ramp and followed a barely used track to the southwest. An old, mould-clouded signpost to his left pointed to a gun club and shooting range, but there was no other traffic along the road, and he figured anyone driving in this direction might be heading for the same place as was Noddy.

He dropped further back. It would be embarrassing if Noddy asked why he was following him. He wasn't even sure why he was doing it himself, except that something was not right. Rainforest overhung the road, but the track was well maintained, and Jack slowed again, wondering if he should keep going. The last thing he wanted was to drive into the back of Noddy's Ute. How would he explain his presence here? Had it been anyone else he could have said he was a lost tourist, but Noddy knew who he was and wouldn't buy it.

He drove on, taking each bend at a snail's pace until the road straightened and he could see it clear ahead. He was in the shadow of the Range now, any further and he would be in the Wet Tropics World Heritage zone. Jack navigated the next bend and saw a double gate made of dark blue Colourbond corrugated iron.

On the gate, a painted sign announced this was *Paramount Holdings. Private property. Keep out. Trespassers will be prosecuted.* He pulled over to the side of the road, staring at the gate. There was no indication of what might lie behind it and Noddy was nowhere to be seen. He got out the car and walked towards the gate. He pushed, but it was locked. He contemplated climbing over it, but a dog began barking. He turned back to his car. Perhaps he should just leave and ask Pete about *Paramount Holdings*. Or perhaps his father might know what Noddy was doing there. He had promised to visit this weekend. He could ask Barry then.

Jack drove back along the tracks he'd come in on. Then he left Bramston Beach to head back to the office. The drive back to Cairns took him an hour, but by the time he arrived at the office, Pete and Tad had left for the day. It was Friday afternoon, and Pete's secretary, Noreen saïd, they had taken an early mark for the long weekend. Jack had forgotten Monday was a holiday.

He gave up work for the day, and drove to his penthouse apartment, picked up a change of clothes and returned to the office to collect the portable gas analyser he had bought with the project money *Green Synergy* had received to investigate the fish kill. Then he drove up to the Atherton Tablelands.

Since drinking that $10,000 bottle of Samantha's whisky on his last night in Winton, he and Sophia had been seeing each other. At first infrequently, but after her locum stint was done in Winton, Sophia had taken a job at the Atherton hospital. Now, Jack saw her every weekend. He planned to stay the night with her and then tomorrow he would head on over to Barry's farm, to do some of the heavy work his dad could no longer manage.

He had brought the gas analyser on a whim, for he had a hunch that the rocky hill on the farm was an upthrust from a fault line that had produced the earthquake that had damaged the kennels last year. It was a long shot and most unlikely, but he wanted to follow a line from the upthrust to the kennels to make sure there were no traces of either methane or carbon dioxide leaking into the atmosphere on his dad's farm.

That night, Jack took Sophia to meet Ed and Tess for dinner at the Baron Valley Hotel, an old country pub that served the best steaks in town. For some strange reason, he wanted Ed to give his blessing to his relationship with Sophia. Why, he didn't know, except he thought he might be falling in love for the first time in his life, and it scared the crap out of him. Somehow he associated love with failure, and he couldn't afford any disastrous relationship dynamics right now. He felt he could trust Ed's judgement better than he trusted his own. You only had to look at his recent track record with Samantha, to know his judgement wasn't good when it came to dating women.

As it turned out Sophia and Tess got on so well that Jack and Ed barely got a word in. When the two women went to the ladies, Jack said, 'So, what do you think?'

'About what?'

'About Sophia, you clod.'

'Clod! Just because Sophia is not uppermost in my mind like a certain smitten bloke I know.'

'Smitten?'

'Yeah.' Ed grinned. 'It's obvious, but she seems nice. I'm happy for you and it's about time.'

'Time?'

'You settled down.'

'Bloody hell, Ed. I'm not getting married.'

'Why not? She's beautiful, intelligent, has a recession proof job. You like her family, and she doesn't seem crazy. Overall, I'd say you couldn't do better. You'd better snap her up before one of the other lovelorn blokes in this joint does.'

'I think she might have the majority say in all of this.'

'Who might have a say...'

Jack looked up at Sophia standing at his shoulder and felt his neck getting hot. 'Ah, nothing. Anyone want another drink?'

Tess sat next to Ed, a grin splitting her face from ear to ear. 'What were you two scheming?'

Sophia looked at Jack with curiosity written across her face. 'Go on, tell us?'

Ed said, 'I was just telling the poor, simple, dolt to snap you up and marry you before someone else did.'

'Shit, Ed!' Jack got up and walked toward the bar, his ears on fire. He would just order another round whether or not they wanted one and take his time about doing it.

When he got back, the conversation had moved on, much to his relief. Tess was in the middle of a story about a set of books she had been required to go through recently. Apparently, Ed was not the only law enforcement officer in the group, and Tess was following the trail of some local money laundering scam.

Later that night, Sophia said she wanted to go with him to meet his father. Jack could feel his heart rate jump up and begin thumping in his throat. He could scarcely breathe.

'What for?'

'Why can't I meet him? You met my family.'

'Sophia, my dad...' What could he say? 'My dad's not...doesn't cope very well.'

'That's okay. It'll be fine.'

Jack didn't sleep that night for worrying. He couldn't take Sophia. What would she think of Barry? He certainly couldn't expect her to stay overnight in the house, in his mouldy bedroom, with its rickety single bed and sagging mattress. How was he going to get out of it?

He wasn't. She wasn't going to let him off the hook. The next morning, he rang his father and said he would be bringing Sophia for a visit. They would stay at the local pub, and he would come to the house after lunch and show her around, and then they would all go to the pub for dinner. Surprisingly, his dad readily acquiesced.

When they arrived at the farm, the place looked worse that it had the last time, if that was possible. The gates hung off rusty hinges and grass brushed against the car windows. Maybe selling the last of the cattle wasn't such a good idea. It hadn't occurred to him that his dad would not cut the grass once there were no cattle to eat it. The place would be overrun by snakes.

He was relieved to see a mown strip from the house to the kennels. That was something, at least. A surge of guilt overtook his battered ego. He said aloud, 'I will have to find time to get up here more often. Dad's getting too old to manage the place. I wish he would contemplate selling and moving into town, but he won't.'

Sophia said, 'How old is he?'

Jack thought for a moment before he said, 'He married my mother when he was thirty, I think, so about sixty-five or six.'

'That's not so old. My dad's 68.'

Just then, Barry came down the veranda steps, and Jack sucked in a breath. He looked like a man of 80. He had lost so much weight his skin fell in sagging folds from his once mighty arms.

Jack got out the car. 'Hi Dad. Are you okay?'

'Why wouldn't I be?' Barry grumbled. 'Who's this you've brought to meet me? Getting married are you?'

'Ah, no...I mean this is Sophia Barnett. Her dad has a cattle station out Julia Creek way. I met her when I was out there. Actually, we met before...' Jack realised he was gabbling and took a breath. "Sophia, this is my father, Barry Fallon.'

Sophia took a step towards Barry and shook his hand. Then she drew in close and kissed his cheek.

Barry looked pleased and gave her his arm.

Jack glanced around. Something was wrong other than his dad's gaunt frame, but he didn't for a moment know what. Then he realised. 'Where are the dogs?'

'Got rid of them.'

Jack stared at his father. He never thought he would see the day when his father would be without his dogs. 'Why?'

Barry shrugged. 'They were getting too much to look after and I'm too old to hunt now.'

'Dad...'

Barry held up a hand. 'Come inside. I have tea and cake.'

Jack couldn't believe his eyes. The house was as bad as ever, but Barry had found one of Molly's trays and on it was laid out Molly's best tea set, along with a shop-bought cake. Jack's eyes stung as he watched Barry pull out the chair for Sophia to sit at the dining table, an old Formica topped affair bought decades ago from a second-hand store.

When the tea was poured and cake cut and served, silence fell, and Jack racked his brain to find some safe topic to talk about. He said, 'I brought a gas detector, thought I would check out that earthquake, make sure it's safe.'

His dad just grunted, but Sophia said, 'What earthquake?'

Jack said, 'A while ago there was a quake here, did some damage to the buildings, mostly the kennels. I just wanted to make sure there was no methane leaking anywhere. He didn't want to begin explaining his theory about what Roy had been doing in his area in relation to fracking, but there was a possibility if they were pushing huge amounts of pressurised carbon dioxide waste down old wellbores, anything might be leaking to the surface.

When he'd been in Roy's area before he left MGEE he had found that some of Roy's wells were a up to three thousand meters deep with horizontal fractures extending up to one and a half kilometres from the main well. Such fractures could trigger earthquakes with an intensity of 4 or more on the Richter scale, particularly if they were near fault lines, which Roy's were. Those same fault lines ran from Roy's area to this, some perilously close to the farmhouse.

He suspected a similar scenario had killed the fish, although that was a long way from the furthermost extension of Roy's horizontal fractures. Still, if it was causing small earthquakes, who knew what gasses were leaking through the capstone to bubble along the many fault lines in the region. Besides, an earthquake in one region could place pressure elsewhere, causing slippages hundreds of kilometres away.

'What do you expect to find?'

'Nothing I hope. Finish your tea and we can go and have a look. Do you want to come, Dad?'

'No son. Run along. I'll wash up.'

'I'll do it.' Sophia volunteered.

'No, my sweet girl. You go with Jack. I'm still capable.'

Jack and Sophia walked back along the driveway, but Jack stopped at the long grass. 'Perhaps you should wait while I wade through this lot.'

Sophia looked at the grass and her sandal clad feet. 'I'll go back to the house and help your dad.'

'Okay. I won't be long.' He pointed to a rocky outcrop about a kilometre away. 'I'm heading for those rocks.'

Sophia turned back to the house. Jack watched her go before he started the equipment and, holding the monitor in front of his body, ploughed through waist-high grass, zigzagging back and forth towards the uplift, covering a broad swathe. After thirty minutes of slow walking, he'd found nothing, but as he came closer to the rocky outcrop, he found higher traces of CO^2.

He turned back, not wanting to risk walking into a pocket of the stuff without breathing apparatus. The coast was at least 60 kilometres away and Roy's nearest well was the same again. But if the sequestered carbon was leaking CO^2 from cracked capstone here, could the same be happening elsewhere, even as a natural phenomenon? Could it have caused the fish kill? There had been several undersea earthquakes clustered around the Gibson Reef. Methane or CO^2 may have leaked from gas or oil reservoirs beneath the ocean floor.

Speculators theorised there were large untapped deposits out there. Tad had been at the forefront of the push for exploration under the reef, around the time Jack was writing his dissertation on the continental shelf. Yet, although there had been a concerted effort to obtain mining licences, the Great Barrier Reef remained off limits, no matter what Tad Hinckler and his ilk had hoped.

Jack walked back to the house; a quicker return than the slow zig zag he'd done towards the fault. Inside, he found Sophia sitting at the table. The used teacups and cake plates pushed aside but unwashed. The remaining cake uncovered. She was holding Barry's gnarled old hand in hers. Jack could see the blue veins through Barry's leathery skin.

Sophia said gently. 'You have to tell him Barry. He has a right to know.'

'Know what?' Jack felt a cold fist squeeze his intestines.

Barry glanced up at his son, his blue eyes cloudy, the whites yellowed and a little blood shot. He took a breath then said, 'I'm dying mate.'

'What?' Jack sat down with a thump. 'Who told you that?'

'It's cancer...'

'Pancreatic.' Sophia added.

'All the grog, I guess.' Barry grimaced.

'Maybe,' Sophia conceded, 'maybe not.'

'Doesn't matter,' Barry said.

'Yes it does. Why the hell didn't you tell me?'

'Telling you now, aren't I?'

Jack looked back and forth between the two of them, not knowing what more to say.

Sophia said, 'You look terrified, Jack.'

'Big girl's blouse.' Barry grinned and winced. 'I guess I don't have long. Wanted to get things sorted. Didn't want you worrying, but...Anyway your girl winkled it out of me.'

That night they stayed at the house despite Jack's protests. Sophia found something to cook and some musty, but relatively clean sheets for the bed. She hung them out in the sun to air. The next day, Jack got out the old tractor, checked it over and then slashed the grass. All Sunday and Monday, he and Sophia worked to make the place liveable, while Barry grumbled and complained. Sophia seemed to have a way of twisting him around to her way of thinking, making Barry seem mellower than Jack could remember, at least since his mother had vanished.

Jack was grateful. If he'd been here alone with his dad, he would have left by now, consumed by guilt but unable to cope with Barry's insults and complaints. When they left at the end of the Monday public holiday, Jack tried to persuade Barry to move into his flat in Cairns, but he wouldn't budge.

Sophia suggested she might return with Jack the following weekend.

Barry actually smiled. 'I'll look forward to that,' he said.

Jack wanted to weep. In the car on the way back to Atherton, he said, 'I don't know what it is, but you seem to be able to make my old man nicer to be around.'

'Jack, he must be in pain and would have been for a while. Poor bloke, no wonder he's so bad tempered. Wouldn't you be if you were in pain all the time?'

Jack fell silent. He should have noticed, should have spent more time with his dad, should have done a lot of things he hadn't, but he'd do them now.

Follow the Money.

On the Tuesday morning, Jack took the fire escape to the top floor of the *Green Synergy* building and found his way along the corridor to where Tad's secretary had her desk. She sat directly across the hall from the elevators, presumably so she could keep a close eye on who arrived and departed.

When Jack arrived, she frowned. 'Where did you spring from?'

He smiled at her and asked, 'Is Tad in?'

'He's not. I can make an appointment.' She picked up a pen and opened an appointment book. 'What do you want to see him about?'

'Where is he? I was kind of hoping to see him this morning.'

She sighed. 'Well, I guess you can't. He's in Canberra.'

'What's he doing there?' Jack's face took on a bewildered look.

She tapped the pen on the desk. 'If you read your morning news bulletin, you would have seen he's gone there for discussion with the Federal Government over more money for the fish kill project.' Then her face tilted to one side. 'Aren't you the project manager for that?'

Jack blinked. He knew nothing about more money. Surely, the cash they had already secured was more than enough to keep projects like this running for the next ten years or more. It was in the hundreds of millions, from what the media had said, although he wasn't privy to the exact amount. Tad kept that sort of thing close to his chest. Although Jack was in charge of the project, he had no access to the money. Tad had told Jack the environmental consulting world did things differently. That difference seemed to Jack to be a case of style over substance, but what did he really know about it?

'Thanks.' He stepped away.

'Don't you want to make an appointment?'

'Another time.' He took the lift down to the floor where Pete's office was located, walked along the corridor, and stuck his head around the office door. 'Got a moment?'

'Yeah sure, come in. I have a client coming in fifteen, but we can chat until then. Noreen, bring Jack a coffee.'

'I'm good, thanks Noreen.' Jack smiled at her.

It would be awful working for Pete. He treated the people who worked for him like personal servants. Jack wondered why Noreen, a competent secretary with a good brain, put up with it. Maybe Pete paid well by way of compensation. He walked into the office and over to the wall map. 'Do you know of any current applications for exploration in the reef area?'

'Course not. Its protected. You know that.'

'Yeah.' Jack pointed to the pin indicating *Paramount Holdings*. 'What's this pin represent then?'

'That's a proposed luxury tourist retreat, held up because the land straddles a Cassowary corridor. Although there's a dispute about whether the corridor runs across the national park area or the adjacent vacant land. Haven't been there for years but the whole project was sunk in a mire of red tape. The owners are probably sitting on it waiting for a more friendly State government. What's this about Jack? Something to do with your project?'

'Who owns *Paramount Holdings*?'

Pete pursed his lips, silent for a moment. 'If memory serves, it's a company registered in the Cayman Islands.'

'Dodgy?'

Pete looked indignant. 'I don't do dodgy, only very legal tax havens.'

'Isn't that a contradiction in terms?'

Pete laughed. 'You always were a bit of a smug bastard.'

Jack stared at Pete, trying to see if he was hiding something behind his genial smile. 'So, who are the directors?'

'Jack...' He dragged the name out. 'Even if I could remember, I wouldn't tell you. You are asking me to divulge client information.'

'How do I find out then?'

'Write to them and ask.'

'Surely there must be a register somewhere.'

'Maybe, but it might not tell you what you want to know.'

'What are they hiding Pete?'

'What are you looking for?'

'I'm looking for what caused the fish kill. That's my job.'

Pete turned away. 'You're chasing shadows, Jack. Forget it. Look, I have to go, my next client...'

'Sure.' Jack turned to go.

Pete stopped him. 'Let's catch up for a drink after work. We haven't seen much of each other lately, and I heard you are now dating my ex.' He smiled.

Jack became still. 'Is that a problem?'

'No mate. No hard feelings, hey.'

Pete put out his hand and Jack took it, trying to smile at his old friend, although it felt more like a grimace. 'Sure mate. See you later.'

As Jack walked back to his own office, he wondered how Pete knew about him and Sophia, but he was soon distracted by a need to access some aerial photos of the area around Bramston Beach.

He could use some of the project money that was earmarked for exploration of the fish kills. It would be an expense that wouldn't go unnoticed and Jack, although he was the project manager, was still required to run everything through the Chief Finance Officer. Maybe he could ask Henry Morrison to fly him over, although he didn't have the right gear for aerial photography, nor did he have any idea of its technicalities. He would need a professional to carry out the job.

Jack went back to his office. A copy of the *Cairns Post*, lay on his desk. He groaned as he read the newspaper headlines. The Prophets had travelled to Cairns from all over the country and some from as far as New Zealand and America. They claimed there would be a revelation in four weeks, on the night of a perigee moon and the equinoctial king tide. They were gathering together to celebrate the impending moment.

He put the paper aside, picked up the phone to make an appointment to see *Green Synergy's* CFO, but his secretary said his first availability was 4.30 pm on the following Friday. Who made meetings on a Friday at knock off time? But Jack agreed because he would do anything if he could get the cost of the aerial photography equipment approved.

Over the next few days, the soil, water, and fish testing reports came in with inconclusive results, leaving Jack with only two avenues left to explore.

One was the aerial reconnaissance across the coastal fringe, and the second was over the sea floor. Both were prohibitively expensive, but the grant money was more than enough to cover such expenses.

The CFO, Mike Hatten was always difficult about spending money, as if it was his personal wallet he had to open. He was a man in his fifties, pale skin, colourless wispy hair, and pale blue eyes behind rimless glasses. Despite living in Cairns, he looked as if he had never ventured into the sunshine. He treated Jack like he treated everyone, with the suspicion they were attempting to waste the firm's money. It didn't seem to matter that the government was getting nervous about the lack of progress on the project.

Surprisingly, the media didn't blame *Green Synergy* for that lack of progress. Instead, they blamed whichever side of the political spectrum they were against. The left blamed profit-taking; the right blamed the woke, whatever that meant. The cane farmers were furious at inuendo they were causing the fish deaths through fertiliser run-off. Tourism operators claimed it was the fisheries. Fishing trawlers and fish farmers ignored jibes about their practices, pointing the finger at Council's effluent disposal. The Prophets claimed it was the third angel of the apocalypse *pouring blood out of the rivers*. Other environmentalist groups claimed it was too many tourists using sunscreen products.

The fishery and environmental people were doing all they could to help Jack. But as they kept telling him, what they needed most was more money. Tad remained firmly on Mike Hatten's penny-pinching side.

When Jack argued they had barely scratched the surface of the grant funding Tad had laughed, and said, you don't know much about how these things work, do you Jack? There are expenses, margins, salaries, and other payments outside of the expenditure of your little project. People like you don't come cheap.

What the hell! Was Tad blaming Jack for the lack of money? He wondered if it was all about profit-taking because Jack was kept on a very tight budget. What was worse was that Tad was pressuring Jack to finalise his report, and it seemed he was angling for an inconclusive result that would specify unknown but natural causes. Jack wasn't ready to go there just yet.

He picked up the phone to call Vernon. When he answered, Jack said, 'Have you heard anything further?'

Vernon sighed. 'They won't have it Jack. It's too expensive, and the university has had another funding cut.'

'Even going 50/50.'

'Yes. It's all or nothing, I'm afraid.'

'Damn.'

'You've checked the 2019 Geoscience bathymetric data, haven't you?'

'Yes. Look, I will try to get the money again, but Vernon, thanks for trying.'

On the following Friday afternoon, Jack got up from his desk to go and do battle with the CFO. He picked up the project file and took the fire escape stairs up to the floor above his level. To his great surprise, the battle turned into a minor wrestle, and he was told the aerial reconnaissance would go ahead.

He was exultant. 'I'll purchase the equipment immediately, and travel on the plane with the pilot to make sure we get the right shots and angles, so we waste nothing.'

Mike Hatten pursed his bloodless lips. 'Ah...I don't think so. Tad has already made arrangements.'

'What arrangements.?' No wonder this was so easy.

'He and a friend are travelling by light aircraft to Townsville this weekend. He said he would get the photos.'

'What with? His phone camera.' Jack ran his hand through his hair. 'Tad doesn't know the first thing about geological formations, nor, I imagine, aerial photography. We need a professional.'

'Nevertheless, those are my instructions.'

Jack raced up to Tad's office, but his secretary said he had left for the weekend.

He fumed as he drove home to his apartment. There was nothing for him to do except grab his bag, pick up some supplies he'd bought for the repairs needed on the farm, and head up to Atherton. At least he would get to see Sophia and could forget his job for a night or two.

That night, he and Sophia stayed at the house she had rented near the hospital. Ed was on duty so their usual dinner at the pub was swapped for Sophia saying she'd cook dinner for Jack. She promised it would be more than supermarket chicken and salad, but Jack didn't care what it was.

Aside from a very large bed, the house was even more sparsely furnished than her Winton house had been. At least there, she had the use of the doctor-in-residence's house, which had some furniture. Since she'd been in Atherton, she had slowly begun to accumulate furniture, but she refused to buy commercial stuff, so, there was still very little other than the bare necessities.

Her idea of furnishing a home was to slowly collect pieces with a history that spoke to her. That had amused Jack, no end. He'd grown up hankering for the modern commercial stuff he saw in other people's homes. While Jack was embarrassed by Barry's furniture, Sophia exclaimed over the Formica table and its uncomfortable chairs. He had always considered them old junk. But if she loved them, they couldn't be that bad.

She said, 'Think of the stories they would have to tell.'

If only they could explain what had happened to his mum, but he also realised she was making him see the world differently, and he wasn't sure if that was a good or a bad thing.

That night, she cooked a pasta con pollo, her mother's recipe, and when Jack had finished eating he sat back, trying to remember a time in his life when he had felt so content. There wasn't one.

After dinner, he took out his laptop and opened the Google Earth app. He imagined the aerial photos he'd get from Tad would be no better than the satellite photos. The Google satellite image was six years old, without clouds, but there was not enough resolution to see anything beneath the tree canopy, not even where there were gaps in its cover.

Deeper into the rainforest from where *Paramount Holding's* gate was located was a lighter patch. It looked like it had once been cleared and now the scrub was growing back. That would fit Pete's description of a delayed development project.

'What are you looking at?' Sophia stood behind him and peered over his shoulder.

'Just trying to work out what might be down there.'

'Trees,' she said.

He nodded. 'Looks like it.'

'What's bothering you, Jack?'

He blew out a lungful of air and ran his hand through his hair. 'Everything.'

She sat next to him. 'Tell me.'

'I'm not sure of any of it. All I have are theories with no evidence other than a gut feel. But I think the increase in earthquakes in the region is happening because of either carbon sequestration practices, or wastewater disposal in old wellbores.'

'But you said the earthquakes they caused were small, and not usually dangerous.'

'I know, but they might place pressure somewhere else and cause a larger quake in a built-up area. That would be dangerous.'

She touched his cheek. 'But there's more, isn't there? I can tell you are worried about something more.'

He laughed. 'Isn't an earthquake bad enough?'

She shook her head. 'Get it out.'

He took a deep breath and glanced at her. 'You'll think I'm crazy.'

'Tell me anyway.'

'Okay. Here goes.' He pointed to the laptop screen. 'You see this reef here?'

She nodded.

'Well, in the last year there have been a spate of minor quakes, so small most were under 2. The biggest was a 2.6 but they seem to be following a line from here to here.' He ran his finger in a northeast direction.

'What's this?' She pointed at the place just southeast of where his finger line had started.

'It's the Gibson Reef.'

'And here?' She pointed to where his finger line had ended just east of another reef.

'Noggin Reef.'

'So, what's significant about these earthquakes?'

'Nothing really, except they have increased in frequency over the last few years although most are still not much more than tremors.'

'What's causing them?'

'Now, that is the million-dollar question.'

'Jack you are not making sense. Why are you so worried about this.'

'Ah. Over here...' He pointed at some blue coloured wrinkles on the map. 'This is the continental shelf. East of the shelf the land drops away steeply into the Queensland trough which has a depth up to 2000 metres below sea level, all caused eons ago by activity between continental plates parting in a sort of rift.'

'Like the Great Rift Valley in Africa.' I learned about that at school.'

'Sort of.' He gazed at her for a minute and then said, 'The shelf here at the end of Noggin Passage has an area about 5 k's squared that is eroded and has the potential to slip.'

'Okay.' She shrugged. 'How far is that from Cairns?'

'About 70 or so Ks.'

'So, what does it mean if it slips?'

'It may cause a landslide, and if the slip is big enough it could displace monumental amounts of water that would trigger a tsunami, with a wave estimated to be somewhere between 7 to 11 metres.'

'Holy shit! Is that possible? 'What will make it slip?'

He took her hand and squeezed it. 'It's relatively stable for the moment and we don't really know what might cause a slippage, maybe a big earthquake, maybe gas hydrate-bearing sediments that further destabilise the area. A team of researchers found the area in 2012, and there were signs of historic slippages along here, but it might be a thousand years before it slips again in this particular spot.'

'Unless something triggers it. That's why you're so worried.'

He nodded.

'Jack, you have to tell someone.'

'I'm working on it.'

'No, you just have to tell everyone. Cairns is in danger.'

'Not just Cairns. It's all along this coast. The wave is not the biggest in history but can still do a lot of damage, and who knows how far a tsunami that big might travel. Wave movement is not my area, but it could reach as far north as Papua New Guinea, and south to Noosa or maybe even Brisbane, and east to the Solomon Islands.'

'Oh my God! Why don't we know this? Why aren't you telling anyone?'

'It was published in the papers after the original research team found it. No one worried about it then and I don't have any evidence it's going to get any worse.'

'You said the earthquakes were increasing.'

'Yes.'

'That's evidence.'

'Not really. They are mostly small and could be put down to natural factors. I spoke to my previous firm MGEE's, about the increasing seismic activity, because I wanted to see if we could find out if our drilling activity was causing it. That's when I began to suspect that Roy was carrying out less that ethical practices.'

'Why didn't you dob him in?'

'What do you think? They didn't buy any of it. In fact, they were thoroughly discouraging and after that, I wasn't allowed anywhere near Roy's wells.'

'You have to tell Tad and Pete.'

Jack frowned. 'The trouble is, I suspect there is something they know and don't want me knowing.'

'What?'

Jack saw a flash of scepticism in her eyes. 'You see...'

'No, I don't see.'

'You think I'm nuts.'

'No, I don't. I know you don't trust Tad, but Pete's been your friend for ages.'

'Would you trust Pete?'

'Well, no... But it's different, isn't it?'

'I don't see why. Someone is either trustworthy or they are not. I know Pete's my friend, or was, but his moral compass points in a different direction from mine, along the same line I reckon as Tad's.'

'Tell Ed then. You trust Ed right? And he's a police officer.'

'It's no good telling anyone unless I have evidence. A hunch is useless. Look, he pointed at the computer screen to where Bramston Beach was located. Over here is a property I think that has something going on that might help me understand it better. Or at least give me some proof to take to the authorities. Can you see now, why no one would believe me? I asked you what you saw, and you said trees.'

'Okay, I get it. But what do you expect to find?'

'Don't know, but I am wondering if they are planning to drill here? Or have begun drilling. The puzzling bit is that Google Earth shows nothing like that, but the photo might be too old. Tad's getting new aerial photos, but if he's hiding something, I won't hold my breath, expecting that I'll get to see anything.'

'Have you spoken to your old uni supervisor about it?'

'Yes.'

'What did he say?'

'He reckons I might be onto something, but agrees I need more data. No one will believe me without evidence. I would be totally discredited as a scientist and an engineer, and I would achieve nothing. All it would do is ensure they hide their tracks, and I would be out of a job.'

'Why don't you just take a look?'

'I've been contemplating it, but it's trespassing. So, same deal about my reputation and my job. Still, I seem to have run out of options. Will you visit me in gaol?'

'You won't go to gaol.' She kissed him and ran her hands down his chest, slipping them under his shirt. 'Maybe we can look again tomorrow.'

Her face held all the invitation he needed, and he shut the laptop and followed her to the bedroom.

At four o'clock in the morning, Jack's phone rang. He tried to ignore it, but it persisted. Then someone banged on the front door. Jack sat on the side of the bed and rubbed his face. Who the hell was at the door? His phone rang again, and he answered it.

Ed said, 'Open the door Jack.'

Sophia woke up. 'What happening?'

'It's Ed.' He spoke into the phone. 'What's up Ed.'

'I need to speak with you face to face. It's not good news, mate.'

'Okay, let me get some clothes on.' He turned on the bedside lamp and made an apologetic face at Sophia. 'I'll just find out what's put a burr in Ed's hide. Go back to sleep.'

He dressed in shorts and a tee-shirt and went to the front door. Ed was in uniform, another man in a suit standing behind him. Jack stood back to let them in, then followed them through to the living room.

Sophia came into the room. 'Hello Ed, what's the matter?'

Ed took a deep breath. 'I'm here in an official capacity, Jack. This is Detective Senior Sergeant David Langley.' He turned to Langley and said, 'This is Jack Fallon a friend of mine, and Sophia Barnett is a doctor at the hospital. Barry Fallon is Jack's father.'

Jack looked from one man to the other, wondering what this was all about. 'Has Barry done something?'

Sophia said, 'Is he okay? He's sick, really sick.'

Ed said, 'Sit down Jack, Sophia.'

Jack thought his friend looked strung out.

Langley nodded. 'Okay Morrison, I'll take it from here. Would you like to take a seat, Mr Fallon?'

'Doctor,' Ed corrected him.

Langley looked confused, opened his mouth to say something. Changed it and said, 'Have a seat, Dr Fallon.'

Jack shook his head but went and sat at the dining table, anyway. Sophia sat next to him and grabbed his hand.

Langley said. 'I am sorry to inform you that your father has passed.'

For a second, it was Jack's turn to look bewildered. 'Passed? Do you mean he died? They said it would be a year.'

Langley frowned and Ed intervened. 'Barry had cancer.'

Langley nodded. 'My commiserations, but his death was not the result of natural causes. It seems your father may have been murdered, or he took his own life. If he was dying, maybe the latter is more likely. The forensic team will be able to tell us more in a day or two.'

Jack put his head in his hands. He couldn't take it in.

Sophia asked, 'What happened?'

Langley said, Neighbours from across the valley called in a fire, and they had heard gunshots. The Fires put out the fire, so it didn't reach the house, just burnt some kind of outbuilding.'

Ed interrupted again. 'Burnt down the kennels, Jack.'

Langley continued. 'They found your father deceased, so they called us in.'

Ed said, 'Barry had a hunting rifle lying next to him when we found him. So, it's likely he took his own life.'

Langley asked, 'Did he have any enemies, or anyone who would have wanted him dead?'

Jack shook his head. 'I don't know, but I wouldn't think so.'

Langley opened a notebook. 'I have to ask, sir, where were you this evening?'

Jack stared at the detective. 'I was here.'

'From what time?'

'I arrived at about six I guess, drove up from Cairns after I finished work. You don't think I...?'

Ed said, 'No mate, just have to ask, you know. Part of the job.'

Sophia said, 'I can vouch for him. He's been here since about ten to six and we haven't left the house.'

After Ed and the detective left, Sophia made coffee as Jack sat in a daze.

When she put the cup down in front of him, he said, 'I should have been there.' He put his face in his hands.

Sophia sat down next to him and put her arm around him. 'We'll go when the sun gets up.'

The next morning, Jack and Sophia were unable to gain access to Barry's farm while the forensic team were on site. They had sent Barry's partially burnt body to the coroner's for examination to determine the cause of death. There was nothing Jack could do, and Ed could tell them little more than what they already knew.

For want of knowing what else to do, on the Monday morning Jack went back to work. The story of his father's death was all over the news, and he was confronted by condolences, pity, and whispers. It was a repeat of his mother's disappearance, and he wanted to smash a fist through the gossip. No one knew what had happened, but it seemed most people had come down on the side of suicide because Barry had cancer.

On the Wednesday following Barry's death, Tad called him into his office. 'Sit down, Jack.'

Jack sat in front of Tad's desk on a chair fifteen centimetres lower than Tad's. It had always amused him that Tad played these sorts of power games, but today he had no time for them.

Tad said, 'I'm sorry about your father, Jack. Truly I am. It must have been an awful shock. To take his own life like that. Lucky, you went to your girlfriend's place, and it wasn't you who found him.'

Jack clenched his jaw and felt his fingers curl into fists as they rested on his knees. 'They don't know if he took his own life. The forensic team are still investigating, and if I had gone there instead of to Sophia's he might not be dead.'

He spoke more sharply than he had intended. Shame washed across him in waves, and he realised he had always taken the path he'd wanted and never considered what his father might want.

'Whoa pal. Look, take the rest of the week off, sort yourself out.'

'Thanks, but I'd rather work. There's nothing I can do anyway until they release my father's body and allow me back on the farm. I might need some time off then, but now I need to get the project wrapped up. Did you manage to get the aerial photos over the weekend?'

Tad looked affronted. 'Yes I did, but I assumed... Never mind. I'll email the photos although what good they'll do, I have no idea. I had a good look flying over the area and all I could see was trees, sand, and water. Maybe you can find something.' He paused. 'But if you can't, the report still goes ahead. If we have to find the results are inconclusive, so be it. You need to wrap up the project as soon as possible or hand it over. If you need time off, I can give it to someone else to finish. Do you understand me Jack? This is no time to play silly buggers and express your wild theories.'

'What does that mean?'

Tad stood up. 'How long will you need for the report?'

Jack shrugged. 'Maybe another week. Much of it is already written.'

'Good, have a draft by Wednesday next week then. I'll take a look before its finalised.'

'Can we make it the following week? I would like to get more photos of the places we've tested already.'

'Okay, two weeks today, but that's it.'

'Sure.' Jack left to go back to his office, where he picked up his keys, laptop, and phone. Then he got into his company car in the parking basement and drove along the Bruce Highway. He was not sure what he was going to do, but he had a vague idea of calling in to see if Noddy was at *Paramount Holdings* on the pretext he was there to talk to his father's friend about Barry's death. That way, he might get to look around without having to trespass. It was worth a go.

He took the same winding track he'd followed last time, past the old shooting range sign, and arrived at a cleared area where he had previously seen the corrugated iron gates with *Paramount Holdings* written on them. Or that is where he thought he was, but somehow he must have taken a wrong turn. There was a cleared area on the side of the road, but no fence, and no gates.

Jack retraced his journey back to the road that led to the boat ramp at the southern end of Bramston Beach. He turned around and worked his way back, looking out for an alternative road he may have missed. There were other gravelled roads including the one to the shooting range, but he was certain none of them was the narrow track he'd taken when he had followed Noddy. He arrived back at the same cleared area on the side of the track. Ahead of him was just rainforest.

He parked, got out of the car, and walked to where he thought the gates had been. He couldn't see any signs of gate posts. He walked towards the tree line. The grass here looked odd, and he knelt down to examine it more closely. He was no expert, but it looked like it had been recently laid down in clumps, the way turf was laid, except this grass wasn't neatly mown turf.

He walked towards the tree line. The trees closest to him were mere saplings, growing close together. He pushed through them for about six meters before he found a track with deep wheel ruts. He followed the track deeper into the rainforest. The ground he walked on began sloping upwards and he figured he was at the base of the Seymour Range. Then the track hit a T junction. He turned right and followed the track for about a 100 meters and found a demountable building in a large clearing. Jack walked up to it, holding his breath. Then he figured if he was really here honestly looking for Noddy, he would be bold in his approach.

He called out. 'Hey Noddy? Its Jack Fallon. Hello. Is anyone home?'

Silence fell in the forest, a silence that hadn't been there before. Even though he hadn't been particularly conscious of any sounds, they were there, in the myriad of noises made by birds, cicadas, frogs, the odd forest wallaby or cassowary. But since his call, the buzz and hum had fallen away to an ear pressurising nothingness.

He remained still, listening until the sounds of the forest came back, slowly, and hesitantly at first, and then settled into the hum he'd taken for granted. There were two steps up to the demountable veranda and Jack took them in one stride before knocking on the door. There was no answer. He tried the handle. The door was locked. He peered through the windows, but blinds prevented him seeing inside. He walked around the back, to where a patch of lawn separated the house from the rainforest.

In the centre of the lawn was a Hill's Hoist with clothes pegs still attached. At the far edge of the lawn, next to the forest, was a small garden shed that looked ready to collapse in anything more than a light breeze.

The demountable had a back door. It opened when Jack turned the handle, and he looked around once more before stepping inside. Whoever used this demountable, still lived here. One room was a bedroom with a roughly made bed. The kitchen, with a kettle and mug on the bench, was part of a larger living room that included a television, a sofa, and a dining table. Another door opened into a bathroom with a threadbare towel hanging over the shower rail.

Jack ran his hand over his jaw, his eyes seeking out information. At one end of the kitchen cabinet, a closed drawer showed the corner of a sheet of white paper sticking out, presumably caught when the drawer was closed. He opened the drawer and found several pay slips made out to one Harold Noddington.

Was that Noddy's real name? Jack had never known, but who else could it be? It seemed he was still here. A caretaker's job, he had said when he took Barry's puppy. Damn, he had forgotten the dog. If Noddy was around, the dog would have a piece out of him, particularly if it was anything like its sire.

He left the demountable quickly, casting about to make sure he had not left traces of his visit. Then he followed the track back the way he'd come, crossing the T of the pathway to the left track, pointing in the direction of the sea. He must have walked two hundred metres when he came to another cleared area with two large mounds about eight to ten metres high. The hillocks were covered in grass and bushes.

There was something odd about them, human in construction rather than natural. He walked up to the first one and caught a whiff of rotten eggs. He wished he'd bought the gas reader. He held his breath and climbed to the top of the first mound, to where the edge of a metal roof was visible through soil that had slid away, perhaps due to heavy rain.

The smell of sulphur was strong. He took some photos with his phone and decided he should get out of there before he was either asphyxiated or discovered. At least he now had evidence.

He quickened his stride, going back the way he'd come in. Just as he reached the car, his luck ran out. A Ute drove up and stopped next to him.

Jack said, 'Noddy, I'm glad to find you. I was told this is where you were but couldn't find anything here. Thought I had the wrong place.'

Noddy looked suspicious. 'Who told you?'

'Barry mentioned it some time ago. But I came to give you some bad news mate, Barry's dead.'

'I heard already.'

'Yeah. It seems he might have gone and topped himself, cancer you know? Didn't have long and he was in pain.' Jack felt a twinge at betraying his old man. 'Anyway, wasn't sure if you knew and you were always his best friend, so I thought it was the least I could do.'

Noddy's face relaxed a little.

Jack said, 'The Coroner has his body, but I'll let you know when the funeral is. Do you have a phone? Save me a long trip out here.'

Noddy nodded. He reeled off the number and Jack pulled out his phone to record it.

'Thanks. Hey, is that the pup you got from Barry? He's grown into a fine animal, although maybe a bit long in the tooth. Must be nine, ten years now.' He put his hand out, and the dog snarled.

'He'll have your hand off.'

'Oh yeah, guard dog, I forgot. Well, I'll be seeing you, Noddy. Take care.' Jack got into his car and drove down the road. In the rear-view mirror, he could see that Noddy hadn't moved. It looked like he was on the phone. Then Jack remembered he should have asked where he lived, given there was no sign of any habitation from the road. Would Noddy find that suspicious? Too late now. Jack would just have to hope he hadn't noticed.

Jack's phone rang and the automatic hands-free, picked up. It was Ed's voice, crackling over a bad line, made worse by the hands-free. 'Hang on Ed, I'll pull over.' Jack pulled up on the side of the track, took the phone off hands-free and said, 'Got you now.'

'I have more news and it's bad.'

Jack became still. What could be worse? 'Has something happened to Sophia?'

'No. Where are you?'

Jack let out a breath, then grimaced at his sudden surge of panic when he thought something might have happened to Sophia. 'I'm down near Brampton Beach. What's the news?'

'I'm sorry to have to tell you over the phone mate, but the forensic team found another body.'

'Where?'

'In the kennels.'

'Who?'

'We don't know yet, not for sure, but it has been there for a long time, not much left.'

'How long? How did no one notice? I would have seen a body Ed. Sophia and I were there a couple of weekends ago, and I went into the kennels. I was worried about the building's structural integrity since the earthquake.'

'That's the thing. There were repairs done to the concrete where the quake cracked it. The new patch of concrete was broken up and partly turned over. That was how the remains were found.'

Jack screwed up his face. 'Why? I don't get any of it.'

'Jack we think someone was trying to get at the concrete when Barry took a few shots at them.'

'I thought it was Barry who was shot.'

'No mate. Barry's head was staved-in, maybe by a shovel. There was one in the kennel. They're checking it for traces of blood or DNA at the moment.'

Jack shook his head. 'Who did it? And whose body did you find?'

'Nothing is certain yet, Jack. They are still doing the forensics. Sometime these things take time, but it seems there is a probability it was a woman. Langley is speculating that it might be your mother, Molly.'

Jack dropped the phone and scrabbled on the floor to find it. ' 'Oh fuck. Ed, Ed, are you still there? Say that again. Who killed her?'

'Don't know Jack, and we don't know anything for sure, just... There's a body, but the length of time it's been there fits with Molly's disappearance.'

'Shit. Did Barry kill her Ed?'

'Don't know mate, but if it's her, I promise we'll find out who did, but I need you to come up and give us a DNA swab, when you can, okay.'

'I'll come up right now.' When Jack hung up, he put his phone back in his pocket and stared out the window. His mind looping around possibilities, scenario, memories of Molly and Barry. How she had been; how they had been together.

Jack was certain Barry believed she'd run out on him. Maybe she did and he killed her because of it. Now he was dead, Jack would never know. But if Barry hadn't killed her, he would never know she hadn't run out on them either. He wanted to howl.

He started the car, put it into drive and was just about to pull out onto the road when his windscreen cracked as if a stone had been thrown up by a passing truck. But that was impossible. Crack another hole appeared with crazed grass surrounding it.

Bloody hell, someone was shooting at him. He thumped his foot down and shot down the track, wheels spinning for traction as he tore at high speed along the winding track. Was he on the shooting range? He thought that sign was a long way off, but maybe all this land belonged to the gun club. Or was someone actually aiming at him? The only person who knew he was here was Noddy.

A Question of Proof

Jack drove up the Gillies Range Road to Atherton, taking the winding bends at an unsafe speed, but desperate to find out what was going on. His life was imploding around him. He was beginning to realise that nothing was as it seemed. *Paramount Holdings* wasn't a tourist project, of that he was certain, so why did Pete lie? Undoubtedly, Noddy knew more than he was letting on. Did he fire those shots or was it random bad luck that someone was using the range as he drove past? Nothing added up, yet he was certain both Pete and Noddy knew more than they were letting on.

Then again, there must be something wrong with the logic systems of his brain circuitry. How could he have believed all these years that his mother had walked out, never to be seen again? How could Barry have believed it to such an extent that he'd become a bitter old man, who drank his life away? How could they have not known there was a body under the concrete in the kennels all these years, even if it wasn't Molly's body? And who had killed Barry? Maybe Ed would have the answers.

An hour later, Jack walked into the police station and asked for Ed. Then he took him outside and showed him the bullet holes.

Ed stared at Jack. 'What the hell are you into here?'

Jack said, 'Come and have a coffee and I'll tell you the whole story.'

'I'll just get someone to write up a report on your car damage and get some evidence for the file. Where did the bullets exit?'

Jack shrugged. 'I didn't think about that. Maybe they are still in there.'

Ed pulled a face. 'Lucky it wasn't through you.' He opened the back door and pointed to the back seat. 'Definitely a lucky bastard. Both rounds must have travelled between the front seats to hit here and here.' He pointed to rips in the leather covered headrest of the back seat. 'Look, I'll get someone on to it. If they can find the rounds, we'll know what kind of weapon it was, and can track it down.'

Jack waited while Ed organised his people to examine the car, and then they walked to a nearby café.

While they waited for the coffee, Jack said, 'Tell me about my mother, Ed.'

'We don't know it's Molly, Jack. It just might be.'

'What did you find?'

'Not much. Bodies don't last long up here. Acid soil and tropical rainfall. Besides it was how many years ago?'

'Twenty-five. What did they find?'

'There were just fragments. Bone, part of a shoe sole, cloth, oh, and a gold charm bracelet, but that wasn't on the body. It was found half a metre away.'

'That was Molly's.' Jack nodded his head, tears prickling his eyelids. He remembered the bracelet, and how every birthday Barry would get her a new charm. Even when there was no money for anything else, there was always a new charm. Jack knew Barry had sometimes bought them from the pawnshop in Cairns, but Molly hadn't known that.

He pushed the memories aside. Molly and Barry were gone, and Jack had more immediate concerns, ones that didn't require using up time on rear vision guilt, grief, and self-flagellation. Concerns that held serious consequences for the future. After the coffee arrived, Jack repeated his fears about increasing earthquakes from gas fracking, and the mysterious *Paramount Holdings* site. .

'But I think I have proof now, Ed. I went to the site, and there are two wellbores, disguised, and obviously capped, but one of them is leaking, what I think, without testing, is hydrogen sulphide.'

'So, what does that tell you?'

'Well, two things. One: its lethal to fish, and two: if they have been pumping sea water down a fracked wellbore to maintain pressure, they may have promoted growth of the bacteria that causes it. It's a common problem for offshore rigs, and they need to be well maintained to prevent it.'

'So that might be what killed all those fish?'

'Yep, and any fracking might be causing earth tremors.'

'But you said the wells were de activated. When were they last in use. Are we talking historical stuff?' Ed shook his head. 'And why shoot at you?'

Jack scowled. 'I don't think this is historical, and drilling in the marine park isn't permitted, so they are operating illegally.'

'If it was historical, they wouldn't need to hide it, right?'

Jack nodded. 'The wells have been operational, at least until recently. The vegetation covering them and at the entrance has all been newly planted, I reckon, as camouflage, particularly from the air. Close up, it might fool someone who didn't know what they were looking at. The bit I don't know is who... This outfit, *Paramount Holdings*. They're registered offshore, but I can't get a handle on the directors. The whole secrecy thing is what strikes me as most problematic. I'm not a lawyer or a copper, but I would take a bet that this is criminal activity.'

Ed scratched his neck. 'Sure, sounds like it, at least the way you describe it, but I've never heard of anything like it. Why would they do that?'

'Money.' Jack paused, thinking about how Tad had once said that he would get the government to approve oil exploration in the Great Barrier Reef. And he had nearly done it. He said, 'Some years ago, the Premier of the State government tried to approve exploration and mining in the reef area. The Federal government stepped in and scuppered the decision.' Jack paused. 'So, either money or an ideological belief to prove a point.'

'Two good motives.' Ed said. 'What can I do?'

'Can't you raid the place?'

'On what grounds?'

On the grounds of an illegal activity hidden in the rainforest on the edge of, if not encroaching on, a world heritage site, with a wellbore that probably runs into rock under the Great Barrier Reef. But you have to keep my name out of it.'

'This is beyond my pay grade, Jack. How do I say I know all this without bringing you into it?'

'Tell them it was a tipoff. I'll send you some photos and some words, but make sure my name doesn't get connected with it.'

'Why can't you get involved?'

'I was trespassing, I guess, and that wouldn't do your case any good. I'm also pretty sure I would be fired. I already have two bullet holes in my car, and I have to explain them to my boss. Please Ed. Just try. I don't know where else to turn. Maybe your dad can help?'

Ed shook his head. 'He's still in South Africa. Do you think your boss is involved?'

'Maybe, and I suspect my previous boss Chad Myers.' Jack told Ed about Chad's pen with *Paramount Holdings* engraved on its side. 'Not that it's definitive proof. I also think Pete Macalister might know something. He set up the offshore company.

'There you go. Ask him about it.'

'I did. Pete said he couldn't remember and wouldn't tell me, anyway. It's some kind of legal client-confidentiality thing.'

Ed rubbed his face. 'This whole thing is wild, Jack. If it's that serious, they are shooting at you, you will need to take care.' He exhaled heavily and got up. 'I've got to get back, but let me think about how I can do this. People are going to think I've lost the plot and become one of those doomsday prophets down in Cairns.'

Jack nodded. 'I know. That's what scares me most, too.'

'Aside from earthquakes, tsunamis and people shooting at you? Ed raised his eyebrows at Jack.

Jack laughed. 'That too.'

Ed got up to go and then stopped as if a thought had struck him. He sat down again and said, 'Hey how long do you think this has been going on?'

'I have no idea. Why?'

'Remember your car accident?'

'Oh crap, was that also about this?' Jack ran his hand across his neck.

'Well, you said a mining truck rammed you off the road.'

'And I was convinced they had covered it up.'

Ed nodded. 'They sent the witness off on holiday so we couldn't ask him any questions. And still he has not returned. I checked last week.'

Jack said, 'Chad had the car crushed.' He paused. 'And, I was burgled, my laptop stolen.'

'You weren't sure if it was connected.'

Jack frowned. 'I thought it was a side issue.'

'I figured it was just kids.'

'But maybe they wanted to know what I had on my laptop because I had been asking awkward questions in Roy's area.' He shook his head. 'Seems a bit farfetched doesn't it? Like some kind of conspiracy.'

Ed raised his eyebrows 'No kidding, and you want me to step right into the middle of it? If it was anyone else...' Ed got up. 'But mate, I'm really sorry about Molly. Never knowing all this time and all...'

Jack watched Ed choke up and turn red in the face as he tried to express his sympathy. A memory flashed to the surface. Molly's bracelet charm. It was still in his drawer. 'Ed, wait a sec.'

He told Ed about coming home and finding the charm on the floor. Then going to the police station with his dad to report her missing.

'We know all that. It's on file.'

'You didn't know about the charm.'

'True.' Ed stopped. 'You think it broke off in a scuffle?'

'Well, you said the bracelet wasn't on the body, just nearby.'

'Barry?' Ed asked.

Jack shook his head. 'Noddy!' He pressed his lips together and a muscle in his cheek jumped. 'He did a lot of work on the kennels and he's a weasel, but I didn't give him enough credit for being able to kill my mum. He was always sliming up to her, paying her those extravagant compliments, annoying the crap out of her, but killing her... Mum couldn't stand him, but surely she could have swatted him off.'

'Who poured the concrete at the kennels?'

'I don't know. I think it was poured while I was at school, but whatever happened, my Dad was supposedly in Georgetown buying cattle when she disappeared and Noddy was most likely the last person to see her.'

'Yeah, Barry's alibi checked out. But now we have a reason to pay Noddy a visit. Give me a statement Jack, and we can go and talk to him. You say he lives on the site near Brampton Beach. I'll get onto Langley right now. Then I'll go with him and while he's talking to Noddy, I will discover the wells all by my clever self. After all, I should know something about mining, having picked up so much from my own father.' Ed pulled a face. 'Dad would be proud.'

'I'll give you a statement and draw a mud map of where you can find him.'

They walked back to the police station, and after making the statement, Jack gave a DNA swab, then picked up his car to take it to the windscreen repair shop on the outskirts of the town. It probably wasn't worth the hassle of reporting it at work. Too many questions. He'd just pay for it himself.

The bloke at the repairers looked at the windscreen. 'Those look like bullet holes, mate.'

Jack nodded.

'I'll have to report them to the police.'

'Already done.'

'Do you have the report on you?'

Jack pulled some paper from his glove box and showed it to the man.

The repairer looked sceptical, but said, 'Okay. It'll cost you. Do you have insurance?'

Jack shook his head. 'Just get it fixed, mate. I'll pay.'

'I can't do anything about the upholstery...'

'Just the windscreen will do fine.'

While the windscreen was being replaced, Jack phoned the marine biologist, who was examining the dead fish that had washed up on the beach.

When he answered, he said, 'Jack I was just about to call you.'

'Have you found something?'

'Yes, It's a bit weird.'

'Hydrogen sulphide poisoning.'

'How the hell did you know that?'

'Lucky guess. I was phoning to ask you to check it out.'

'Some guess. Can you explain how the fish came into contact with it.'

'I can, but I need a while to get more evidence.'

'Okay, well I can have a preliminary report in the morning if you want to call in.'

'Thanks, about 9 am okay.'

'Sure. See you then.'

Jack wandered back to the workshop to see how the windscreen repair was coming along. It was nearly done, and he glanced at his watch. Nearly knock off time. No point going back to work now. He'd just go and see Sophia.

He felt a surge of happiness at the thought of seeing her, staying the night, not having to wait for the weekend. It should be like this all the time. He should be able to come home every night and spend it with her. He wondered if she would feel the same. He'd ask her tonight. There was a lot to tell her.

When he arrived at her house, she rushed out to meet him, waving an invitation above her head. 'Fergus is getting married, and I'm a bridesmaid. The wedding's at home in Julia Creek. Do you think you can get time off to go Jack?'

'Sure.' He held her close to his chest, her hair tickling his cheek. He could stand there forever, so long as she was with him. He wondered if Barry had felt this way about Molly. He thought he might have. A surge of emotion welled up in his throat and he closed his eyes.

The next morning, Jack drove down the range to Cairns and went back into his office. He would finalise the report before he asked for leave to go to Fergus's wedding. He couldn't ask until that was completed to Tad's satisfaction.

An hour later, his face creased in concentration, he stared at a row of desk paraphernalia lined up in front of him. He was using things, like the stapler and pens, as props to help him make connections. A noise outside broke through his concentration. He got up from his desk and walked to the window, looking down onto the street below.

The Prophets filled the street with placards exhorting people to repent before it was too late. He noted they had taken to wearing grey robes and sandals. Jack could not believe they had once been part of a sane group of environmentalists, who had genuinely protested human extinction through climate change. What had sent them through this worm hole? He had read somewhere that *The Prophets of the Apocalypse* cult arose when one man, calling himself Elijah, a man with a straggling grey beard and lank hair, claimed to have seen a vision, in which God had said it wasn't His Will to stop climate change. Elijah claimed that heating the planet was God's tool of chastisement.

He reasoned that trying to prevent global warming by reducing emissions was useless. Unless multinationals and governments repented their lies, corruption, and gave away their financial profits the earth was doomed. Consequently, the only means of stopping God's retribution was to repent.

Many fell for the con and followed him. The belief spread across the internet like wildfire during the pandemic lockdowns. Apparently, there was no turning back from God's will. The only survivors would be those who had repented, born again into *The Prophets of the Apocalypse*. The world was doomed, and they alone would be saved by God's intervention.

The consequences of the cult were that the Prophets had made the vast climate protester network, a laughingstock. If the climate activists had been infiltrated and ransacked, it could not have been a more effective measure to sideline their movement. Now genuine climate protesters were treated with ridicule as God-bothering conspiracy theorists.

Jack sighed; short-term greed determined what kind of society we lived in. It was no different from the people of Rapa Nui or Easter Island who destroyed their own environment, and consequently their own society, in search of the perfect statue to their gods. You could excuse them, he supposed, for they could not have understood the science the way it was understood today, but some of the Prophets were no better, and were probably just as superstitious as the people of Rapa Nui.

In Jack opinion, human greed was the architect of the world destruction and there were no gods or conspiracies needed, either to make it happen or to save it. Only humans with evidence-based government policy ,premised on the greater good for humanity, could do that. If it wasn't already too late.

He went back to his desk and rearranged the desk objects. Each one represented some aspect of what he was trying to include in his report. A bundle of pens represented the dead fish, a drink coaster the wellbore site, rulers ran from the wellbore site to an A4 paper sea. Jack wondered if there was a pipeline for pumping up water, or if it came from one of the well bores. That would make sense of a kind. Pumping sea water up from one and down the other at pressure, no waste to store in tailing dams. What did they find? Oil or gas. How had it been transported away? There were no tanks on the site that he had seen. Of course, they might have been moved already. Alternatively, oil or gas could have been pumped via a pipeline, but he had seen no sign of one.

The bores were key to all of it. But if he could not access them, he had no proof to place in the report, just conjecture. Clearly there had been heavy vehicles using the road, judging by the rutted ground he'd seen, but that was only on one short stretch. Maybe the road had been graded. That was a lot of work to hide a site. When had it been done and why? Was it because of his questions?

He wondered if the wellbores were capped safely. Wellbore integrity was a multidisciplinary endeavour and Jack didn't have a hope in hell of getting anyone to let him check their safety, let alone the depth and direction of the wellbore. Neither could he check when it was last used, or if abandoned, if it was properly plugged or merely rendered safe for suspension. There were so many technical aspects to consider for a check on wellbore integrity, he would need Tad to okay it. Then he could establish that it was indeed the source of the hydrogen sulphide that killed the fish, if not the cause of the seismic activity off the coast in that area.

He pulled up Tad's aerial photos of the region. As he had expected, they were useless, showing little other than an overview of the forest and the coastline. He noticed there was a good shot of each of the villages and towns along the route, but the area of the wellbore site was a little out of focus. That alone spoke volumes, but it was not something he could put in his report, nor could he ask anyone. He had to find the source of the hydrogen sulphide some other way, one that would lead to a full and independent investigation of the site.

He picked up his phone and rang Ed. 'How did it go, mate?'

'We found Noddy at home and took him in for questioning. Of course, he denies everything, but we took DNA and fingerprints. Also found an old photo of your mum in his possessions.'

Jack felt vomit surge into his throat. He didn't want to hear stuff like that. 'But DNA and fingerprints won't help, will they? There was a fire and anyway the whole case is too old now.'

'You never know what will turn up Jack.'

'What about the wellbores?'

'Ah. Noddy said they were an old water well and sewage system for the proposed resort, but were closed up temporarily, when the resort was mothballed a few years back. It sounded plausible Jack, and Langley bought it and let him go, pending further investigation.'

'So that's that is it?'

'No. I persuaded Langley there might be more bodies down there. I told him to climb to the top of the mound and see if he could smell sulphur. He said he could.'

'Can you smell sulphur from buried bodies?'

'How the hell do I know? I just know you said you smelt something like that, and I figured it would make him curious. Anyway, long story short, he reckoned the mounds' revegetation was too recently done to fit what Noddy claimed, so they will be excavated.'

'That's great. When?'

'Not sure Jack. There's a process. I'll let you know when I know. Oh, and I checked on the gun club. It hasn't been operational for years, so those weren't stray bullets. We did find a rifle, locked in a trunk in the garden shed at the back of Noddy's house. He said it wasn't his, and he knew nothing about it, but he would say that, wouldn't he? Especially if the bullets match the slugs we took from your car. We'll have enough to arrest him, soon mate.'

Jack hung up, and a surge of adrenalin rushed through him. Now he knew how to write the report. He pulled his laptop closer.

On the following Tuesday, Ed phoned to say that the excavation of the mounds had been approved and a company had been appointed to begin work on the site. They were still trying to trace the owners. Although *Green Synergy* was listed as local agents for *Paramount Holdings*, they claimed only to communicate via mail, with the secretary of an offshore company somewhere in the Caribbean.

Jack said, 'Have you noticed everything seems to lead back to Tad?'

'Yes mate, but there's more. The company contracted to excavate the wells is a subsidiary of your old firm in Townsville. Apparently Tad told the Inspector, MGEE's were the only firm with the expertise to do something like this safely, and so close to national and marine parks.'

Jack groaned. 'That's it then.'

'Patience Jack. You never know what fate might cough up.'

The next day, Jack emailed his preliminary report to Tad, then sat back and contemplated what he had written. He had laid the blame for the fish kills squarely on an unknown source of hydrogen sulphide, explaining how the gas was produced. It often occurred through organic material decomposition, but more readily through human activity such as seawater in connection with wellbores in offshore gas or petroleum drilling. It could also arise in sewage treatment plants, tanneries, animal waste, but as there were none of these activities in any volume in the area of the fish kills, the source remained unknown.

Water testing from rivers and the nearby Eubenangee Swamp, an important and environmentally significant bird habitat, as well as the runoff from farms, found no traces of the gas in the quantities required to induce mass kills of sea dwelling fish. He made a point of specifying the location, at the southern end of Bramston Beach, offshore of the Ella Bay National Park, which was a significant cassowary habitat, and recommended further investigations in the area.

He suggested a seabed exploration for natural seepage from geological faults and stressed the importance of finding the source to prevent further damage to the environment, to marine life and to human health. He explained how seepage from a fault or an old gas pipeline, or wellbore may have poisoned the fish.

He also noted an observed increase in seismic activity around Gibson Reef, which lay about thirty-five kilometres offshore from Bramston Beach. Now all he could do was hope that was enough to frighten any reader who understood a little geology. Throughout the report he had included pictures and diagrams showing the places tested, and diagrams of likely sources of contamination.

Overall, while the cause of the fish deaths was identified as hydrogen sulphide poisoning, its source was unknown. Jack felt he had met Tad's requirements for an inconclusive report. He just hoped he had given enough detail for a curious scientist somewhere in the Commonwealth Public Service to examine things more closely. At this point, it was all he could do.

The next day, Jack received a copy of the coroner's report. It stated that Barry's death resulted from a craniocerebral trauma caused by bunt force. In other words, a blow to his head. Barry's body was released to the funeral agency for burial, and now his report was in, Jack requested bereavement leave to take care of his father's funeral arrangements. Molly's remains had not been released as investigations into her murder were still ongoing.

The funeral was a small, sombre affair. Only he, Sophia, Ed, Tess, and Mrs Morrison and a few of Barry's oldest friends attended. Noddy didn't turn up although Jack had texted him the time and place.

Jack knew Barry wanted to be buried rather than being cremated. He wished he could have buried Molly at the same time, but the next best thing was a plan to place them side by side by side in the local village cemetery. At least they could rest together in death. He had gone over everything he could find about his mother's disappearance, even searching through old newspapers in the National Archives, until he began to dream about it.

He badgered long-suffering Ed with his theories and talked to Sophia about his memories of his mother. Sophia soon winkled out buried emotions, until the protections he had built around Molly's memory broke and rolled out the corner of his eyes to drip onto her lap, while she combed her fingers through his hair. But at the end of it, he was certain Barry had not killed Molly. It was just a matter of time until the police found evidence that would pin the murder on Noddy.

Jack was as certain of that, as he was that Tad Hinckler and Chad Meyers, were in some form of diabolical partnership, and had been experimentally drilling under the Great Barrier Reef, looking for oil or gas, placing pressure on fragile geological systems, and redistributing pressure that caused the earth to tremble. At least now, with the added scrutiny of police suspicion, they had been forced to stop.

Yet despite his musings, he always came back to the point of realisation that no matter what he believed, he still had no proof for either his theory about his mother's death, or that Tad and Chad's activities had caused the earth tremors. Then Ed rang to say they had an eyewitness report of Noddy driving in the vicinity of the farm the night of Barry's murder, although he had sworn he was in Brampton Beach at the time. Enough for an arrest at any rate. The news hadn't surprised Jack, although what had taken place in the kennels was still a mystery.

Did Barry discover Noddy had killed Molly and buried her under the concrete? Or was there some other reason for him being at the farm that night? Ed suggested Noddy might have been covering up evidence by setting fire to the place when Barry confronted him. Whatever the reason, it would come out in the investigation.

While Jack was on bereavement leave, he stayed in Atherton with Sophia, even though the forensic team had left the farm. He wondered what he should do with it. The land was free title, unencumbered by debt, which was more than he could say for his flat in Cairns, and Barry, surprisingly, had left a will. Yet, there was still paperwork to complete before the property could be transferred to him. Just another thing he had to do. He pulled the laptop towards him and began filling in forms. He had just finished the last form and emailed it off when Sophia arrived home from work.

She came in through the front door and kicked off her shoes. 'Wine in the garden, I think. What a shit of a day. You'll never guess who came in for a Covid vaccine booster...'

'Who?'

Jack got up, found an open bottle of chilled wine in the fridge, poured a glass for Sophia, and took out a beer for himself.

'Elijah the bloody Prophet, the man who says intervention in God's will is pointless. Ironic little man. But would you believe he admitted that he came up to Atherton because he didn't want his followers to know he was vaccinated? He said he had vulnerabilities. It would be laughable if it wasn't so bloody dangerous. I felt like telling him to piss-off but what can you do?'

'The Hippocratic Oath.' Jack handed her the wine.

'It's called the Declaration of Geneva now and I actually think that Elijah is the one in violation of human rights and civil liberties. Maybe I should have told him to piss-off and catch Covid for all I care.' She sighed. 'God, I'm tired.'

Gas Lighting 101

On the following Monday, Jack returned to work and found a message from Pete asking him to come up to his office. Jack found his friend had moved to the top floor next to Tad's office. It looked like he was still unpacking boxes into filing cabinets.

Pete came around the desk and shook Jack's hand. 'How are you feeling mate? Really sorry about your father. I would have come up to the funeral, but things got a bit hectic here.'

'That's okay Pete. You didn't even know him. What happened here, then?'

Pete put on his fake, modest look. 'I finally made partner.'

'Congratulations. That's what you wanted.' Jack couldn't get enthusiastic for Pete, although he tried to show he was.

Pete raised an eyebrow. 'It's been a busy weekend for us, working out what policy platform we will advocate for before the federal budget. It would have been good if you had been here.'

Jack grimaced but said nothing.

Pete paused and looked at Jack for a long minute. 'You will have to get involved Jack, even though I know you hate politics, but this is a political job, mate. We need to get out and lobby for our interests, and you will need to start acting like a team player, especially since the fish kill project is finalised. You had that one handed to you on a plate. Your job now is to go after new projects and lobby for the funding.'

It struck Jack that Pete was now talking to him like he was an employee, not a friend, and he knew he had to be very careful about what he said next.

'I haven't yet had any feedback on the draft report I sent to Tad about the fish deaths. I should probably wrap that up before I begin any new projects. I'll go and see Tad now.'

'No need. I dealt with it, and it's been submitted. In fact, I think the Federal Environment Minister will be making an announcement in a few days.'

Jack frowned. 'Do you have a copy of the finalised report?'

Pete looked around his office as if expecting one to be sitting in plain sight. 'I'll have Noreen send you one.' Then, out of nowhere, he said, you're not depressed are you? You can have more time off if you need it for your mental health.'

'What? I'm fine. What made you say that?'

'Considering your dad's death and your mum's... Anyway, let me know... You look pretty glum.'

Jack shrugged. 'My natural expression, mate. Can't help it.' He forced a smile. 'But thanks for asking.'

Later that same morning, when Jack received the report and began reading it, his face registered his growing horror. None of it reflected what he'd found, nor what he'd written. The aerial photos Tad had taken were now included, and arranged like a tourist brochure, interspersed with the photos Jack had included of the sites they had tested.

The section about the hydrogen sulphide and its possible sources was gone, replaced by a section that said, *hydrogen sulphide resulted from the microbial breakdown of organic matter, and a consequential absence of oxygen, which occurred naturally in swamps, such as the nearby Eubenangee Swamp.*

Jack almost choked. He flicked over to the section on risk, to find it too had been modified and turned into legalese gobbledygook. As he read, blood thumped through his arteries, the muscles in his jaw twitched, and his head felt like it would explode. When he finished reading, he sat back in his chair and stared out the window.

The report was nonsense; worse than nonsense, it was misleading, and it had his name on it. He printed off the report and walked slowly up the fire escape stairs to the top floor. With every step, his pulse slowed as he gained ground on his rage. He took a deep breath and opened the fire escape door to walk down the carpeted corridor to Pete's new office.

Noreen wasn't outside, but he could see through the open doorway that Pete wasn't in either. He turned back to head in the opposite direction towards Tad's office when a thought struck him. He turned back again and walked into Pete's office, quickly scanning the half-unpacked boxes for the file he was seeking. He found it in one of the lockable drawers that now stood open. He took the papers out of the file, returned the file to its slot, then quickly returned to his office to secrete the papers in his desk.

Leaving his office once more, he retraced his steps to Tad's office, this time taking the lift, which opened within sight of Tad's secretary. She told him that Tad was in conference with Pete. Jack made an appointment, went back down in the lift, and walked back to his office and sat at his desk. He opened his drawer to lift out the papers from the file in Pete's office when his mobile rang.

An unfamiliar voice said the speaker was Dr Michael Finley, from Geoscience Australia. He wanted to discuss Jack's report.

Jack sat forward, and said, 'Sure what is it you wanted to discuss?'

The report says you are a qualified, geo-physicist and a geotechnical engineer.

'That's correct.'

'Did you write the report we have received regarding fish deaths off the Queensland coast?'

'No.'

'That's odd. It has your name on it. Do you know who did write it?'

'I have just returned from bereavement leave. The report I wrote was a draft. The report you have received is not my work, but I have only discovered this fact a few moments ago and have not yet had time to understand how this came about.'

'That is unfortunate.'

'You're telling me. Look Dr Finley, there is something odd happening and I would like some time to sort it out. I can send you my draft and you will see where I was heading with the final report, but I would ask you to keep this quiet for the moment, until I have more information.'

'That's very irregular, Dr Fallon. If there is something problematic about this report the Minister should know...' He paused before saying slowly, 'However, the report was not sent directly to Geoscience. A colleague in the Department of Agriculture, Water and the Environment sent it to me because he couldn't make sense of it. He checked out your qualification and, thinking a fellow geo-physicist might understand it, he sent it to me.

Of course, his minister is different from my minister although they are connected under the larger ministerial portfolio.'

Jack realised the man's long-winded explanation was code, for *he was giving him time before he reported anything*. 'I'm not familiar with how the public service works, but you should tell your colleague that I think an environmental lawyer called Pete Macalister wrote the final report that you have received.'

There was silence on the phone, and Jack waited until Finley absorbed that bit of information.

Then Finley said, 'I will wait for clarification, but if the Minister is at any risk of this thing blowing up, it's my duty to inform him.'

'Look, give me your email address, and I'll send the correct draft version immediately. And please try to hold off on publishing anything regarding the report you have, especially associated with my name. I will call you the soon as I know more. Oh, and Dr Finley, thanks for calling me directly to check. You cannot know how grateful I am for that.'

As soon as Jack hung up the phone, he sent Finley his draft with *Private and Confidential* written in the email subject line. Then he saved Finley's phone number to his contacts. He hoped that was enough.

His phone rang again. It was Tad's secretary, saying Tad was free now and would see Jack.

By the time Jack went upstairs, he was glad of the delay. His pulse rate was now normal, and he had the beginning of a plan forming in his mind. Instead of blowing his top, he was going to be much more strategic about fighting this...this...whatever it was.

When he entered Tad's office, Pete was still there, along with a petite woman with a stiff blonde bob. He tried to remember her name and failed. They had only met briefly when he had first started with the firm, but he knew she was the human resource manager.

She stood by the window, arms folded, the pointy toe of one shoe tapping the carpet in rhythmic impatience, matched by the tap, tap of long red fingernails against her upper arm.

Jack stopped, and looked from one to the other, waiting for some indication as to why the H.R. manager had been called in.

Tad said, 'Ah Jack. Good to see you back with us. My commiserations once more for your tragedy. Terrible.'

'Thanks, but I'm fine.'

The H.R. manager took a tiny step forward. It was possibly all her tight skirt and high heels would allow. Her face was creased in earnest concern. 'Are you really though, Jack? It would be quite understandable to be a bit shaken by events.'

Pete intervened. 'I explained how down you looked this morning, mate.'

'Perhaps you should take more time...' She crooned at him.

A chill ran across his shoulders. 'I don't need more time off. I need to discuss this report.' He shook it in Tad's direction. This wasn't turning out as he'd planned.

'The report's done. The project's finished.' Tad had an echo of finality in his voice.

'It's not done though, is it? This is not my report. It is a load of rubbish, but it has my name on it.'

'That's the report you sent me, Jack. You should have said, if you thought you had made a mistake. We would have understood. I know you've been under a huge amount of pressure.'

Jack shook his head. 'You know I didn't write this report.' He swung around to stare his old friend down. 'But I suspect you did Pete.'

Pete glanced at Tad, a worried frown rumpling his forehead.

Tad raised his voice. 'Jack, I see you are still overwrought, not yet fit to return to work. Take two weeks, but before you return, I want a doctor's report to state you are fit enough to work. As your employer, I am liable for your health. If we know you are suffering a mental illness, we have a duty of care to act. This is nonnegotiable. Do you understand?'

Jack stared from one to the other. What the hell was going on? The H.R. manager smirked. Pete's face was fixed in a ridged frown and Tad was trying to stare Jack down. It dawned on him then that they wanted him out the way for some reason other than just the report.

What could he say? 'Fine, but I want it on the record that this report is all wrong. It cannot be submitted in its current form.'

The H. R. manager took his arm. 'It'll be fine Jack; you are not to worry.' She handed him a card. 'I want you to go and see this man. He is very good with workplace burnout.'

'Burnout? What is it, burnout, trauma, or grief you think I'm suffering from.'

'All of them, Jack. Take the card. He's expecting your call.'

Jack was escorted by the H. R. manager to his office, where she said he should collect his things before he went home but should leave any company property, like his mobile and laptop, behind. He remembered the contents of the file in his drawer and managed to slip them into his resume file before adding that to his small inventory of personal items. Otherwise, he didn't have much in the way of personal stuff at work. He had never owned much anyway and didn't see the point of all the knick-knacks and photos, people like Pete, littered across their desks.

All the data on his laptop and phone was saved to his private cloud, a precaution he'd always taken, but after Vernon's place was ransacked, he'd set up a system that uploaded every bit of new data instantly. He picked up his car keys, and she held out her hand.

'You're kidding. Am I being sacked?'

'No, but I am just protecting company property, Jack. You should not be driving in your current state of mind. Just go home and rest. I understand you have a flat within walking distance, or I can call you a cab.'

He shook his head. What did she know about his state of mind, but what did it matter? He was never going to go back to work for Tad again. It was just a question of time, to get the proof he needed to screw the man to the wall, and then he'd have resigned, anyway.

On reaching his flat, he let himself in and opened his C.V. to take out the papers from Pete's file. He scanned them and saw the company directors of *Paramount Holdings* were listed as Tad Hinckler and Chad Myers. He noticed Pete Macalister was the company Secretary as of last Saturday's date. No surprises then as to how he'd achieved his sudden promotion. Jack was jubilant. He had his first real piece of evidence. Now he needed to put the papers in a safe place, but where? If Pete reported them missing to the police, the first place they would look would be his flat. He couldn't stash them here.

He walked through to his bedroom and pulled an overnight bag from his wardrobe. Then he packed a change of clothes and placed the papers between the folded clothes. He collected his apartment keys off the hall table where he'd left them just ten minutes ago, and walked out with the bag, locking the door behind him, but leaving the security gate unlocked. He'd always considered the gate overkill for a place like Cairns. Then he walked into town, bought a phone and a laptop, downloaded his contact numbers from the cloud and called Sophia and Ed before he found a cab to take him to the Cairns domestic airport.

Jack was done taking Tad and Pete's shit. He was going to fight back, although he was not sure what he was pitting himself against. One thing he was sure of was that Tad and Pete were not going to ruin Jack's reputation with their lies. He'd go down fighting them to the last breath, but first he was going to pay Dr Finley at GeoScience Australia a visit.

The Australian Capital City

It was late when Jack arrived in Canberra, after a stopover and change of planes in Brisbane. For a capital city it was a hard place to fly into unless it was from one of Australia's state capitals. A cab took him to a moderately priced hotel somewhere in the city. It was his first visit to the place, and he had no idea of the city's layout. When he'd had the opportunity at school to take an excursion to visit the Australian Parliament, Barry couldn't afford it, so Jack stayed home while his classmates went.

After Jack checked into the hotel, he unpacked, took out his new laptop, connected it to the hotel's Wi-Fi, and studied a map of the city. Canberra was laid out with several centres linked to the main centre in a spoke and wheel design, with Lake Burley Griffin, a long, narrow body of water stretching roughly east to west, at its centre. The main centre, where his hotel was located, was south of the lake, and the Department of Agriculture, Water and the Environment was just across a bridge to the north. Geoscience was further south from the city centre.

The next morning, he rang Finley, explaining he was in Canberra and would like to meet up and discuss the report. Finley suggested a café in Manuka, which wasn't far from Jack's hotel. Then he asked if Jack minded if his colleague tagged along as it was he who was interested in the report. Jack figured he had to trust someone, so he agreed and an hour later found himself sitting with two earnest scientists, over very good coffee and pastry, at a pavement café in a busy shopping precinct.

After the northern warmth, Jack was glad of his jacket, but still shivered as a breeze whipped around the corner. Yet, the sun on the pavement was warm, and the colour of the trees along the avenues showed him that the autumn pictures he had seen in magazines weren't photo shopped. He wrapped his hands around the steaming mug, while he waited for one of the two men to comment on what he'd just told them.

Dr Finley blew air out between his lips and said, 'What you have told us is mind blowing. Criminal even, but if you don't mind my saying, it's a bit unbelievable. If I hadn't checked out your credentials, and spoken personally to Professor Prentice, I would think you were perhaps a little challenged. But he vouches for you, and your sanity.' Finley grinned, then looked sober. 'The question is what do we do about it? What do you think Ben?'

Ben Anderman frowned. 'Look, I don't know anything about geology but the fish dying of hydrogen sulphide poisoning makes sense to me. From what I can make out that's what the report said. The whole project funding was based on finding out what killed the fish, but if we want to prevent it happening again, we have to find the source. Your draft gave an indication of that source, but the final report suggested it was a natural phenomenon from the Eubenangee Swamp. My Minister is braying for something to announce. The fishing industry has her on the ropes, and she wants to have some policy or grant to calm their agitation.'

'Okay, but what about the possibility of oil exploration under the barrier reef or the increase in seismic activity?'

Ben pursed his lips. 'Sorry. Outside my area of expertise.'

Finley said, 'It will have to be investigated.'

Jack told them about the police investigation already occurring. Of course, it meant him telling them all about the connections between his father, his mother and Noddy, and what Ed had told him about Tad saying, MGEE, the only company with the expertise to excavate the site, was involved up to their necks with *Paramount Holdings*.

Both men looked at him in astonishment. Ben said, 'The story becomes wilder and wilder.'

Jack remembered the *Paramount Holding* registration papers and took them out of his jacket pocket, smoothed them out and showed the two men the directors' and secretary's names. Then he carefully refolded them and returned them to his pocket.

Finley's eyebrows almost met in the middle as he stared at Jack. 'I think you need to speak to the Australian Federal Police, Dr Fallon. This is way beyond mere public servants.'

'Do you know anyone I can talk to? If I go into the AFP with this story, they'll have me sectioned for a mental health assessment.' It dawned on him, that this was exactly what Tad had been setting up, with his suspension from work on mental health ground. His shoulders sagged. What the hell was he supposed to do now? He paused and stared at the table. He had to tell them. They had gone out on a limb for him, but he'd lose credibility. What the hell...He took a breath. 'It just occurred to me my boss is setting me up.' Jack explained his suspension from work pending a mental health review of fitness to return to duty.

Ben said, 'I am not sure I should be seen talking to you.' But he smiled for the first time, which gave Jack some encouragement.

Finley said, 'As it happens, I do know an AFP officer, my brother's wife. Unfortunately, she is way down the food chain, but I can tell you one thing, you are absolutely correct. If what you are saying is true, the first people the AFP will check with, is the local police, then the company excavating the site, and your place of work.'

'I'm screwed aren't I?'

Ben said, 'Not quite. I have an idea. What's always a popular news story?'

Jack shook his head, but Finley was grinning. 'Go on tell us, Ben.'

'Dirt on politicians.'

'But this isn't about politicians.'

'Oh, isn't it? Your company, over the term of this government and the one before that, has received millions in grant money, while the public service is hollowed out until the buildings echoes with protests against the private sector running off with public money, making enormous profits and producing nothing for the country.'

'Poetic,' Finley said. 'Ben's becoming a socialist.'

'I've always been a socialist, a well-educated, and well-heeled socialist, with not one but two doctorates, and one who cannot claim working-class roots, but nonetheless I subscribe to democratic socialism as a fairer way of running society.'

'Particularly given your father is a venture capitalist, and you attended King's School in Sydney, before clashing with the political right at Sydney University.' Findley turned to Jack. 'I met Ben when he had to move from Sydney to the National University in Canberra. I was his tutor for a while.'

Ben scowled. 'That little escapade with those fascist bully boys, now in power mind you, ruined any chance of promotion and yet I cannot bring myself to leave and work for the pirate sector.'

'You mean the private sector, don't you?' Finley corrected.

'No. I mean what I say. Nevertheless, this government's focus on so-called big society and small government is radicalising me further to the left. Canberra is crawling with multinationals sucking at the Australian government teat.'

'So, what do you suggest?' Jack asked, a little taken aback by Ben cynical assessment.

'Me? Nothing. I am just having a coffee with a friend of a friend, who is new to Canberra and might want to join us at a party I am throwing for my partner's fiftieth on Friday night. That's if you will still be here. Of course, I should warn you it will be full of National Press Club people.'

Finley said, 'Ben's partner, Nick, is an investigative journalist.'

Jack paused and glanced from one man to the other. Was this what he thought it was? They were offering a path forward. 'I'll be there, thank you. Thank you both.'

'Sorry we weren't much help.'

'On the contrary.' Jack pressed his mouth together. He'd need to prepare his assault.

Ben said, 'I'll send you my address. Let me have your telephone number.'

For the next few days, until the night of Ben's party, there was nothing Jack could do, so he played the tourist, watched television, and wrote a complete account of what he'd discovered and what he had theorised from seismic data. He tried to write in layman's terms, imagining a news article explaining the issue. It was complicated so he added diagrams, drawings, photos, map references and scanned images of the *Paramount Holdings* registration paperwork. He left nothing out, explaining which was educated guesswork, and what was a fact. He also figured there would be too much to explain to a journalist at a party, so he saved the document to a thumb drive as well as to his private cloud storage. That way, he could show a brief presentation of the issues on the thumb drive, and later, if Nick agreed to exchange information, he could share the private cloud file with the raw data with the journalist.

On the Friday night, he pocketed the thumb drive and went to Ben's house. When he arrived, the party was in full swing, noisy, and bright with an overwhelming number of famous faces, many of whom he recognised from television. No one paid him the least attention, and he was glad to be an invisible man. He found Ben in the kitchen and was introduced to his partner, Nick.

Now, he realised who Nick Ralding was. He was a tall, ruggedly handsome man who had been a war correspondent until he copped a bullet to his thigh, somewhere in the Middle East. Ten years ago, he had come home and taken up investigative journalism, winning two Walkley awards since then.

He limped towards Jack and shook his hand, his grip resolute. 'Come into my study. Ben's told me what he knows, but I need to ask some questions, and it will be quieter in there, away from the madding crowd.'

The study had the cosy feel of a library. Books lined the walls, and a glass-panelled door led into a small garden. A desk held a lamp and a laptop, with a notepad and pencil beside it.

'Have a seat. Can I get you something to drink? I have a very good bottle of Bourbon whiskey hidden in the drawer. I should have asked earlier, but I can fetch you a beer from the kitchen.'

Jack shook his head. 'Maybe later, thanks. He took the thumb drive from his pocket. 'I've written it all down and I can share some of the data and photos with you through a shared cloud file to which I can give you access, if you let me have your email address.'

Nick's eyebrows lifted. 'Wow, that's great. Wish all my sources were so organised.' He put the drive into his laptop and opened it. 'Crikey, you are thorough.'

He picked up his note pad. 'First of all, a little background. Ben says you have a PhD. in Geophysics...'

Jack spent two hours in the study answering questions, until Ben came in and said, 'Enough. This is your party Nick, and people are beginning to gossip about you hanging out in here with this handsome hunk.'

Jack blinked with surprise at being referred to in that way, but got up and said, 'I really appreciate what you are doing. I'll go now, but I'll leave you my number if you want any more information.'

'Stay and enjoy the party.'

'Do you mind if I don't. All these famous people are a bit intimidating.'

Ben laughed. 'I understand entirely.'

Nick shook Jack's hand. 'I'll be in touch. Take care my friend. It was nice meeting you. I hope everything works out well. You deserve it, standing up for right like this. Many people would have averted their eyes.'

Jack called an Uber to take him back to the hotel. He sat back, thinking about the night's events, when the car's radio broadcast penetrated his brain.

The Minister's announcement yesterday into the sustainability of the Reef has been welcomed by the Queensland State Government.

'Can you turn that up, please?'

The Uber driver obliged, but the announcer had already moved on to another story.

When he got back to his room, he opened his phone, found the ABC app, and there was the story. He read the press release and saw that the government was promising millions more dollars to look at what they called the sustainability of the Great Barrier Reef. The article outlined how the Great Barrier Reef supports 70,000 jobs and contributes almost $7 billion to the Australian economy.

Global warming is contributing to acidification of the coastal swamps and beaches, killing forests and marine life as the recent report on the massive fish die-off has attested. Constant bleaching of the reef is placing tourism and fishing industry jobs in jeopardy, which will have a significant impact on the economy not only of Queensland but also of for the whole of Australia.

The Minister said, 'We must plan for the future and find new ways to live with a warmer climate; that is why the Federal Government is promising it will allocate an extra two billion dollars to developing sustainable solutions for alternative jobs in the region. This will be part of the National recovery program as we move into and find ways to manage living in a changing world.'

Jack stopped reading. This was why they wanted him out of the way. Tad had persuaded the government that they should permit gas and oil exploration in world heritage sites, an underlying code for alternative jobs for the region. UNESCO would never allow it, but what could they do except declare the heritage areas in danger, which it was already? Perhaps they would rescind world heritage status, but by the time that happened, it would be too late, anyway. Tad and Chad were going to have their criminal activity made legal. He couldn't believe it. He copied the URL of the news story and texted it to Nick. Then he rang Sophia to tell her he was coming home.

He went to sleep that night, feeling his mission to expose this environmental vandalism was hopeless, and perhaps he should leave he world to go hang itself. He could marry Sophia, if she would have him, and become a farmer. He'd be content with that. What was he trying to save, anyway? Major sea currents were slowing, affecting weather patterns around the globe. Carbon emissions were increasing at an alarming rate. Plastic particles polluted everything, including the Antarctic. Animal extinctions were out of control. The world was already screwed. How would his attempt to stop further environmental vandalism change any of that?

A Small Triumph

On the Saturday, Jack flew home still harbouring a sense of failure he couldn't seem to shake. He arrived late in the afternoon and took a cab to his flat. He paid the driver and then went into the building. His flat was on the eighth floor. There were only two penthouses in the block. Who owned the other one? He had no idea. He'd never seen anyone going up to it. Perhaps they were absentee landlords of vacation accommodation like he'd been for so many years. He was lucky he had bought the place off the plan when the housing market was at its worst. If he had had to buy it today, he would not have been able to afford it.

The large landing space outside the lift doors, all marble columns, tiled floors, and mirrored walls, led to his front door. The security gate was a fancy black wrought iron affair, never locked. He had always thought it was more for effect that a necessity, although now he realised he'd been a fool. The gate was standing open, and the front door gaped. Where the door lock had once been, the wood was now a splintered mess. He walked inside, his throat tight as he peered ahead in case someone was still there, but the silence told him otherwise.

He had half expected this when Pete discovered the missing paperwork, although he had anticipated a visit by the police coming to his door with a search warrant. It would seem that wasn't how Tad and Pete operated. Perhaps they didn't want the police knowing what was in those papers either.

The flat had been ransacked. Most of its contents had been removed including television, washing machine, dryer, fridge, and microwave, even the three-piece lounge suite, carpet and his dining table had gone. The only thing still there was his bed, but the mattress had been ripped to shreds. Clothes and books were scattered all over the place. Perhaps this was just a burglary after all. Surely taking the furniture was a bit over the top, even for Tad.

Wearily he went out to the rooftop veranda and gazed out toward the marina, while he rang the police. A yacht, white and gleaming, was anchored out in deep water. He'd never seen anything quite so massive and wondered if it was the same yacht he'd seen sailing off Bramston Beach. From this distance he couldn't see much except that a motorboat had left the yacht and was coming in towards the Marina.

That was the way to live. Difficult for burglars to ransack a yacht although he'd heard that pirates were a menace in some areas around the world. He'd never been sailing. Maybe he would give it a go one day. He sighed and spoke to a woman who answered the phone, explaining his flat had been broken into.

On the weekend, after the police had finished dusting the place for fingerprints, Sophia, Tess, and Ed came down to help him tidy up and give the place a clean, and a new coat of paint. He was so glad to see them, he decided instantly to put the flat on the market and move up to the Tablelands. He didn't care if he didn't have a job. He had a tidy amount in savings and the sale of the apartment would realise a large amount of the equity he had tied up in it.

The next day, he rang a real estate agent and was told property sales were booming. It was hard to come by a new property, especially a penthouse so close to the sea, and she wanted to bring in a buyer that same day. Jack told the woman he needed to make some repairs before he could have people viewing the place.

He still needed a new front door, but he could do that in a day. He agreed to an appointment for an inspection on the Wednesday. Then he went to buy a utility pickup. If he was going to become a farmer, he'd better forget driving fancy four by fours, besides a Ute was cheaper. On his way home, he picked up a front door, took it home, installed it, painted it, and fitted a deadlock.

On the following Wednesday, he waited downstairs at a café while the agent showed a buyer around. She had indicated the house-showing would take about an hour. He looked at his watch. Still 40 minutes to go. He got up and walked along the road, looking in shop windows, stopping at a jeweller to examine the display of engagement rings. He had no idea what Sophia would like, but he knew it would be nothing like the glitz he saw in the shop window.

He glanced again at his watch. The inspection should be over by now, safe to return. He retraced his steps only to find the buyer, a burly man with a heavy accent, waiting for him.

'I'll make you an offer right now.' He pulled out a cheque book.

Who still used cheque books? Jack glanced at the agent.

She said, 'There are other buyers wanting to see the place.'

'I'll offer 20 grand above the asking price. I have to have this. My wife says it's perfect.'

The wife stood a little apart from the man and, as if on cue, she said, 'The view is to die for.' She too, had a foreign accent. Scandinavian, Jack guessed.

The man frowned at her, and she walked away.

The agent said again, 'There are other people interested.'

The man said, 'Fifty grand on top of the asking price.'

'I am perfectly happy to get an extra fifty grand, thank you.' Jack smiled at the agent to take the sting from his words. 'I say yes, let's do it. I want to sell they want to buy. You get your commission, so where's the problem?'

She took Jack off to one side and said quietly, 'Other buyers may offer more, and I am not sure these people are even Australian citizens, or if I can sell to foreigners.'

'Wouldn't you have checked that before you showed them around?'

'They said they were.'

'Well, that's it then. It's a good deal.' Jack turned back to the man. 'It's yours mate.' He shook his hand.

The agent sighed. 'Congratulations.'

Jack was jubilant, and the following weekend he took Sophia out to celebrate. Before they left, he had cleaned out the new Ute and found he still had the second set of keys for the new front door of the flat. He reminded himself to return them to the estate agent next time he was in Cairns and placed them in the glove compartment.

The following week, the story broke just as Nick Ralding promised it would, in a low-key way, in an online national newspaper. The copy was hedged about with caveats and possibilities, rather than statements of fact. Jack wasn't surprised as he read the article. Nick was a good writer and had got it right, neither sensationalist nor inaccurate, just the known facts, along with probabilities and some possibilities.

Jack understood that Nick couldn't claim too much in the face of so many uncertainties. Yet the article juxtaposed what was known, what was fact, and what was conjecture in a way any reader must surely be able to understand the potential dangers, without pointing a finger at the likely culprits. The account began with increasing earthquake activity in the north and cited corroboration of this fact from both Professor Vernon Prentice and Dr Finley of Geoscience Australia. Then it explained how Jack, a whistle-blower, had brought it to media attention after failing to have his report to the minister submitted in its original form.

The Minister, whose announcement of an extra two billion dollars to develop sustainable solutions for alternative jobs in the region was, in Jack's estimation, premised on false information. The article explained what Jack's team had found regarding the massive fish kills off the Cairns to Innisfail coast, outlining how the report Jack had submitted had been altered before it was given to the government although it didn't say by whom.

Nick had also explained Jack's qualifications, and work experience in the area of gas and oil extraction and the qualifications of the multidisciplinary team working on the project under his leadership. He cited several of the team's findings. Then he outlined how gas and oil extraction could not only cause earthquakes, as they had indisputably been doing for some time in America. There was also the potential for damage to the environment through pollution from chemical leakage or escaping gasses, including methane, CO^2 and the hydrogen sulphide, which was what was found to have killed the fish.

Nick mentioned the discovery of the wellbores by the police in connection to an investigation into a cold case murder, citing Detective Senior Sergeant David Langley, saying they had taken into custody the caretaker of an area of private land near Brampton Beach, on which were found two illegally sunk wells.

While Langley acknowledged little was known about the origin of the wellbores or what they were used for, or when they were last operational, the area of land on which they were situated belonged to a firm called *Paramount*

Holdings. Nick explained that *Paramount Holdings* was an offshore registered company whose directors included the well-known environmental defender Tad Hinckler, and also Chad Myers, who was currently MGEE's, regional manager.

To his disappointment, Nick didn't include Jack's fears for the Noggin Block's stability from increasing seismic activity. Perhaps he thought that was a step too far, although it didn't matter. So long as any further exploration, sequestration or extraction was stopped, the Noggin Block might remain as it was for decades into the future. Jack conceded it was possibly better that the article only dealt with the issue of the fish kills, his report being altered, and its linkage to a coverup of potential gas or oil extraction in the Great Barrier Reef Marine Park.

Despite some omissions in the article, Jack felt a sense of jubilation that the story was at last out there, and he had done all he could to expose what was being hidden from the public. They had a right to know. Now he could shut down his past life and embrace the life of a farmer with a clear conscience. He chuckled. Who would have imagined he would ever have looked forward to living on the farm?

He wondered if this was how his dad had felt all those years ago when his father had died, and he took over the farm. Jack had been a toddler and had no memory of his grandfather. It seemed strange that his dad had become a builder to get away from the farm, and Jack had gone mining to get away, but somehow both men were drawn back to their roots although he hoped that was the extent of the similarities between their two lives.

Disaster

Jack spent the next two weeks at the farm, mowing grass, fixing fences, sorting out his dad things, patching up the house, cleaning windows, walls, and floors before repainting the whole house, inside and out. Sophia joined him for the weekend. On the Friday night they sat outside on an old blanket, drank wine, and gazed in awe at the Milky Way, with Sophia exclaiming and pointing at each shooting star.

Fireflies flickered above the mown grass as Jack told Sophia about his dream for a life on the farm. He spoke about how he would improve the house, adding a study and a library. He'd put in a kitchen garden to grow veggies and rejuvenate the orchid. There would be a healthy herd of Drought Master cattle, and chickens, and children running freely across the grassy paddocks.

She raised an eyebrow at him and said, 'Are you planning to farm children? The Child Safety Department might have something to say about that.'

Jack laughed and fished about in his top pocket. Earlier that day, he'd gone through his father's things looking for the ring, hoping it was as good his childhood memory said it was. It had belonged to Barry's mother and before that, his grandmother, who had been born on a farm in the Glen Innes region in New South Wales. Sapphire country. After Barry's mother died, Jack was only about eight, but he remembered Barry giving the ring to Molly. She had cried and said it was too precious to wear on the farm. Barry had suggested she sell it, but Molly wouldn't hear of selling a family heirloom, as she called it, although Jack thought that was probably too grand a name for the ring.

He took it from his pocket and held it out to Sophia. It was an old-fashioned table-cut cobalt blue sapphire, surrounded by what looked like tiny diamonds, but it didn't look like any engagement ring he'd seen in the Cairns jeweller's shop window. Yet, it did have a story, and he hoped Sophia would like it.

She did, and she said yes, and he slipped the ring onto her finger. Then he went to the fridge and took out a bottle of champagne he'd bought just in case.

In the early hours of the following morning, Jack got up for a drink of water and a headache pill, wishing he had drunk less wine. The night was stygian black, but he knew his way around. He wandered through to the kitchen and felt about on the wall for the light. Nothing happened when he switched it on. He walked along the passage to the meter box, and then realising he'd need a light to see if a switch had tripped, he turned back to the bedroom for his phone.

As he made his way along the dark corridor, a heavy blow glanced across his shoulders, and he stumbled forward. Before he could recover, someone leaped on his back and an arm slid around his throat, squeezing his airways. He twisted, but the man hung on grimly. Jack fingers dug into the man's arm, trying to loosen his grip, but the fingers were like steel traps. Panic rose as his breath depleted. He was losing consciousness. On his last bit of oxygen, he gave one mighty heave backwards, slamming the man into the wall of the corridor.

A grunt and the chokehold loosened. He twisted to face his attacker and brought his arms up to break the grip, kneeing him hard in what he thought might be the man's groin area. He caught what might have been a thigh. The man grunted and slid away. Jack gasped for air and tried to yell, but his voice wasn't working. He tried again and this time the sound came out as a croak as he shouted for Sophia to call the police. Then, in the dim light at the end of the corridor, he saw the man. He gave chase, bolting through the open front door and out onto the veranda. He caught sight of a wiry figure running down the driveway.

Jack thundered down the stairs and raced after him, gaining ground until he stupidly tried a flying tackle, something he hadn't attempted since his uni rugby days. He brought the man down by landing heavily on top of him. The fall winded him. While the man kicked and wiggled to escape, Jack tried to suck in a breath, all the while hanging onto the fighting fury with grim determination.

A flickering light caught his eye. Flames were leaping up the curtains inside the sitting-room window at the front of the house. He pushed himself up, leaving the man on the ground, and raced back to the farmhouse.

'Sophia,' he yelled and ran into the house and along the corridor, bursting open the bedroom door. She was still asleep. He bent to pick her up.

She awoke fighting him. 'What the fuck!' she shouted. Then she looked down the corridor and saw the flames licking out from the sitting-room door. 'Oh my God!'

Jack let her down and grabbed her hand. 'We have to run through it. Ready?'

She had the presence of mind to grab her phone and keys, and together they ran towards the front door. Smoke billowed from the sitting room into the corridor and Jack pulled his tee shirt over his nose. He tightened his grip on Sophia's hand and charge through the smoke.

Sophia fell onto the grass, her long hair smouldering where the flames had singed it. He ran his hands over her head, smothering any bits still sizzling. Then he grabbed the hose, but the water pump was electric, and the power was out, or had been turned off by the intruder.

Sophia shivered. 'What happened?'

'A burglar, I think. Are you okay?' Jack asked.

She nodded.

'I'm just going to check around.'

'Don't leave me.'

'I won't go far.'

'Jack the house is burning.'

He shrugged. 'Nothing I can do. There's no water.'

'I'll call the firies.'

'No signal. Sophia, I have to catch the bastard.'

He ran up the driveway and heard the sound of a motor starting, reaching the gate as a Ute, its wheels spinning on the gravel road, took off. There was no way he would catch it. He walked back to where he had left Sophia.

She had moved to small rise where they could sometimes get a phone signal and was already talking to the emergency operator.

When she hung up, he said, 'Better call the police as well.'

'The operator said they would send the police with the Firies when I mentioned the burglar. Did you see him?'

'He took off in a Ute but I'm pretty sure that was Noddy. I must have surprised him, and he clobbered me with something, felt like a steel pipe, then jumped me. I nearly had him out here, but then I saw the fire and let him go.'

'I thought the police had locked him up.'

'So did I. I'll call Ed. Damn! My phone's still in there.' He pointed to the conflagration that was once his home.

'Here.' She gave him hers.

The fire truck arrived, and the fire officers put out the blaze to prevent a grass fire, but it was too late to save the old wooden house. When the police arrived, Jack explained what had happened, saying he was certain the intruder was Harold Noddington.

The police officer asked if he knew why Noddington would come back here and set fire to the house. That gave Jack pause. It seemed arson was Noddy's modus operandi. After all, he had set fire to the kennels to cover up Barry's murder, but why had he tried to burn down the house, now? Did he know Jack and Sophia were inside? Was he trying to get rid of Jack, or was there some other reason for the fire, like covering up clues to his culpability for Barry's murder?

He shook his head. 'Sorry, I have no idea.'

When Ed arrived almost an hour later, he explained that Noddy was out on bail. It seemed Pete had posted it on behalf of *Paramount Holdings*, Noddy's employer.

Jack and Sophia followed Ed back to Atherton. They stopped off at Sophia's house for a shower and change of clothes, chucking their soot blackened tee shirts and shorts into the bin, before going onto the Morrison's. Ed had phoned Tess, and breakfast was waiting for them. As the sun rose, they recounted the night's events, but Jack still couldn't figure out why Noddy would come to the farm or what he might have had to gain by setting fire to the house.

Mrs Morrison said, 'He obviously wants you out of the way. You are a witness to your mother's disappearance all those years ago. Who knows what you might say in court?'

'Or...,' Mr Morrison said, 'maybe he was paid to do it and make it look like an accident. You have created a hornet's nest with that news article.'

'You saw it did you?' Jack was pleased. 'What did you think?'

'Jack, have you watched the news in the past week?'

'No.' He shook his head. 'Been busy and the signal at the farm is terrible, so I don't get online much. I will have to get a satellite connection installed.'

Ed said, 'A satellite connection won't be much good without a house.'

Jack's shoulders slumped. 'Bugger. It really has gone.'

Morrison said, 'You have bigger problems than a house Jack. That article created a storm. It's made the headlines in every newspaper here, and even stateside. Your face is grinning all over the internet, and the government sure are riled. Their own fault, in my opinion, especially after they doubled down on their promise to fund development in the national park, but they began back-pedalling when there was a public outcry. The opposition has seized the moment, throwing their hats in the air, and hollering for an inquiry. The public has not been confronted by so many scientists and engineers giving their opinion on talk shows since the start of the pandemic. Sophia, you must have seen it.'

'I never watch the news or listen to talk shows. It's too depressing.'

Ed's eyes narrowed. 'But is that enough motive for a contract killing? This is country Australia not down-town Tijuana. Are you sure it was Noddy, mate?'

'Pretty sure.' Jack rubbed his throat. It was bruised from the hold Noddy had him in. He couldn't believe the man he'd always thought of as a bit of a runt, could be so strong. Or maybe he just knew the right techniques. Jack had never been much of a fighter. At school, Ed's presence kept most of the bullies at bay, and since school he hadn't moved in company that resorted to that kind of fisticuffs. If this was going to keep on happening, maybe he should learn.

Morrison interrupted his rumination. 'You'll be pleased to know the Prophets now have your picture and name writ large on their signs. They are calling you a hero and demanding that the Australian Federal Police arrest the Minister.'

'You're joking.'

Tess said, 'It might be funny if it wasn't so serious.'

'There's more.' Ed said. 'That reporter who wrote the copy was interviewed on the ABC. He was asked where you were, and he said he didn't know, but he told them about your concerns about the Noggin Block.'

Jack sat forward in his chair. 'And?'

Tess said dryly. 'The press has gone nuts over the name Noggin Block. Bloody typical; miss the point and focus on the sensational or absurd.'

Sophia said quietly, 'I think a tsunami threat is pretty sensational?'

'Yeah, but they can't get their heads around that one.' Ed smiled at her. 'Your hair looks interesting, sort of flyaway.'

'Ed! Show some sympathy.' Tess frowned at her husband.

Sophia touched her singed hair. 'I'll have to have it cut off.'

Jack said, 'Why didn't you tell me, Ed?'

'Tell you what?'

'About the media.'

'Jeez, I like that! For one, I haven't seen you, and secondly, I thought you knew. I figured out that was why you were hiding away at the farm. I didn't think you wanted to see them so, I told the press I didn't know where you were, and Langley said the same.'

Mrs Morrison exclaimed, 'Oh my goodness!' Everyone turned to look at her. She was staring at Sophia's hand. 'You're engaged.'

Sophia looked at the ring as if in surprise. 'Yes, last night. It seems like a lifetime ago.'

Mrs Morrison jumped up and hugged Jack then kissed Sophia. 'I am so happy for you. Now we'll need to forget all this nastiness and organise a party.'

'You will have to fight my mother for that.' Sophia smiled. 'I'd better call her. Maybe we should go out to Julia Creek for Fergus's wedding a week or two early. Neither potential contract assassins nor the press will find you out there.'

Jack shook his head. 'I think I have to speak to the media. I started this; I can't just leave Nick Ralding to carry this shit-can. Can you give me the name and number of the people who contacted you Ed. I'll give them a call back.'

The Media

Two days later, Jack was back in Cairns sitting in a local television studio, a subsidiary of a national commercial network. He sweated under hot lights while two women fussed about him. One dabbed a makeup brush at his face. 'To stop the shine,' she said.

He didn't care about shine and put up his hand to try and stop her, ending up with powder-flecks on his shirt.

'Oh, now look what you've done. Try to sit still, please.' She immediately attacked the power marks with a different brush.

Jack gave up and tried to remain still.

Another woman fixed a lapel mike to his shirt, a more relevant task in his opinion. An engineer was busy checking sound and someone else fiddled with a camera on a stand, pointing it into his face and adjusting the focus.

Another woman poked her head around the door and said, 'Two minutes.'

Jack was about to be patched into the Sydney studio to participate in a live interview, and his gut churned.

The woman fixing his mike said, 'Just relax. It's like talking to a friend on facetime. There's nothing to worry about.'

He resolved to follow her advice.

She stepped away, and suddenly he was live, with the interviewer giving a background to who he was, his qualifications, where he worked and how he had become involved in the project investigating the fish deaths off the Queensland coast.

The interviewer then spoke directly to Jack, thanking him for taking the time to come on National television, and clarify some issues. First he asked about the report that was submitted to the government, and how he came to find out the report was altered.

Jack hadn't expected that question to come up first and stumbled over his words. 'Ah, I discovered the switch when I returned from leave. My friend Pete gave me the report that had been submitted to the Government. I reviewed it and realised it wasn't what I had written...'

'Your friend... That is Pete Macalister the eminent environmental lawyer?'

'That's right, we were at uni together.'

'Am I right to say he recruited you to the firm?'

'That's correct.'

'So, he was your boss?'

'I suppose...'

'You suppose, or he was?'

'Well, he wasn't when I started the report.'

'But he was when he gave you the completed report?'

'Yes.'

'So, is it true that you gave Tad Hinckler the first draft report to approve?'

'Yes.'

'And is it true that Mr Hinckler asked you to give the report to your immediate boss Mr Macalister, but you were unhappy about Mr Macalister's promotion, a promotion you thought was rightfully yours? You were jealous of your friend's promotion to Partner.'

'No. That's not right.' Jack frowned. What the hell was this?

The interviewer then changed the subject, and his voice modified to one of concern. 'You mentioned you had recently returned from leave. That was bereavement leave, wasn't it Dr Fallon?'

'Yes.'

'My condolences, but I understand you have suffered two traumatic events recently.' He turned and spoke to the audience to explain. 'Dr Fallon's father was found murdered, and a cold case involving Dr Fallon's mother's disappearance, several years ago, was also found to be a murder.' He turned back to Jack. 'That would have been a considerable shock, and I imagine the news would have placed you under significant stress.'

The interviewer paused, but as he hadn't asked a question Jack didn't volunteer any comment.

The interviewer narrowed his eyes as if trying to see something inside Jack's mind, then said, 'This awful news, coming on top of a tough job in charge of a stressful project, would have been difficult.'

Again, there was no question.

The interviewed continued. 'Your stress levels caused you to become increasingly demanding of your team when they could not find the causal factor in the fish deaths. Is that not right, Dr Fallon?'

Fear rose in Jack's throat. He was being set up. 'No, that's not right.'

'You became frustrated, didn't you, Dr Fallon? Which is why your firm suggested you take time off to attend to your increasingly erratic mental health.'

Jack shook his head, his throat tight with anger. 'No...'

'Isn't it also true, Dr Fallon, that Mr Hinckler and Mr Macalister were so concerned about your mental state they ordered you to take mental health leave. I understand you were referred for counselling; an appointment you did not attend. Perhaps you can tell us why you did not attend that appointment Dr Fallon?'

The interviewer didn't wait for Jack's response but turned back to the audience and began talking about the importance of gas to the Australian economic recovery after the pandemic and bemoaned the current trend of mine-bashing.

Jack leaned forward and said in a low voice, 'Try to discredit me if you will, but my warning stands, the area is vulnerable with increasing earthquakes from gas fracking...'

'Isn't it true Dr Fallon that an earthquake occurs somewhere in the world roughly every 30 seconds?'

'There is a fragile spot on the continental shelf...'

'Yes, we know about that, Dr Fallon, a spot the research team who found it said would likely remain stable for thousands of years.'

'Unless an earthquake destabilises...'

'Thank you Dr Fallon. We will go to a break now and hear from our sponsors.'

Jack recognised the futility of trying to persuade the audience, without making a further spectacle out of himself, and he left the studio. It was just as well his mental health wasn't as fragile as they made out, or he would have gone out and topped himself. He'd never been made to feel this much of a failure in his entire life.

He stepped out the front door of the building and his phone rang.

Nick Ralding said, 'Should avoid talking to the media, Jack.' He laughed. 'Or at least those bastards. Not really media, just shock jocks. How are you feeling?'

'Terrible.'

'Don't take it to heart. Look on the bright side.'

'Can't see one.'

'It's there. Now we know someone is doing something to cover up and there is big money in it, enough to get the shock-jocks to carry out their bidding.'

'Is that what was happening? Someone might have warned me. The whole world will think I'm off my trolley. No one will listen to me now.'

'Give it a week Jack and everyone will have forgotten. Let me do a bit more digging. I am trying to get Four Corners interested. So, let's just take a breather okay?'

'Sure.'

'We'll talk again soon. Don't despair mate.'

Jack walked down a short flight of steps and made his way towards his car. He should have spoken to Nick first, instead of making a mess of the whole thing. If only he'd been a bit more media savvy. Maybe it was stupid to agree to talk to them. Now he just wanted to go back to Atherton, collect Sophia and head west to Julia Creek.

The sound of chanting pulled him out of self-castigation, and he looked up to see the Prophets bearing down on him. They were in their grey robes, gathered at the waist with rope. Most of the men wore wild and untrimmed beards. The women were dressed the same way, without the beards. Many were barefoot. Jack decided to cross the road to avoid them and stepped off the pavement.

One of the placard bearers shouted. 'There he is. God's messenger.!'

Jack had no idea the bloke was referring to him and glanced behind. Within seconds, three men and two women reached him and stopped, looking indecisive about what they should do next. The man, who looked a bit like the newspaper photo of the leader Elijah, muttered to the others before edging closer to Jack.

He bowed and said, 'My Master.' Then he grabbed Jack around the waist and bent to place his shoulder against the tops of Jack's thighs.

Confused by what they intended, Jack tried to leap away, but another man tackled his other leg. Jack struggled and half fell to the ground, one knee on the road. As he rose, one of the women wearing a long, grubby robe tried to grab his arm. At the same time, the two men got a grip on his legs and lifted him lopsided into the air. The woman tried to help but stumbled into one of the men who had Jack's leg. He found himself hopping along the road while another man scrabbled to push him up to shoulder height. Eventually they managed to hoist Jack onto their shoulders to a great deal of huffing and grunting.

Jack shouted for them to let him down. But once they had him aloft, they re-joined the rest of the Prophets and paraded Jack along the road. He might have fought them, but didn't want to hurt anyone, including himself, so he pleaded with them to let him down.

Passers-by stopped to watch, grinning, and cheering Jack on. He saw phones focused on him and knew the whole charade was being videoed by strangers. He didn't quite know whether to laugh or be terrified. What a mess, but it seemed a fitting end to his interview. He was about to become the laughingstock of Australia.

Eventually, he managed to persuade them to put him down and once he was standing on firm ground he straightened his clothing, pulling down his shirt that had been pushed up to his armpits in the scuffle. The crowd of Prophets gathered around him in a semicircle, blocking the road, and gazing at him expectantly. Blocked traffic began tooting horns. Jack moved to the side of the road and the Prophets moved with him.

Elijah said, 'Speak to us, oh messenger from God. Give us a sign to take forth to the people.'

Jack wanted to flee, but he didn't think he'd get far so he said, 'Look mate, it's really decent of you to be so supportive, but I'm really not a messenger from anyone. What I'm talking about is just science, geology and seismic activity, earthquakes, and stuff.' He ended lamely.

'God works in mysterious ways brother.'

'Okay, but... oh hell'. He raked his hands through his hair, hoping for inspiration. 'Look, if there are any more earthquakes, I just want people to know what's happening so they can save themselves, especially from the sea. An earthquake out there, he pointed towards the Coral Sea, could create a tsunami. If you hear a tsunami warning, you should get to higher ground, even up in those buildings.' He pointed at some high-rises along the main road. 'Get to the highest floor, above level four even five, if you can, as fast as you are able.'

'Amen to that, brother.' Elijah turned to the others and held out his arms. 'We will call people to higher ground to be saved before the end.'

The others repeated. 'Call them to higher ground.'

Dismayed, Jack realised there was nothing he could say that would deter the Prophets.' Around him the crowds pressed in closer, phones videoing everything he said. Someone shouted, will the buildings withstand a tsunami.

Jack nodded. 'They should, and it's better than being caught in traffic jam, like the last time.'

Several people conferred, remembering that awful and confusing event. Jack had been at university in Townsville in April 2007 when a magnitude 8.1 earthquake struck at a depth of 10 km beneath the sea off the Solomon Islands. It had generated a significant tsunami, devastating communities in the Solomon Islands and creating panic in Australia. When the alert was announced memories of the Indonesian tsunami of 2004 were uppermost in people's minds, and in Cairns, families and friends piled into their cars to head for the Atherton Tablelands.

As it turned out, by the time the tsunami had crossed the Coral Sea to reach the Australian coast, the wave was less that a metre high and had little impact. Most of the problem was the panic it set off. No one knew what to do. Ed had told him the Kennedy Highway all the way up the Kuranda Range was like a car park. After that, the Council had put out maps showing people the high ground within Cairns City, a shorter distance to drive but still high enough for safety.

Jack added, 'But the buildings should be your last option. There are lots of places of high ground, in and around Cairns, check the council maps.' He tried to walk away, but the Prophets took up positions behind him and began following.

Then Elijah began chanting, 'The end will come from the sea. God's prophet calls on you to move to higher ground to be saved.'

Jack increased his pace and once he had escaped into his car and driven away, he began smiling. As he drove up the Kuranda Range, he chuckled every time he recalled some small detail. At least the television interview had paled into insignificance by the time he arrived at Sophia's house.

Retreat

Jack was glad to be back in Western Queensland. Cairns had become a proverbial mine field, where he could no longer walk down the street without someone recognising him and commenting on his grilling by the Sydney television show. He'd been made to look like a deluded fool, rather than a credible witness.

The debacle afterwards with the Prophets hadn't helped, with video footage of him speaking to them going viral. It was played on local television stations as well as on social media, ad nauseum. He'd stopped watching television, and never wanted to see anyone from the media again. Out on the Barnett Station he was unlikely to run into any reporters.

He and Sophia had decided to keep their engagement low profile so as not to detract from the focus on Fergus and Barb's wedding ceremony. But the moment that was over, Isabella began planning another party for the following Saturday to celebrate their engagement. Jack suggested that, given all the effort Isabella had already put into the wedding, which had accommodated the entire district in its invitation list, they might forego a party and just let people know they were engaged. Isabella wouldn't hear of it.

Saturday afternoon saw early guests arriving, some erecting tents in the paddocks, others merely rolling out swags on the back of Utes. Isabella had invited Vernon, Shelia, the Morrison's. They all had rooms in the house because, aside from Mr Morrison, none of the others had travelled this far into the outback before and didn't know the customs. Besides, Tess's belly was becoming round as a football, a sure sign of a boy according to Isabella.

Mr and Mrs Morrison flew in, landing in a paddock cleared for that purpose. They were not the only ones, and light aircraft were lined up like rows of toys. Ed and Tess drove out from Atherton, and Vernon and Sheila had driven out from Townsville.

By 6 o'clock that evening, Jack was surrounded by a crowd of locals, all of whom wanted to know why he was warning the nation of catastrophe after MGEE's had persuaded them that drilling on their land was safe. Jim Barnett had anticipated this and warned Jack to be straight with the landowners. Jack could see they were confused. Yet, if they were still willing to give him the benefit of the doubt, he would do his best to explain what had happened as honestly as he could.

He knew they weren't going to be fobbed off by any glib comments, but he also worried about how he was supposed to explain the geological and scientific intricacies. It was that detail that created confusion, but there were no shortcuts. Trying to explain things had dogged the whole criminal enterprise all the way through. People just didn't understand what the hell he was banging on about.

He sat on the veranda steps and took a breath as he tried again to explain. 'There are two considerations. First, when I first began drilling in this region, I said what I believed to be true, and still do. If you drill in the right place and take precautions not to wreck the environment, you can extract oil and gas, safely. The trouble is that burning fossil fuels is cooking the earth, which is why I gave up my job in mining to join an environmental firm.

I believed *Green Synergy* was trying to bring about clean energy reform in a fair way for everyone.' He paused for a moment. 'Well, that is the first part of this story, simple and straight forward. Like many people in Australia, I earned my living from an industry that was hazardous to human health, and I didn't want to lose my livelihood.'

He stopped and looked around at the faces. They were all farmers and would understand a farming reference better, perhaps. 'Remember how angry farmers were when the Queensland government prohibited growing tobacco because its use in cigarettes was a health hazard?'

There was a lot of murmuring and nodding of heads from the crowd.

Jack said, 'We know burning fossil fuel is a health hazard, but none of us wants to lose our income, so we latch onto other excuses. I had my existential crisis about the excuses I had made when I read that an Antarctic ice sheet had collapsed. I could no longer look in the mirror and convince myself the burning fossil fuels was okay. I have good qualifications and could find a different job. I know it's not so easy for others, especially when it's your only means of earning an income. I get that.' He shook his head.

One man said, 'Why are we listening to this rubbish? What he said is not what happened. I saw the telly, mate. Your firm had to put you on leave because you told lies in a report to government.'

Jim held up his hand. 'Give the lad a chance to explain.'

'He's had a chance and he's banging on about a load of rubbish, nothing to do with the issue.'

Jack ran his hand over his mouth. 'I said there were two things. I have only explained one.'

Another man shouted, 'Well, get on with it then. The beer's breeding mossies waiting for you to get to the point.'

'Okay. The second thing is my new job.'

'Make it a short story this time.'

'I'll try. When I took the job, I believed I was joining a firm of environmental defenders, but I soon discovered my firm was covering up environmental vandalism. When I challenged them, they first set out to shut me up, and when that didn't work, they tried to discredit me.'

'That's a big claim, mate. Tad Hinckler's been around for a long time, and you are calling him a liar. If he's a liar, you will have to prove it.'

'That's what I've been trying to do.'

'So, what's he supposed to have done then?'

'To cut a long story short, I think he's been illegally fracking a region of the north Queensland coast. He's either extracting oil or gas, or he is forcing carbon beneath the reef as a means of sequestration to meet environmental offset targets. Perhaps both.'

'What wrong with carbon sequestration? That takes carbon out of the atmosphere, doesn't it? Isn't that a good thing?'

'Not if its leaking out to poison sea creatures like the fish, and not if the extra pressure of forcing carbon into the sedimentary or igneous rock is exerting added pressure on fault lines, and consequentially contributing to an increase in earth tremors in the region, which I think it is.'

'There are always earth tremors around the world every few minutes. You told us that yourself.'

'That's true, but over the last decade or so there has been a significant increase, particularly around the wellbore regions around Greenvale, and more recently between Innisfail and Cairns. Basically, any earth tremors in the right spot could cause a risk to the stability of the continental shelf.'

'That Noggin head thing...'

'The Noggin Block.'

'Yeah whatever... What's the odds.' The man turned to the crowd. 'Best have good odds for the betting shop, hey boys.'

A few laughed. One man said, 'All this science stuff is way above my head.' He walked over to the ice tub and cracked open a beer.

Another followed him, saying, 'It's too far from here to worry about, anyway. Give us one of those, mate.'

Someone else said, 'We have a professor from the university here. Why don't we ask him? Hey professor,' he called to Vernon, who stood back in the shadows with some of the others. 'Is he telling the truth?'

Vernon stepped into the light. 'He is. Everything he said is correct.'

Mr Morrison stepped forward. 'Many of you will know I am an oil man from the dinosaur age, but what you don't know is that I have known Jack since he was a kid. He and my boy Ed grew up together and what Jack has just told you is the god-awful truth. I am ashamed to admit it, but the man's right and has a moral backbone stronger and more upright than mine. You can trust what he said is true.'

Jack's gratitude towards these two men pressed hotly against his eyelids and to his relief the crowd began breaking up, some discussing the issue and what they knew about it, and some just heading for the beer or the women, most of whom had not bothered to join the men. This was with the exception of a few, including Isabella and Sophia who stood on the veranda listening.

Jim Barnett winked at Jack, then he turned to the crowd. 'Let's get this party started.'

By 2 am the party was beginning to slow down. Dancers hung onto each other barely moving around the dance area, drinkers swayed next to the glowing coals of dying fires, and many of the guests had already taken themselves off to bed, including Vernon, Sheila and the Morrisons.

Jack and Sophia sat beside a campfire with Ed and Tess, barely speaking but comfortable with each other's silences.

Eventually, Tess yawned and got up. 'Come on Ed. Time for bed.'

Jack's phone pinged in his top pocket, and he took it out and squinted at the alert. He jerked, looked harder at the screen, then breathed, 'Oh fuck no.'

'What?' Sophia leaned over. 'What are you looking at?'

Tess and Ed paused, waiting for Jack's response before heading to the house.

Jack moaned, 'Shit... no...'

'What. Tell me Jack. You're scaring me.'

He held the phone for her. She shook her head. 'What does it mean?'

His thumbs flashed around the screen, typing in another seismic monitoring site's URL.

'Jack what's up mate? Ed asked.

Jack shook his head. 'Hang on, just checking. Oh shit.' He looked up at Sophia, and Ed and put his palm over his mouth.

'Jack...'

'Innisfail's been hit.'

'Hit? What does that mean?'

Jack's voice became harsh. 'Innisfail's been hit by an earthquake.'

'Shit, how bad?' Ed asked.

'6.1 and really shallow.' Jack said.

'What does that mean?'

'It means it's bad.'

'Has anyone been killed?'

'I don't know, only the size, location and depth are recorded on the app. I'm seeing data from an automated monitoring station, anything else will be speculation.'

Ed said, 'They will need everyone on deck to help. Maybe I should head back.'

'You've had too much to drink to drive,' Tess said. 'We'll go to bed. Your dad can fly you back in the morning.'

Sophia said, 'That goes for me too. Come on Jack.'

'I'll have to call in,' Ed said.

'Hang on a minute, I need to think.' Jack reflected on the process. 'There is a 24/7 GeoScience/Met Bureau earthquake warning centre. They make the call if they think an earthquake will cause a tsunami threat. Then the Met

Bureau puts out the warning to emergency services. This earthquake appears to be inland, so no tsunami. Outside of Innisfail and the Bureau, I doubt anyone even knows what's happened. If you call in, they may not know what you are talking about.'

'Well, they soon will.' Ed took out his phone, walked off a little way and rang a number. When he hung up he walked back and said, 'You were right they didn't know, but they do now. The warning came through while I was on the phone to them.'

Jack flicked through some news apps. All he could find was a short news alert on the ABC. He read aloud.

'In news just to hand there are unconfirmed reports that an earthquake has struck an area North-East of Innisfail's CBD at a depth of about twelve kilometres. Innisfail is a small town on the Northeast coast of Queensland, about 80 kilometres southeast of Cairns. The town lies on the confluence of the North and South Johnstone Rivers, approximately 5 kilometres inland from the coast. The town has a population of approximately 10,000 people and is reputed to have one of the best collections of art deco buildings in Australia. More information on the situation will be posted as it comes in.'

Jack looked around at the remaining party goers. It was pointless telling them. There was nothing anyone here could do and by tomorrow, it would likely be all over the news. He followed after the others and went to bed.

There was no way he could fall asleep. Eventually he got up so as not to disturb Sophia, made coffee and went to sit on the veranda, looking out over the now silent vista with its onyx and silver sky arched over ghostly Utes, the dull glow of wood coals, rows of light aircraft, shadowy tents and sleeping cattle, all scattered haphazardly across the pewter coloured earth. He wanted to cry-out at the unfairness. Why Innisfail? Why not some uninhabited stretch of land that would hurt no one?

By six am, as the household began stirring, Jack was on his third cup of coffee as he read the news.

This morning at 1:53 an earthquake with a magnitude of 6.1 struck the small regional town of Innisfail. The quake was felt in Cairns and Townsville. Innisfail is located inland from the coast at the confluence of the North and South Johnson Rivers. Dr Michael Finley, from GeoScience Australia, said there is no risk of a tsunami from the quake although he warned residents that there may be aftershocks.

We have unconfirmed reports that many people are injured, but at this point it is not known if any lives have been lost or what the eventual damage might be, but it is expected to be in the millions of dollars. From unverified reports the damage is extensive. Buildings, strengthened for cyclones, have reportedly crumbled into the streets. The Mother of Good Counsel Cathedral, the historic Art Deco Council Chambers and the Innisfail water tower are reported to be destroyed. The Johnson Rivers, both North and South, have broken their banks, and it has been reported that large parts of the town experienced a wave of river water rushing through streets and inundating buildings.

Dr Finley said, while a magnitude 6.1 earthquake is relatively large for the region, it is not unprecedented. The largest recorded earthquake in Queensland was a 6.3 magnitude which hit Gladstone in 1918. He said that it's likely that the quake would have been amplified by soft sediments deposited from the North and South Johnston Rivers. He explained that he had recently begun monitoring the increase in seismic activity in the region, after being alerted to it by Dr Jack Fallon's report on seismic activity possibly being instrumental in the fish deaths in the area.

Jack stopped reading and headed for the shower. He had to get back and speak to the press. This was his opportunity to get his point across without appearing to be a ranting conspiracy theorist.

GREENWASH

An hour later, just as he and Sophia were getting ready to leave, Jack's phone rang. When he answered it, Nick Ralding said, 'The ABC want you on Four Corners Jack. How soon can you get down to Sydney?'

Revenge

The Four Corners team worked furiously to put the show together so it could air on the following Monday. Jack had to sign all sorts of papers, wavers, exclusive rights and so on. Then he sat around for two days, occasionally being grilled by an interviewer, or giving direct face to camera information for the Four Corner's team to release to ABC news and 7.30 advertorials.

The team ruthlessly checked sources, data, and Jack's claims, calling on one expert after another, including Michael Finley. For the first time, the press actually contacted the marine biologist who had found that the fish had indeed died from hydrogen sulphide poisoning. Other news channels picked up the story. The Innisfail disaster was the story of the moment, and they played his snippets endlessly with each new bit of information the TV channels unearthed.

On the Tuesday afternoon, Jack was told he had done his bit and he could take the rest of the week off. He might return home but should remain on call in case the team needed more information before the following Monday when the program would go to air.

He caught a cab back to his hotel and rang Sophia. Both Ed and Sophia were involved with the disaster response teams and when Sophia didn't answer, he figured she must still be working, so he left her a message saying he'd be back the next day. Later that day he rang Ed, who agreed Sophia was bound to be at the hospital, working around the clock. All the region's hospitals were overwhelmed with the injured.

Jack was desperate to go and have a look around the Innisfail area, particularly along the earthquake zone. That afternoon he learned that an investigation team was to be deployed by GeoScience to the Bramston Beach location to assess the wellbores, but it wouldn't get there for another month in case of aftershocks. Jack asked to be part of that team, but Finley said it would be better if he wasn't involved, given all the controversy. Jack wasn't satisfied. The perpetrators would get off scot-free if the investigation was derailed by political interference.

Already news channels were producing drilling experts to say the Innisfail earthquake was a completely natural phenomenon. Tad Hinckler and Chad Myers were claiming that the wellbores on the Bramston Beach property were unknown to them. They pointed the finger at the caretaker, who had vanished, it seemed, into thin air.

Noddy had not been seen since the night he'd set fire to Jack's house and Jack was determined to track him down, not only to answer to two murder charges, and burning Jack's house to the ground, but also because he was key to who knew what about the wellbores.

Ed warned him against it, saying leave the police to do their job.

The whole thing was becoming a charade where no one was to blame for anything. Any source of earthquake activity was hard to prove and if the police didn't find Noddy, not only would his parents murders go unpunished, but like the Old Testament goat laden with others' sins and sent out to die in the desert, Noddy was becoming the scapegoat for the environmental vandalism that Jack was certain had brought about the earthquake in Innisfail.

Over the past few days, TV channel after channel played scenes of Innisfail from the air, or close up. The town had been difficult to access with the bridges either side of Innisfail damaged by the quake, but now the press was there in force, and everything was seen as worthy of a photo opportunity or an interview.

On one channel Jack's face had filled the screen. He turned up the sound.

'They were warned,' the announcer said. 'But they didn't believe.'

The camera panned to a bearded man in a grey robe standing on a street in Cairns, holding up a poster with Jack's face on it and a biblical slogan scrawled below.

He heard the sound of the trumpet and did not take warning.
Ezekiel 33:1-33

Jack changed channel. He had never imagined that rather than his warnings, he would become the story. The seismic activity should, and must, be the whole focus. Already the death toll was at fifty, and hundreds more were injured.

Then came the first aftershock, magnitude 5.4 and Innisfail was once again evacuated, the Press the first out of the town. Police roadblocks prevented anyone from travelling into the region surrounding Innisfail, including Bramston Beach.

While all this spilled out of the television into his hotel room, Jack packed his bag in readiness to go home. His phone pinged, and he ran his thumb across the screen to open the message. It was from a private number, maybe Sophia. Because of her work, she often hid her number. He opened the message.

If you want to see your girlfriend alive again, withdraw your media claims now.

He stared, unable to blink, his brain scrambling to form meaning. Seconds passed as his mind thrashed about, looking for a reason. It was a scam, a joke.

While his gaze was still glued to the screen, another message popped up.

Tell 4 Crns you are lying, or Sophia dies.

Jack remained frozen as fear curdled his stomach. Then another message came through.

Bring in the police and she dies.

He could feel his heart hammering and struggled to take a breath. What the hell was he supposed to do? Was this real? He thumbed through his contacts for Ed's number.

'Mate. Have you seen Sophia?'

Ed sighed. 'You asked me that already. We're busy Jack. Everyone's under the pump. I only answered your call because I'm on a break. She'll be working. There are so many injured...'

'I know, but I have this weird text on my phone.' Jack relayed the message.

'Holy shit! I'll go and check on her right now.'

Jack glanced at his watch. He had three hours before his flight left and there wasn't another that could get him home earlier. He rang the Four Corners producer and asked to meet with her urgently. On his way to the studio, he rang Nick Ralding and asked him to meet him there also. His every action was now driven by some unconscious plan of pursuit, and he watched himself from a distance, marvelling that he could operate at all. He really hadn't a clue what to do about the messages, didn't know if they were real, but if they were and someone had taken Sophia, he needed as much help as he could muster. Whoever was behind all this wasn't going to get away with it.

The Four Corners producer called in the AFP, a man by the name of Adrian Lister. Apparently she knew him well and said they could trust him, whatever that meant. Together they devised a plan of sorts. But until Jack was contacted again by the texter, it seemed there was no leads into where Sophia might be. Jack was certain Pete and Tad were involved, but as Lister pointed out, he had no proof. At the moment, she was a missing person, or at least might be a missing person and that was a local police matter.

'Except for the threatening texts.'

Lister had nodded, with a level of indifferent scepticism that got right up Jack's nose.

'You'll need proof, Dr Fallon.'

Lister's phone rang. He listened for a second, then hung up. 'Good news. We have traced the texts. They came from Dr Barnett's personal mobile.'

'Why is that good news?'

'Is it possible she sent them?'

'What? No! Why would she send something like that?'

Lister shrugged and glanced at the producer.

Jack wanted to punch in his smug face. 'It also might mean they are using her phone. Someone has kidnapped my fiancée to shut me up.'

After a bit more discussion, all going nowhere, Jack said, 'I will have to do as they demand and pull out.'

The producer said, 'You can't. You signed a document.'

'Fuck that.'

Eventually, she agreed to a delay the scheduled program airing. They put out a statement that there were some technical difficulties with the following Monday night's program and another program would be aired in its stead. But they had no real intention of withdrawing the program. If they could lull the kidnappers into a sense of triumph, where they might make mistakes or even let Sophia go, they would keep up a charade until the final moment.

'Unless,' the producer clarified, 'Jack was going to make a statement that he'd lied.'

Did no one believe him? Although it was obvious they thought there may be something in Sophia's disappearance despite their scepticism. The AFP kitted out Jack's phone with a transmitter that would carry his conversations to Lister's team. Jack also planned to confront Pete and try to get something incriminating to hang on him. The Four Corners producer told a story about a previous incident that bore some similarity when she was stationed in Lebanon. She said confronting Pete might work. Lister wasn't optimistic about that tactic, but Jack had to do something.

He made his flight to Brisbane with ten minutes to spare before boarding, then from Brisbane he flew to Cairns. He picked up his Ute from the airport car park and drove straight up to Sophia's house and pulled up in the driveway. Her car was in the carport next to the house. Relief flooded through him until he realised the car being there meant nothing.

He leaned over to scrabbled in the glove compartment for her house keys, the second set she had given him. Instead, he found his flat keys; the second set for the new door he had installed. He had never taken them back to the agent. He chucked them back into the glove compartment and took out Sophia's key.

Inside, the house was dim and smelled of disuse. All the curtains and windows were closed as if Sophia had just shut up the place to go on holiday. A pain stabbed at his chest, and he rubbed the spot as he glanced around. There was no sign of a struggle or forced entry. Then he remembered his mother leaving. The first thing the police asked was, *did she take any clothes,* but Barry hadn't checked.

Now Jack stalked purposely towards the bedroom and wrenched open the wardrobe doors. Clothes were missing, along with her overnight suitcase. In the bathroom, he found toiletries missing. He staggered out backwards as an overwhelming sense of déjà vu clouded his brain. He stumbled to the bed and thumped down, his heart pounding as if it would burst out from his chest, his stomach nauseous, skin clammy. Head in hand, he tried to calm his thrashing pulse.

As he regained control, he saw the edge of a blue Chux kitchen-cloth poking out from under the bed and bent to pick it up. It was folded in a wad and emanated a sweetish scent. Jack stood up and turned back the bedcover. Sophia was a neat freak when it came to making the bed, hospital corners the works, but the blanket and sheet beneath the cover had been roughly pulled up over the pillows. He ripped all the covers back and searched the bed. A small clear plastic syringe cap, the kind that is usually placed over the sharp end of the needle, fell onto the floor.

He rang Ed. 'You have to get round here quick, mate.'

Part Three

Without a Clue.

J ack remained at the Morrison's home while the police searched for evidence of the crime in Sophia's house. He glanced at his watch, expecting Ed home soon, but time seemed to be standing still. He checked the grandfather clock near the library door. It was the same as his watch.

The Morrison's library had always been his favourite room. It held memories of his childhood where he could forget his home life, and his mother's disappearance for hours on end. It was where he and Ed used to do their homework, watch telly, or read. At least he read. Ed wasn't that keen, but Jack had read most of the books on the shelves. Now, to distract himself from the ticking clock, he ran his finger across each spine in an attempt to reminded himself of their contents. As a distraction it wasn't working.

He stepped over to a window overlooking the garden, his mind seething. Where the hell was Sophia? Was she alright? Her disappearance had been made to look like she had walked out, but he knew Sophia would never do that. Yet, the scenario was eerily familiar with all the hallmarks of his mother vanishing all those years ago. This could not be happening to him again, but he wasn't going to make the same mistakes his father had and believe the decoys. He knew Sophia better than that.

Besides the messages he'd received on his phone in Sydney, indicated she'd been kidnapped, but by whom, and why? This kind of thing didn't happen in Australia. People weren't kidnapped to stop a television show airing. Yet, the only people who had anything to fear from the Four Corners program airing were the directors of *Paramount Holdings* and their illegal exploration and extraction activities, if indeed that was what they were doing.

As directors, Tad and Chad had a problem on their hands. Pete as well. Yet, the AFP officer, Adrian Lister, had said it all seemed highly circumstantial, and not something they might prosecute without further evidence. But if they had kidnapped Sophia, that was another matter entirely, and although the messages had come from her phone, the police hadn't been able to trace it.

Since those first texts, there had been no more messages, and no further information, just the lingering threat. If it wasn't for the fact that Sophia was missing, he'd have put the messages down to trolls, but she had definitely disappeared, and from the evidence he'd seen in her house, she had been taken. All his hopes were pinned on Ed finding a lead. Until then, she was classified as a missing person, just like Molly. No. He couldn't think like that.

Whenever Jack stayed with the Morrison's he stayed in the main part of the house, in the guest bedroom because Ed and Tess had the annex. Although the annex had a sitting room, bathroom, and kitchen, there was only the one bedroom. The block of land Ed and Tess had bought was still waiting for the builders to begin their house, but Jack didn't think Ed was in any hurry to move out. His parents' home was too comfortable and once the baby came, they would have a full-time babysitter in Ed's mom. Besides, every time Ed mentioned moving into their own home, Mrs Morrison began crying. It was an old joke that they would have to carry Ed out feet first.

Jack heard a car drive up to the house, picked up the newspaper article he had torn out from *The Cairns Post*, and raced out the library towards the entrance hall just as Ed opened the door.

'Did you find anything?'

'No mate. The place was wiped clean, but you were right about the Chux and the needle cover. Looks like whoever took her did it when she was asleep. Gave her the chloroform, then a needle of something to keep her out for the count.'

'It was Noddy. I'm sure of it.'

'Mate, if Noddy is still in the district, I'd be surprised. We've been looking for him since he set fire to your house, but there's been no trace.'

'Doesn't mean he didn't take Sophia. He's made it look like she left on her own accord, taking a suitcase. That's what happened to Molly too, and I'm certain Noddy killed my mother.'

Ed nodded; his face creased with weary sympathy. 'We'll find Sophia, Jack.'

He walked into the living room and Jack followed, remembering the police officer saying a similar thing when Barry reported Molly missing. What if Sophia was already dead. His breathing faltered, and a pulse thudded in his neck.

'What if it's too late already? If they run the Four Corners project, she's done for. The producer said they'd hold off, but that's not a cancellation. Even though I threatened to say it was all a lie, she said it would make the story more interesting.'

Ed's phone rang. He said, 'Sorry I've got to take this.' He listened for a minute and a smile spread over his face. When he hung up, he said, 'You were right. It was Noddy and we have a print on a hanger in the wardrobe that puts him in Sophia's house, where he had no reason to be. It seems he wasn't as thorough as he thought he was. But then you picked it. Maybe you should join the force and become a detective.'

Jack said, 'Noddy's working for *Paramount Holdings*. Pete's the company secretary. He must know more than he's letting on. I'm going down to Cairns to find out.'

'Don't do anything stupid, Jack. Let this play out.'

'We don't have time. I have to confront them; they know something for sure. Everything links back to Noddy and *Paramount Holdings*.'

'They'll admit nothing, and it could get you into more trouble if you barge into their offices.'

'As far as I know, I'm still employed there.' He held out the article from the paper. 'Tad's been given the job of recovery coordinator for Innisfail. He'll need my expertise.'

'You're joking!'

'Tad told me to take two weeks, but I'll say it took longer for me to see the light, and now I have, I can be of use to him. Besides, it's the only way I can get anywhere near Innisfail. It's still off-limits to the public since that last aftershock.' Jack frowned. 'While I'm there, I'll have a good look around the Bramston Beach site.'

'She's not there, Jack. There's nothing to see but broken buildings and ripped up roads. The residents have all been evacuated and there may be more aftershocks.' Ed shook his head. 'Don't try to side-track me. You know Tad won't let you into the building and if it's Noddy who took her, who's to say it was not on Tad's instructions?'

'I want to see Pete's face. I've known him for a long time. I reckon I will be able to tell if he knows where Sophia is.'

'And then?'

'I don't know. Maybe I'll beat the crap out of him until he tells me.'

'It's not much of a plan.'

Jack ran his palm over his face. 'I know, but I don't know what else to do. I don't know where to begin looking for her.' He looked pleadingly at Ed. 'Mate I'm dying here. I can't sit in your house and wait for the police investigation to play out. Not while she's out there. I have to find her, and Pete and Tad are the obvious starting points.'

'Any further texts?'

Jack shook his head.

Ed said, 'I guess they got rid of Sophia's phone after they sent the first texts, or we would have tracked it down by now. Do you want me to come with you?'

'Thanks, but if you came with me, you'd lose your job. I can't have that on my conscience as well. Better you don't know what I'm doing.'

Ed pressed his lips together. 'Just don't do anything dumb, please.'

'You don't happen to have a handgun I could borrow, do you?'

'That's not funny, mate.'

The next morning, Jack drove his Ute down to Cairns. There are two roads of similar distance from Atherton to Cairns. One is via Mareeba and Kuranda and down the Kennedy Highway over the Macalister Range to Smithfield, a northern suburb of Cairns. A lookout along the route shows a panoramic view over the city suburbs to the City centre, all set along a tourist-perfect-seascape. The other route is through the picturesque market village of Yungaburra. From there, the jungle flanked Gillies Range Road winds down the mountains to Gordonvale, a small inland town separated from the sea by the Nisbet Range, which runs in a long tail through the southern part of the Cairns local government area. The Nisbet Range, with its multiple peaks and protected forests, separates the alluvial plains of the Russell and Mulgrave riverine region from the sea.

Jack chose the Gillies Range Road, and just over an hour later, pulled into a parking space about 50 metres from the *Green Synergy* office tower entrance. In the rear-view mirror, he checked out the day-old growth on his chin. He'd stopped shaving, thinking a beard might give him some anonymity, but his face itched. At that moment, Chad and Samantha walked down the steps from the building's foyer and turned towards where he had parked. He sat stock still, dithering over whether he should duck below the dash or just hope they wouldn't notice him. He need not have worried. Neither of them was interested in their surroundings. Instead, they appeared to be arguing.

After they passed, he got out and locked his Ute and followed them. It crossed his mind that he should go into the office as he'd planned, and confront Pete and Tad, but he was curious about why Chad and Samantha were in Cairns, and why they had visited *Green Synergy*. Of course, there might be many reasons.

Chad and Samantha had begun dating after she'd dumped him, and Chad and Tad had fingers in many common pies. Yet he hoped this might have something to do with the Bramston Beach site. He still thought it probable that it was where they were holding Sophia, despite Ed's assertion it was under police control. The area around Bramston was wild, surrounded by jungles and swamps, a perfect hiding place.

Jack was too far behind to hear what Chad was saying, but he saw him grab Samantha's arm. They crossed the Esplanade, a road that ran the length of the city along the foreshore. Their argument was clearly over for they walked arm in arm, along paths, through trees, and across lawns, past the swimming lagoon in Fogarty Park, and across the car park.

He followed them to the entrance of his old apartment building, by which time Samantha had dropped Chad's arm and taken his hand. Then they entered the building where Jack's old apartment was located. Jack stopped outside the entrance and peered through the glass. Chad and Samantha were waiting at the lifts, their backs to him.

After they stepped into the lift and the door had closed, he went inside to watch which floor the lift would stop at. It was the top floor. Was it possible that Chad had one of two penthouses in the same building in which Jack had lived and he'd never run into him? The coincidence was too much, but perhaps this was where they were staying. Many of the apartments in the building were still managed vacation rentals.

Jack walked along the wharf to a café on the corner facing his old apartment building. He chose a table pushed up against a pillar. A waitress came out to take his order, and he asked for an expresso. From his seat, he could see the entrance to the building, but he figured he'd be partly obscured from the view of anyone exiting. He sat back to wait. Of course, they might be in there all day, but he was in no hurry.

Ed was right. Confronting Pete was probably a waste of time, but Chad might lead him somewhere. It was half an hour before Chad and Samantha reappeared. They passed the café where Jack sat and turned onto one of the jetties that ran perpendicular to the wharf. They were heading towards a massive white yacht, docked on the seaward side of the furthermost peer.

The yacht must be 100 metres long, and he'd seen it before, of that he was certain. Was this Chad's friend's yacht, the British aristocrat. Jack couldn't remember the name. No, it wasn't his yacht in the photograph on Chad's desk. That was just an opportunity for Chad to name-drop. It belonged to someone else. The aristocrat's business partner. Someone with a Russian sounding name, the same as the Russian petrochemical oligarch. Prokhorov, that was it. But Chad denied the man was Russian. Where did he say he was from? Jack couldn't remember.

He hurried back to his Ute, took out the apartment spare keys from his glove box, and then returned to the building. This time he walked into the building as if he still owned the place, pushed the lift button, and alighted at the 8th floor. The elaborate gate was hooked back against the wall leaving the door clear, and he boldly knocked on his erstwhile front door. If someone answered he could explain he was just returning the keys. If no one answered he would go in and take a look around. Perhaps Chad and Samantha had stayed here although he didn't know what he expected to find, just that there were too many coincidences.

As soon as Jack opened the door to the apartment, he caught a whiff of Samantha's perfume. Spicy and rich, as she had always worn it when he dated her. The place was kitted out like a holiday stay, with crisp white linens, blonde wood, and wheat and chocolate coloured furnishings. Jack moved carefully through each room, feeling like a voyeur. The kitchen was the same as when he'd owned it, with the exception of a new double door fridge and an enormous chest freezer. He retraced his steps and headed for the bedrooms. He went into the master bedroom first, but other than some of Samantha's clothes thrown on the bed, nothing caught his eye. The ensuite that led off the room was full of her toiletries.

He walked back to the guest bedroom. There were some men's clothes hanging in the wardrobe, but nothing noteworthy. In the guest bathroom, he opened a cabinet. A few bottles, toothpaste, toothbrushes, and a packet of syringes sat on the glass shelf. He picked up the syringes. They had the same small clear syringe caps; of the kind he had found in Sophia's bed. He took a photo with his phone, replaced everything, and shut the cabinet door, his heart thudding, and his breathing shallow. Then he went through to the open-plan living room and rifled through drawers. He pulled a folder from a drawer in an entertainment unit, just as the front door opened. Jack's heart leapt into his throat, and he stood up, holding the folder to his chest.

'Oh, sorry-sorry. I thought you had left.' A woman stood in the doorway, a pile of towels in her arms, a cleaning trolly outside the open door.

Jack muttered. 'I'm just leaving.'

He brushed past her, and her eyes narrowed, but he kept walking.

She shook her head. 'I think you are not Mr Myers. Who are you?'

'Just running an errand for Mr Myers.' Jack showed her the folder and kept walking towards the fire stairs. He didn't stop until he was a block away from the apartment. His pulse was still racing as he walked into a camera shop to buy a set of binoculars.

Half an hour later, after returning to the wharf area, he found a table outside another restaurant. He laid the file he'd stolen on the table and ordered another coffee before he realised he was at a fancy seafood restaurant, not a café. It didn't seem to matter. The waitress took his order without a murmur and walked to the café next door to get his coffee. Perhaps both places belonged to the same business. There were hotels, restaurants, and cafés set side-by-side all the way along this stretch of the city's seafront and marina district.

The binoculars were not the strongest, merely bird watching 8 x 42 high density, but they were good enough to pick out some activity on the yacht.

He could see people walking along the lower deck. If Chad was on that yacht, this might be where they were keeping Sophia. Although he could not believe Samantha would be complicit in a kidnapping, but then neither could he believe Pete would be, especially a kidnapping of his ex-fiancée. How well did he know either of them?

There was also the possibility that neither of them knew of Sophia's abduction, although surely Chad and Tad were in on it. He reminded himself that all his speculations were just that—conjecture. He had no real information about what had happened to Sophia, nor who might have taken her, nor where she had gone.

The only certain thing was that Noddy was involved. How else could the fingerprint in Sophia's wardrobe be explained? Through the binoculars, Jack could see how big the yacht was. If she was on board, it was possible the others may not know. But then on whose orders was Noddy acting?

Jack would have to search the yacht. He paused. How the hell could he get on the thing. First he needed to know who owned it. He took his phone from his pocket and rang Ed. 'Hey mate, how do you find out who owns a yacht in the Marina?' He described the yacht and his theory that Sophia might be on board.

Ed sounded sceptical but promised to look into it.

Jack's coffee came, and he moved the file so the waitress could place the cup in front of him.

She smiled at him and said, 'On holiday?'

'Not really.'

'Do you live in Cairns?'

'I did.' Jack paused and then lied. 'I'm thinking of heading off to Brisbane.'

'Oh, I love Brisbane. I used to live there before I came up here on holiday and met my husband.'

'Nice.'

She paused and peered at him. 'You're not looking for work, are you?'

He hesitated.

'Because if you are, we have jobs going here, kitchen hand and if you know how to make coffee, we need a barista.'

He smiled at her, then said, 'Who belongs to that monstrosity?'

She looked to where he had pointed and shrugged. 'Some foreign billionaire.'

'Have you seen him?'

She shook her head. 'But I will.'

'Oh yeah. Does he come in here for his breakfast then?'

She grimaced. 'He's having a cocktail party and we're the hired help for the snack and seafood catering. Can you believe it. They want us all wearing uniforms?'

He laughed. 'You'll look good in a frilly apron and cap.'

'I'm serious. If you are looking for work, we're desperate for staff. Since the pandemic, we just can't get people.'

'Okay, maybe. I'll give it some thought. Kitchen hand hey?'

'Or barista...'

'Only experience I have with coffee, is drinking it.'

'I can teach you the machine. It's not difficult.'

'Do I get to go to the party on the yacht?'

'You'll do better than that. You can help load the provisions. You look like you have enough muscle power for lugging cartons.'

'I can probably do that.'

She bit her lip and frowned. 'It's for the job, isn't it? Not just to get onto the yacht?'

He smiled to alleviate her concern. 'Will you be my boss?'

She said, 'We own the place.'

'Right. You and your husband. Must be my lucky day.'

'I'll get the forms; you can fill them in while you drink your coffee. It's on the house.'

It was a pity he'd sold the flat. If he was going to take up the job offer, he had nowhere to live in Cairns. He drank his coffee, then looked through the employment forms and found they wanted superannuation scheme numbers, driver's licence numbers and bank account details. There was no way he could fill in a fake name. But why shouldn't he get a job in a restaurant?

When she returned he said, 'Sorry I'll have to get these back to you. I don't have these details on me.'

She looked so disappointed he wanted to reassure her. 'When do you want me to start?'

'This minute would be about perfect.'

He laughed again. 'I'll be back tomorrow, okay? With the forms.'

She looked doubtful. 'Promise.'

He smiled and got up.

'Hey, your folder.'

'Thanks.' He took the folder from her hand and walked away.

It wasn't until he was back at Ed's place that he looked through the folder. It was full of papers in a foreign language, some written using an alphabet he didn't recognise. There was no way he would find anything useful in that.

There was one document in English, a bill of sale. He scanned it. It was the sale of his flat to a company called *Grecotec Inc*. The name meant nothing to him. He was about to put the file aside when he stopped. Chad and Samantha might have been staying at a rented apartment, but if that was the case, whose syringes were in the second bathroom cabinet? Why would the buyers leave their folder in an apartment they intended to let for vacations?

He opened his laptop and googled how to find details of a private company. He soon found Grecotec was a private equity firm located in Malta. It was registered with ASIC as having an Australian agent, *Green Synergy*. Jack chuckled, wondering if Pete knew that the Maltese company had bought Jack's flat and paid an extra 50 k for it.

He recalled the buyer, swarthy skin and foreign accent and his laughter dried up as he realised this was bigger than he'd first thought. Somehow Tad, Chad and Pete were involved with companies registered in the Cayman Islands, and in Malta.

He looked at the other documents in the folder, then googled the Maltese alphabet. It was based on the same Latin alphabet as was the English language although they had some additional markings, something like the accents of the French language. This wasn't it. He googled types of alphabets and found the closest to the paperwork in the file was the Cyrillic alphabet. It was used in Eastern Europe and Russia. What the hell was *Green Synergy* mixed up in?

There was nothing unusual about a firm being the local managing agent for foreign firms, but Tad's business was supposed to be environmental defence in Australia. Besides which, Russia had become a pariah since its invasion of the Ukraine a few months earlier. Surely, any business relationships with companies using the Russian alphabet in their documents was suspect.

Jack wished he knew more about the law, although none of this was getting him any nearer finding Sophia. The syringes in the bathroom cabinet were his only lead, and they took him nowhere. Had Noddy stayed at the penthouse before abducting Sophia or did he take her there afterwards? Was he acting on his own, or with others? Could anyone rent the flat? He picked up his phone again and rang the agents to ask if they had an apartment in the complex he could rent.

There was a studio apartment on the seventh floor. That would be the floor below his old penthouse apartment. He said he would prefer a penthouse. They regretted that since the pandemic the penthouses were now occupied by their owners. So, Chad's presence there was no coincidence. Somehow he was connected to *Grecotec Inc.*, and it was more than just through *Green Synergy*.

Jack needed somewhere to live while he worked in Cairns, so he said he'd take the seventh-floor studio for a week. It probably cost more than he would earn working at the restaurant, but what the hell. It was right there in the same block and somehow he felt his old apartment was connected to that yacht, and to Sophia's disappearance. Additionally, he still had the spare set of keys to his old flat.

Jack typed *Grecotec Inc.* into his web browser and clicked on a link to a professional-looking website. The company was involved in everything from shipping to new builds, exploration, pipelines, and production of hydrocarbons, to sequestration. It also provided financial and marketing services. They were also into poly-carbon manufacturing, machinery and mechanical appliances, pharmaceutical products, and printed material. It looked like they had fingers in every pie available.

Later that day, when Ed knocked off work, Jack accosted him at the front door. 'Did you find anything?'

'Yes. Let me get inside will you and I'll tell you all about it.'

Once Ed was inside, Jack said, 'Well?'

Ed shook his head in mock exasperation at Jack's persistence. 'The yacht is registered to a Maltese company.'

'*Grecotec,*' Jack said.

Ed pulled a notebook from his top pocket and looked at it, then he raised an eyebrow at Jack. 'How did you find out?'

Jack pushed the folder towards Ed. 'They bought my flat.'

Ed read the document, then looked up, his face a mask of bewilderment. 'Where did you get this?'

'You don't want to know, mate. But I'm going back down to Cairns tomorrow. I have a job that might get me onto the yacht. If Sophia's on it, I will find her.'

'Two questions. What do you mean you have a job? What job? And why would Sophia be on that yacht?'

Jack ran his hand through his hair. 'I got a job as a kitchen hand. As for Sophia... I don't know. Just a hunch. The yacht, my flat, Bramston Beach, Noddy, *Paramount Holdings*, the Maltese firm, my old firm MGEE's, all link to *Green Synergy*, like it's some kind of maypole we're all dancing around.'

'What's this about maypoles?' Tess came through the front door and kissed Ed, then hugged Jack. 'How are you, Jack?'

'I'm fine.'

'You don't look fine. Okay, what are you and Ed into?'

Ed went through a short version of what Jack had found while Tess listened.

Then she asked, 'Who owns *Green Synergy*?'

Jack stared at her. He had never checked, just assumed it was Tad's firm. He walked over and sat at the dining room table to open his laptop.

'It's a public foundation, whatever that means. It says here that Tad is the managing director.'

'It means Tad reports to a Board. So, who's on the board?' Tess stood behind Jack and looked over his shoulder.

Jack peered at the screen. 'The names mean nothing to me.'

Tess looked at Ed, her eyebrow raised. 'Ever heard of any of these guys?'

Ed looked at the screen. 'No, only... The Chair's name sounds familiar. Catherine Fairclough.'

'Google her.' Tess suggested.

Jack typed her name into the search bar. 'Nothing, just her role as chair of this board.'

Tess pulled a face. 'That's really strange. Board chairs usually like to splash their names all over the Internet—marketing themselves for the next big job. Is there a photo anywhere on the Foundation's web page?'

'Nope.'

Ed said, 'I'm sure I've heard that name before. Let me think about it.'

Jack's fingers played out a tattoo on the tabletop. 'I don't get it. If *Green Synergy* is a Foundation, then what Pete told me doesn't add up.'

'Why? What did he say?' Tess placed her hands on her hips, the small football pushing against the material of her dress, stretching it tight over her stomach.

Jack pulled out a chair. 'Here, sit down.'

She sat then repeated her question. 'So, what did he say?'

'He said he'd been made a partner. I thought that meant he had a share in Tad's firm, but if it's a Foundation, how does that work?'

Tess said, 'A Foundation can also own private, or even public companies.'

Jack was already typing into the search bar. 'Ha!' And here it is. There is a subsidiary called *Global Defenders,* registered with the Legal Services Board.

'That's a complicated little set-up.' Tess said.

'Hang on there are more subsidiaries, *Global Energy Solutions*, and *Global Resource Strategies*.' Jack scrolled down the page. 'Makes you wonder why a not-for-profit environmental foundation needs so many for-profit entities hiding under its mantle.'

'Are they all generating money for the parent company to spend on doing good, or for something else?'

Jack shook his head. 'Maybe it's just greenwashing. Which makes me the world's prize mug.'

'What the hell is greenwashing?' Ed was looking bewildered again.

Jack grinned. 'Like money laundering except with fossil fuels, making something dirty, like gas, look clean and green.'

The next day, Friday, Jack reported for work at the café and handed his completed forms to the woman who had recruited him. He smiled at her. 'Told you I'd be back. I'm Jack Fallon, but I'd prefer to be called something else, maybe Fred Smith.' He scratched his two day old beard, acutely aware of the new growth.

Her face fell, and she pushed a lock of hair off her face. 'Shit, I thought you looked familiar.'

'Don't believe everything you hear on the telly!'

'Don't watch telly. Saw you on Facebook saying there would be a tsunami and people should get to the top of high-rise buildings. Is it true?'

'If they can't get to high ground, then yes.'

'Is this building high enough?'

Jack looked up at the hotel rising above the wharf. 'Depends on the height of the tsunami and its run up wave, but it could be if you got onto the top floor or the roof.'

She looked down at his employment papers. 'Is this all fact?'

'Yes.' Jack waited for her to make a decision.

'Why the hell would you want a job as a kitchen hand?'

'I don't really, but you asked, and I'm at a loose end, so what the hell.' He adlibbed. 'After the media debacle no one else will employ me anyway. I was planning to go farming in a little while, but I like you. You gave me a free coffee. I can help out for a week maybe two, give you enough time to employ a real kitchen hand. But... if you don't want me, that's okay too.'

She looked over her shoulder and then back at Jack. 'Fred Smith, hey? Okay, I'll have to explain to my husband, but I reckon you look trustworthy enough and I'm desperate. I'm Jude by the way.' She held out her hand and with some relief, Jack took it.

For the next few days Jack carted boxes, washed dishes, swept, cleaned, and did whatever was asked of him, even learning how to use the espresso machine, and waiting table when the other staff were under pressure.

Both the café and the seafood restaurant belonged to Jude and her husband, Conrad, who was the chef. The front end of the operation looked like two separate businesses, but the back end was one, and Jack worked across both.

During his time off, he schemed about how he would get on to, and search the yacht. He spent hours gazing through the binoculars from the balcony of his rented studio apartment, trying to familiarise himself with each deck, or what he could see of each deck, and making notes about any regular patterns or movements by the staff or passengers.

On the Sunday night before the Four Corners program had been scheduled to run, Jack was finishing his shift. He was locking the sliding glass doors that lead out to the restaurant outdoor seating area, when he saw a bearded man in unkempt grey robes stop at the wharf in front of the café. He switched off the restaurant lights just as the man glanced about furtively.

Jack could see his movements easily from his vantage point because the jetty was lit by overhead lighting, while he was hidden in darkness. At first he thought the man was Elijah the Prophet, although this man had boots on his feet. He was also thinner than Elijah, wirier with a rolling gait. There was something familiar about the way he walked. Jack scratched his beard as he watched the prophet walk hurriedly towards the yacht and step onboard as if he had been invited.

He raced up to his rented studio apartment to get the binoculars. Then he walked out onto the tiny balcony to train them on the yacht. In a patch of light on the access deck he could just make out the prophet talking to another man. As he watched the two men, it began to dawn on him that the man to whom the prophet spoke, was the same man who had bought Jack's apartment.

The men separated and Jack lost sight of both of them. A movement on the top deck showed two men passing each other in what appeared to be a patrol. It told him there was probably some kind of security on board, guarding the yacht. It wouldn't be wise to go prowling around in the dark.

As he prepared to go to bed, his brain looped around questions that had no answers. Why would a member of the *Prophets of the Apocalypse* be talking to a foreign national on board a luxury super-yacht? Unless, the prophet was not Elijah, but someone dressed to look like him, and he had a feeling he knew who it was.

A Lucky Break.

The next morning, when Jack awoke, the yacht was gone. It was Monday. The restaurant was closed, and Jack had a free day. He had planned to get a closer look at the yacht, but as it had vanished during the night he was at a loose end. Clearly, it would be coming back because the restaurant was doing the seafood catering for the party on Thursday night. But in the interim, he had to find out where it had gone.

Not too far from where the yacht had been moored, a fishing trawler was tying up at the jetty. Jack dashed downstairs and walked out onto the jetty towards the trawler. A man was on deck.

When he reached the trawler, Jack said, 'Good catch, mate?'

'Not bad. You buying?'

'Sorry, just taking a walk. Is the fishing usually good out there? I heard there was some problem, dead fish, or something.'

'Whose asking?'

'Just visiting, mate. Passing the time of day. No harm meant. Fantastic yacht here overnight. Saw it from my hotel window.'

The man nodded. 'Passed it on my way in.'

Jack stroked his fledgling beard. 'Heading north, I heard.'

'Must have been a different yacht. The one I saw was heading south-east, off Fitzroy Island.'

Jack raised his eyebrows. 'Maybe a Sydney mob.'

'Maybe. Look, did you want something? Only I have to get on.'

'Sure mate. I'll leave you to it.' Jack turned and walked along the pier. He looked back and the man was still watching him. He took a circuitous route towards a tourist hotel, then doubled back and entered his building from the other side, via the stairs to the basement car park. He got into his Ute and drove up the Gillies Range Road, planning to drop in on Ed in Atherton. Maybe the police had a way of tracking the yacht.

An hour and a half later, he was sitting in Ed's office. On Jack's request, Ed shook his head, his mouth held in a grim line.

'Jack I can't use Government resources to feed you information just because you want to know.'

Jack was silent, knowing Ed was right. Then he had an idea. 'What if you had a tip-off that a vessel was heading for Innisfail?'

'That's still off-limits, even for ships, and I would have a good reason for checking on it.'

'Well...?'

'Are you giving the police a tip-off?'

'Yes, and I think you will find Noddy on board.'

'Why?'

'I suspect Noddy may be disguised as Elijah.'

'The Prophet?'

Jack nodded. 'I saw him, or at least a bloke that looked like Elijah, board the yacht last night, and today the yacht's gone. I asked a bloke on a fishing trawler, which way the yacht had gone, and he said, south-east.'

Ed shrugged. 'South is most of Australia, southeast is the Pacific. It's a big place.'

'Yes but Ed, they can't be going far. They are scheduled to be back by Thursday. We are catering a party for them.'

Ed stared at Jack, blinked, and shook his head. 'There are so many questions that arise from what you have just said, I don't know where to begin. Who is we for starters? What are you catering, and more importantly, why do you think Elijah is Noddy?'

'I promise I will tell you everything, but later, okay mate?'

Ed sighed. 'Okay, that's probably enough information for me to go on. Just go and wait at the café down the road. I'll have a look and join you when I'm done.'

Twenty minutes later, Ed walked into the café and beckoned to Jack, then turned and left the café.

Jack followed Ed outside to a police four by four parked at the kerb.

Ed said, 'You're getting your wish. We're going to Bramston Beach.'

'What's happened?'

'Transpires the yacht's transponder shows the vessel is still docked in the marina. Now, why would it do that unless they have something to hide?'

They drove back down the winding Gillies Range Road towards Gordonvale and turned south towards Innisfail. Most of the villages and towns along this stretch of coast were located on an alluvial plain that stretched from Cairns to El Arish, a village south of Innisfail. The alluvial plain was separated from the sea by various mountain ranges. The beach villages like Bramston Beach were accessible via low lying passes between one range and the next.

After an hour and a half of driving they passed through the small inland town of Miriwinni. Just south of the town was a roadblock. They pulled up and after a brief conversation, the police waved them through. They turned east at Bucklands Road and came to a bridge crossing over the Russell River. It was also blocked off. Ed pulled over, got out the vehicle and spoke to a police officer.

When he returned to the car he explained that the bridge was damaged by the quake. It was navigable on one side only, and they would have to drive slowly to get across. There was also concern about a smaller bridge further along the road. Engineers were assessing it. The police officer hadn't known if they would get through as far as Bramston.

They pressed on, arriving at the next bridge a few minutes later. Again, they stopped, and Ed got out and spoke to the police officer, who consulted the engineer. Minutes later, they were allowed to proceed.

Ed got back into the car and took off again travelling very slowly across the bridge. When they had crossed the bridge, he said, 'I hope the bloody things hold long enough for us to get back again. I also hope this is not a wild goose chase, or I'll have some questions to answer.'

They drove through Bramston Beach, which appeared deserted. It too had been evacuated when Innisfail was. Jack couldn't see a lot of damage, other than some fallen power lines, but he wasn't getting up close to inspect the buildings. There wasn't much by way of infrastructure at the beach village, mostly beach homes hidden among coconut palms and beach almond trees. They drove along the seafront and parked. Both men used their binoculars to scan the sea for the yacht. Ed's police issue field glasses were more powerful than Jack's, but either way, they could see nothing that might be the yacht.

They returned to the car and Ed took the narrow track to the lot registered to *Paramount Holdings*. On several occasions, they were forced to stop and drag fallen trees off the road. When they reached the spot where the gate had originally been, there was no sign anyone had been near the place either before or since the earthquake.

Jack turned to Ed. 'I thought MGEEs was carrying out investigative work on the wellbores?'

Ed shrugged. 'So, did I. Maybe they left after the earthquake and couldn't get back because of unstable bridges.'

The two men got out the car and walked towards the forest, neither speaking. More fallen trees blocked their way, but they were soon through the regrowth, and walking along the track. They went to Noddy's demountable house first, but unsurprisingly there was no one there. Then they walked back to the wellbores. There was no sign anyone had even begun an investigation. The place was as Jack had last seen it.'

Ed shook his head. 'Nothing.' He glanced at Jack. Sorry mate. Looks like this is a dead end.'

'Maybe.' Jack walked around the mounds, peering into the trees. Then he walked back the way they had come, still examining the tree line.

'What are you looking for?'

'I don't know, signs... They disguised the entrance with replanted trees and bushes, so, maybe there is another hidden track somewhere.' He glanced at Ed's face. 'Five minutes. Just humour me please, mate.'

Ed sighed but followed after Jack. When they reached the shed at the back of Noddy's house, Jack ducked through the trees and started to climb.

'Oh shit.' Ed looked at the steep incline and hesitated.

Jack stopped and looked back. He said in a low voice. 'You can stay there. I'll just be a second.'

'Where are you going?'

'This range is only about 85 metres high at this point. If I get to the top, I may get a better view of the sea and maybe spot the yacht. I can also scour the lay of the land surrounding us. If there are any other human-made structures in the forest, I may be able to see some signs.'

'Okay.' Ed sighed and followed behind Jack, although he climbed more slowly.

Halfway up the mountain, Jack waited for him to catch up. Around him trees grew thickly blocking the possibility of a clear outlook. He visualised the map. On the southern flank of this range was the Ella Bay national park. To the west was the Eubenangee Swamp, to the east was the sea.

He took out his phone to check the direction. The signal was good here because it was between two communication towers, one at Bingle Bay, the other on the Bellenden Kerr Range. Google Earth gave him an idea of his location and showed a spur of land running north-south, off the main east-west range. The spur dipped down into the heart of the Ella Bay national park.

When Ed caught up, Jack continued climbing upwards, heading towards a spur from where he hoped to get a view of the sea. He reached the top of the range and followed Google maps until he came to the spur.

In deep shade, rainwater oozed from under a rock beneath which the sodden ground had filled a pool. The water spilled out to gurgle down the slope, creating a stream that fell over the cliff face and down the side of the spur. Over years, if not centuries, the rocky watercourse had cleared a path through the trees, through which he could now see a section of the sea.

A flash of light caused Jack to crouch low, although he wasn't sure why.

Ed saw him. 'What are you doing?'

Jack pointed.

Ed looked and frowned. 'Can't see a damn thing for trees.' He was sweating and breathing heavily. 'Jack if you've dragged me up here for no good reason... Shit! I'm covered in leeches.' He leaned down to brush one off his trouser cuff. It immediately latched onto his hand.

Jack grinned at his friend. 'Thought you rugby players were fit.'

'Sprints mate, not marathons.' Ed squashed the leech and began hunting for more.

Jack said, 'I saw something out there, a flash, glass, maybe binoculars, but I reckon we need to move to a clearer spot. They walked a little way further along the ridge and then Jack saw it.

The Seymour Range tracked west to east, its jungle-clad eastern ridge descending to the sea where boulders protected its base. On the Ella Bay side of the ridge was the spur they were standing on. Below them, Jack could see a river meandering through the national park to empty over a sandbar and into the sea. Just beyond the headland was the yacht, heading east into deeper waters. He raised his binoculars. It seemed to tow some sort of long island covered with vegetation.

Ed was also looking at the yacht through binoculars. 'What the hell is that behind it?'

'Search me.' Jack said. 'But whatever it is, you can be sure it's up to no good.'

'I think we should get back and call this in. It's probably something Border Force will be interested in.'

'I wonder if that's a disguised tanker they're towing?' Jack's binocular'd gaze swept the landscape, but he could see no sign of further human habitation. If Sophia was not here, his last shot was the yacht. Otherwise, he had no idea where they were holding her. He would just have to get on board and find out.

Ed interrupted his thoughts. 'Hey mate. You know that stuff about the Noggin Block. Where is it out there?'

Jack pointed east and slightly to the north. 'Out that way, about 70 kilometres, is the continental shelf, a cliff that drops off from the seabed into the Queensland Trough. The trough is like a trench that runs all the way along the coastline here. It was caused by rifting when the continental plates pulled apart to create the Coral Sea...in the age of the dinosaurs.' He grinned at Ed, remembering how much he'd hated it when his father tried to explain geological formations to him when they were kids. The dinosaur reference was the kind of thing Mr Morrison would say in an attempt to engage his son. 'At the end of Noggin Passage is the Noggin Block, a large area of sedimentary rock on the edge of the continental shelf.'

'I only asked where it was,' Ed said. 'I didn't need the lecture, nor the crack about dinosaurs. I'm not eight.' He glowered at Jack.

'Sorry mate. Look, you know I'm grateful, don't you?'

'Yeah, yeah. You owe me. Come on; let's get back so I can call this thing in and get rid of the leeches before I keel over from blood loss.'

Returning Kindness.

The following morning, while Jack got ready for work, he noted the yacht was berthed back at the wharf. He had a busy day ahead in the restaurant kitchen, so there was not much he could do about it. As kitchen hand, he was not only expected to do the regular jobs but also to help prepare for the yacht party. He had no time to do anything other than the duties allocated.

At about midday, he took some rubbish out to the bins in a back alley area, and found a man slumped against the wall. By the look of his grey robes, he was one of the prophets.

'Hey mate, you okay?'

'The man looked like he'd been crying.' Jack walked slowly towards him. 'Is there something I can help you with?'

'Do you have any food?'

'Sure. Hang on a minute.' Jack went back into the kitchen and looked around. There was a quiche on the bench. Conrad was on the other side of the kitchen and Jack went over to him.

'Hey Conrad, is it okay if I take my break now?'

Conrad nodded. 'No problem.'

'Can I buy that quiche over there?'

Conrad looked to where Jack was pointing. 'You don't want that. It's for the bin.'

'Is it still good?'

'Yeah, it's been in the fridge until five minutes ago. Should be fine, just a bit stale.'

'Can I have it then?'

Conrad shrugged. 'Be my guest.'

Jack grabbed the quiche and went back to the prophet. Then he sat down next to him, broke off a bit of quiche and gave the rest to the man. He could see the bloke was starving.

The prophet wolfed down the pie in several gulps while Jack ate his small portion. It wasn't too stale at all.

After some minutes of silence, the prophet said, 'My name's Saul.'

'Nice to meet you Saul, I'm Fred.'

'Do you work here?'

'Yeah, kitchen hand.'

'I've done a bit of that before I converted.'

'Oh yeah. What do you do now?'

'I follow the prophet Elijah.'

Jack scratched his beard and wondered where the money would come from to feed the group if they didn't work. 'How do you live if you don't work?'

'Elijah feeds us.'

Obviously not very well, Jack thought, but said nothing.

'You look familiar.'

'Well, you've probably seen me around here. I work in the kitchen.'

Saul shook his head.

He looked like he was too absorbed in his own problems to focus on Jack, for which Jack was grateful. Maybe he should go back inside before the bloke's memory improved, but he had an idea.

Saul spoke again. 'Elijah's gone.'

'Gone?'

'Vanished.'

'When?'

'I don't know, a few days. He used to bring us food. When he stopped coming, we were starving, so most of the people went home.'

'I'm guessing you don't have a home to go to.'

Saul shook his head. 'And Centrelink won't give me any dole money because I can't prove who I am. I need a birth certificate or a Medicare card, or a driving licence, but I don't have those any longer.'

'Can't you get them replaced?'

Saul shrugged. No money to pay for them.'

'Do you want a job?'

'Yeah. But who'd hire me? I don't have any proper clothes. Elijah took all our clothes in exchange for these.' He tugged at the robe.

Jack had two ideas brewing. 'Can you get hold of the other prophets?'

'Yeah.' He pulled an old mobile phone from his robe.' I still have this.' Saul grinned.

'Look, I think I know where Elijah is and I may be able to get you a job, if you want one and are willing to work hard and do right by the people.'

Saul stared at him. 'Hang on, I do recognise you. You're that bloke... The one Elijah called the messenger, aren't you?'

Jack sighed. 'Yes, but I'm incognito at the moment.'

'Incog what?'

'In disguise.'

'Oh okay, but where is Elijah?'

Jack got up. 'Come with me.' He walked to the end of the alleyway. From there, the marina was in full view. He turned to Saul. 'You see that yacht, the big white one on the far jetty? I think I saw Elijah on board.'

'Na, you're pulling my leg.' Saul grinned at Jack.

'Seriously. I think he might be a prisoner.'

Saul's eyes took on a troubled look. He hesitated, then said, 'Maybe we should call the police.'

'The police won't do anything, mate. Those people on the yacht own the police.'

'That's true.' Saul nodded vigorously. 'You can't trust them.'

Jack said, 'I have a plan to rescue him, but I need you to help me, and I need you to get the other prophets to help.' He felt a twinge of guilt at manipulating the poor bloke, but he thrust it aside. 'If you do this for Elijah, and you still want it, I will see if I can help you get your identification papers and a job, okay?'

'Okay. What do you want me to do?'

'Can you get all your prophets to come here on Thursday night?'

Jack took out two fifty-dollar notes from his wallet. 'This is for food and phone credit, okay. I'll let you have more if you need it after Thursday.'

Saul gazed at Jack as if searching for some sign of trickery before he took the money and stuffed it into his robe.

'Don't forget.' Jack watched Saul shuffle away and wondered if he would ever see the man again.

Late on Thursday afternoon, Jack, along with all the other staff from the restaurant, waited for Jude's inspection. They were all wearing black pants, white short-sleeved shirts and black closed in shoes. Jude had put her foot down at the request for waistcoats and bow ties. It was too hot; she had objected.

After the inspection, they went to their stations. Jack went with Jude's group, who were to cart the supplies on board and set up. The others would put the finishing touches to the food trays under Conrad's exacting gaze.

While they loaded the van to drive the short distance along the pier, Jude asked Jack about the quiche. She spoke quietly so as the others wouldn't hear. 'Hey Fred, Conrad told me you wanted a stale quiche for smoko. Don't you have money for food? I can give you an advance on your salary.'

Jack smiled. 'Thanks, I'm fine.' He explained about the prophet outside, abandoned by his leader, and who now wanted a job. 'He was once a kitchen hand and has some experience.'

'Oh no, Fred. You're not fobbing off your waifs and strays onto me, especially not those looney tunes.'

'You said you needed staff and maybe he'll be okay. I'll make sure he's scrubbed up and presentable and train him myself. Then if you reckon he's okay, he can take my place. Besides, he's learned the error of his ways and has left the prophets now.' Jack twisted his mouth with the lie, but maybe it would turn out to be true. Who knew? He just hoped after tonight, Jude would not be so angry that she would ban any past prophet members from her kitchens.

'Okay. If he's really left them and reformed his nuttiness, then maybe, but only if he's any good, mind. Here, you'd better take this. It's a barman's friend, in case you need it for opening champagne. It's also got a little blade for cutting the tape on the boxes.'

'Thanks.' Jack slipped the barman's friend into his pocket.

Jude's group reported to the yacht's chief steward, another man with a foreign accent, one that Jack couldn't place. His task was to carry boxes of glasses to set up in the bar. The restaurant staff would be catering to the cocktail party guests, whereas the regular yacht staff would mostly be occupied with the VIP's who would stay on for a private dinner.

The chief steward explained there were five decks on the yacht, and Jude's staff were to remain on the lower two. The one on which they had entered, and the pool deck above, which was where the party would be held. The decks above that were off limits. To set up, they would use the crew mess facilities on the lower deck.

Jack was directed to take his boxes up to the pool deck, and he trotted up a flight of stairs. The deck had a swimming pool and a bar down one end, taking up less than a quarter of the deck. Behind the bar, a double door with glass inserts led through to the rest of the deck.

He raced through his jobs and then took a walk, knowing the rough layout of the vessel from his scrutiny through binoculars. Boating terminology was a mystery to him, but from memory he was at the back of the boat, which he thought might be called aft. To the front of the deck, or the bow, was a large flat area with a helicopter and a hoist to lower and raise the speed boat it held.

On the top deck was what he understood to be the wheelhouse. Numerous gadgets atop the wheelhouse, he guessed, were communications instruments. Below that was an aft deck with a comfortable-looking patio and plunge pool. At the bow end was a smaller seating area. Below that was another deck with a larger seating area. Below that again was the deck he was on. It included a large swimming pool, and then there was the deck below him, where they had come on board.

The size of the yacht was mind-boggling, and he didn't have a clue where to begin looking for Sophia. He took a breath. He had all evening and would just start at one end and go through every part, bit by bit.

The deck on which they had boarded seemed to be the crew area, for it was where the crew mess was located. If it was to be Jude's staff's headquarters for the evening, he should begin there. He would wait until the party was in full swing before he tried to explore the upper decks.

He went down to the lowest deck. There were more stairs that went down to yet another level, seemingly below the waterline. He walked down and came to a laundry area. There was no one about, so he walked along a passage and looked into each room. A laundry, storage rooms, open plan office space with desks, several compact cabins with bunks and shower recesses. None were locked, but neither did any hold Sophia.

In the last cabin, the smallest of them all towards the bow, he found a grey robe folded at the foot of a bunk. This must be the fake Elijah's cabin. It might be a cabin Noddy had used. No wonder the police couldn't find him, but if he was on board, Jack would have to be extra vigilant because even with a beard, his face was still recognisable. The good thing was that no one would expect him to be working as a kitchen hand.

He turned to leave the crew area and just as he reached the galley a woman came down the steps.

'Who are you?' She looked him up and down.

'Sorry I got lost. This boat is enormous.'

Her eyes narrowed. 'You're one of the people hired for the party tonight.' Her accent was European, maybe from one of the Scandinavian countries.'

'Yes.'

'It is forbidden to wander around the yacht. I will show you out.'

'How big is this thing, anyway?'

'98 metres.'

'That's longer than a rugby pitch.'

'I would not know.'

'What do you do on board?'

'I am a junior steward.'

'What does that do then?'

She didn't answer and Jack followed her back up the stairs to the crew mess. Then she turned and said, 'Only this deck and the one above are for the party. Please make sure you do not get lost again.'

Jack ducked up the stairs to the pool deck before Jude saw him. He slipped through the double doors and found himself on what looked like an entertainment deck. A quick scout around showed toilets, showers, a gym, a small galley, a large lounge, and a cinema. Beyond, were four more cabins, all more spacious that those below. A narrow corridor between the cabins led to a door through which he could see the helicopter. In an alcove before reaching the doorway, a ladder ascended to a hatch in the ceiling.

He glanced around, then swiftly climbed the ladder, and lifted the hatch. He was on another deck, where the ladder continued up the wall to another hatch. It looked like the ladder connected all the decks.

He let the hatch close and slid back down the ladder. The deck above was where he suspected most of the inhabitants of the yacht were, if they were here at all. He walked back through the double doors and slipped back into the bar area.

The chief steward was behind the bar. He looked startled to see Jack coming through the double doors. 'What were you doing through there?'

'Just went to the bog, mate. Is that okay?'

The man muttered, throwing a cloth at him, saying something that sounded like polish the tables. Just as Jack was about to ask him to repeat the direction, another man came down the stairs from the deck above. It was the man who had bought Jack's flat.

Jack touched his beard, and began polishing tables furiously, keeping his head down, while the two men had a conversation in another language. The only words Jack understood were Tristan Richards. The only place Jack had heard the name was in association with an Australian member of parliament. Was he coming to the party?

A few minutes later, the noise of the helicopter taking off almost deafened him and he looked out to see it flying north in the direction of the airport. Maybe they were off to pick up the MP.

After the purchaser of Jack's apartment left, Jack tried to engage the chief steward, pretending admiration for his role on board the yacht. 'How do you become a chief steward?'

The chief steward was gruff but answered. 'It takes many years of experience.'

'And the bloke you just spoke to, what does he do?'

'He is the master's butler.'

Jack was taken aback. 'Ho. There are butlers on board yachts?'

'Of course. The yacht is like the master's second home.'

'Who is this master? Some European robber baron?'

The chief steward gave him a sour look and told him to get on with his work.

GREENWASH

The guests began arriving, and Jack became busy. His job was cleaning up after them, making sure there were no spills, no dirty glasses or full ashtrays, or plates left lying around. He stacked a dishwasher beneath the bar and ran up and down stairs, carting trays of food from below up to the pool deck before taking empty trays back down. He dodged out of the way of guests, and men in formal uniform; the captain, and senior officers of the yacht, he guessed. The men in uniform swirled about the pool deck, mingling with the guests, including, he noted, the city's mayor. Luckily Jack had never moved in these circles and knew no one other than having seen some of them in the media.

The helicopter returned, but the MP, if that's who they had gone to pick up, was nowhere to be seen, at least not among the guests on the pool deck. Then Jack spotted Tad arriving on board with his glamourous wife. He had never met her, but she was the only daughter of a media tycoon, set to inherit a fortune if the gossip columns were right. Behind him trailed Pete with a woman on his arm. Jack had never seen her before, but following behind Pete were Chad and Samantha. Why hadn't he thought of this possibility? They were bound to recognise him, beard, or no beard.

The butler, who had bought his flat, walked down the stairs to greet them. To Jack's relief he then escorted the men back up the stairs to the next deck above the pool deck. The woman stayed behind, and Jack watched as the chief steward guided them towards the champagne at the bar. He would have to keep his distance, or Samantha would recognise him.

The party was in full swing, so now seemed like a good time to visit the deck above. He was about to head for the ladder connecting the decks when he saw Saul leading a group of about ten prophets along the pier. Jack breathed a sigh of relief. He hadn't known if he could trust Saul to turn up on time.

He slipped through the double doors and was back in the entertainment area behind the bar and pool deck. He found a secluded niche and sent Saul a text. The text gave Saul directions to the tween deck, where Jack had seen the grey robe. Once the text had gone, Jack sprinted through the entertainment deck to the ladder and began climbing, stopping at each deck to make sure he wasn't seen before climbing up to the next deck until he reached the final hatch. He peered out and saw he was behind the wheelhouse.

The sound of shouting floated up to him and he used the noise as cover to slide out from the hatch. Keeping low he moved to the yacht's rail to glance over the side. The noise grew louder, and he could see two prophets struggling with a security guard.

Jack glanced around. Would the wheelhouse be a good place to hold a prisoner? He crept towards the door and eased inside, his heart hammering against his ribs. To one side was a cabin. It was a large room, functional rather than lavish, a peaked cap hung from a hook by the door. This must be the captain's cabin. It would make sense to be close to the bridge. Jack did a quick scout around the rest of the deck but could see nothing that might hide Sophia.

He left the way he'd gone in and ran silently towards a staircase leading down to the deck below. As he trod down each step he held his breath. He was heading into the heart of the owner's territory, and whomever he was entertaining. At least he knew Pete, Tad and Chad were among those private guests, but he had no way of knowing, who else might be there, or how many staff might be wandering about.

Jack tiptoed along a narrow corridor, glassed in on the seaward side and panelled wood on the inside. To his relief his steps made no sound on the thick carpet. He discovered a bedroom lavishly decorated in gold and onyx. This must be the master suite. Leading off it was a private sitting area, a bathroom, and an office. The whole area was grandly appointed, but held no living being. Outside was a private sun deck with the plunge pool he had seen from his balcony.

He glided down another short flight of steps to another narrow deck. It led to a door with a narrow strip of glass along one side. He sidled up to peek through the glass. Inside the door and to his left, a corridor ran off to one side, but he could see beyond that into a large sitting room with two couches shaped like square brackets, facing each other over a square table.

Tad and Co sat in one bracket, while in the opposite bracket sat an elegant looking man with silver hair, next to a thick set man with thinning dark hair, and the MP Dr. Tristan Richards. A wine waiter filled glasses and a woman served canapes.

Just at that moment a door, at the end farthest from Jack, burst open and the butler hurried in. He leaned over and spoke to the thick set man. As the man turned to the butler, Jack could see a hooked nose, and sallow skin with hyperpigmentation or dark circles beneath his eyes. He got up and Jack ducked.

A minute later he risked another peek. The man now stood at a set of sliding glass doors that opened halfway down the lounge area and which seemed to lead out to a smaller private deck on the side of the yacht. He stepped through the doors and Jack lost sight of him. The others got up and followed.

Jack could still hear the commotion downstairs, caused by Saul and his mates, and assumed the men had gone out to take a look. Just at that moment, Saul burst through the same door the butler had come through.

He waved the grey robe at the two staff members and shouted. 'Where is he? What have you done with Elijah?'

A security guard ran in after him, but Saul danced around the lounge chairs with surprising agility. Jack took the opportunity to slip through the door and make a left turn behind some kind of bulkhead, which led to a passageway. He could still hear the noise in the lounge area but could no longer see what was happening. Knowing he only had minutes at most, he raced to each door and looked into each room. They appeared to be guest suites, although these were more luxuriously appointed than the ones in the entertainment area.

He was becoming desperate. If she wasn't here, where was she? In the last room he stood and gazed around trying to think of what he might have missed. The room in which he stood was located next to the rear sun deck, but there was no door leading outside. He would have to find his way back the way he'd come, which in turn meant passing the lounge area, but that meant the risk of exposing himself. If he was caught, he might claim to be lost again, so long as it was by no one who knew him. Otherwise, at best he'd be thrown off the boat. The ladder would be a better option. He hadn't noticed it on his way in here, but then, he hadn't been looking.

He sat on the edge of the bed trying to visualise the ladder's position in relation to where he now sat. It must be in the corridor. He had probably walked right past it and just not noticed. An item on the bedside table drew his attention. He picked it up and recognised it as the same type of plastic needle cover that he'd found in Sophia's bedroom, and then again in the bathroom cabinet of his old flat.

He slid open the bedside drawer. In it was Sophia's sapphire engagement ring. Sitting alongside it was an elastic band, the kind Sophia used to tie her hair back in a ponytail. It had several hairs still attached. He knew then this was no coincidence. She had left tell-tale clues of her stay here. But where the hell was she now?

He photographed the entire room and the contents of the drawer and sent the photos to Ed saying he was on the superyacht. He added for his friend's sake, he was there in a legitimate working capacity and had come across these items in one of the guest cabins. He then explained the grey robe in the crew quarters that had been uncovered by the prophets storming the yacht. He was convinced the robe belonged to Noddy who had used it as a disguise although the prophets had accused the yacht owner of having kidnapped Elijah, who was apparently missing.

After he pressed send he felt a lot better. He slipped Sophia ring into his pocket. With the photos Ed at least had evidence of his being here, because getting out was going to be trickier than getting in. The men in the lounge would have got rid of Saul by now and would be back discussing whatever they had been discussing.

What if he called on Saul for help again. It was worth a try, so long as they had just chucked him off the yacht and not called the police. He texted Saul again. *Mate, they have me trapped on the third deck. The one you were on. Please help*. He grinned. A second storming of the yacht by Saul would be a distraction, nothing more, but it might give him that edge to get passed the men in the lounge.

'Oh, shit.' He had been so intent on finding Sophia, he hadn't given a thought to what Chad, Tad, and Pete were doing with those other men in the lounge. He should do some eavesdropping before he left. He was just about to leave the room when he heard a noise emanating from behind the wainscoting.

Jack glanced back, ready to flee but the noise came from the wall, not from the corridor. He stepped closer to listen, then tapped lightly. There it was again, a muffled groan. He placed his hands flat on the wood panelling and ran them along the top of the panels, feeling for a gap. He pushed against the bead at the top of the wainscotting in several places, and then ran his palms down the boards.

A click and part of the panel opened. He slid it back and saw Sophia bound and gagged in what appeared to be some kind of luggage storage space. Relief surged through him as he saw she had her eyes open. He peeled the gaffer tape from her mouth as gently as her could and held his finger to his lips. Then he tried to help her out. It was a difficult manoeuvre because her hands and legs were bound. He needed something to cut the ties. He looked around and then remembered the barman's friend in his pocket.

He opened it and hacked at the plastic ties around her wrists until they parted, then did the same with the ties on her ankles. When she was free she climbed out of the space and hugged him. She rubbed her wrists, which Jack could see were covered with bruises and welts. There was no time to worry about that now. He just hoped Saul would launch a new attack on the yacht. If not he didn't know how they could escape.

He whispered for her to follow him. She held on to his shirt as they walked back along the corridor towards the lounge. Halfway along he stopped at a cupboard and opened it. Sure, enough there was the ladder. He opened the hatch and left it open. He whispered to Sophia. 'Escape hatch. Get down it to the next deck and wait for me. If I don't make it, go out to the party on the pool deck and create hell, then get off the boat and go to my studio, floor below my old flat. He pressed his keys into her hand.

She shook her head and mouthed. 'No. I'm coming with you.'

'Please,' he whispered. 'I want to know you are safe.'

She shook her head, pressing her mouth into a firm line.

He knew she would not relent so, leaving the door open, he walked to the end of the corridor and put his finger to his lips, cupping his ear in pantomime.

She nodded. He opened an app on his phone and set it to record along with a real-time upload to the file he had shared with Nick Ralding. Then he did the same with another app, which he left showing on the phone screen before slipping the phone into the breast pocket of his shirt. They remained still, listening to the low hum of conversation in the lounge.

Tad's voice was raised in indignation. 'That wasn't the deal!'

Another voice, British and cultured said, 'It has to be now. Russian oil and gas must have an outlet and you've blown the old deal.'

Someone opened the door from the deck. The same door Jack had entered from the deck above, but it was too late to hide.

The man stopped abruptly and stared. Then he said in a thick eastern accent that Jack thought might be Russian. 'So, you are the one snooping around the wheelhouse.'

Jack walked towards the man, who pulled a pistol from behind his back. Jack stopped. He could hear Sophia's breath quicken.

Jack said, 'If you will excuse me, we are just leaving. We seem to be on the wrong deck.'

The Russian laughed and called out something to the other men in the sitting area.

The man with the dark circles around his eyes came through and said, 'Who is this?' Then he saw Sophia. He glanced back at Jack. 'So, you are the man who causes me all the problems.' He turned to Pete who had followed, along with the others at the meeting. 'You're right. Your friend does have balls.' He turned back to Jack. 'Peter said you would come for your blyat.'

Jack said, 'You'll have to translate. I have no idea what you're saying mate.'

Pete said, 'Blyat is whore, and that's what you've got yourself. A maniacal bitching whore, but if you play nice I am sure we can come to some arrangement. Right, Viktor. That's what we agreed.'

Jack stared at Pete in disbelief. Had he known they had kidnapped his ex-fiancée, and gone along with it?

The man with the black circles called Viktor, chuckled. 'So naïve my friend. This man is a problem, no? Once in Russia, maybe fifty years ago there was a novelist Anatoly Rybakov, who used an expression he attributed to Joseph Stalin, *Death solves all problems — no man, no problem.* It is a philosophy I have always admired.'

Pete's face paled and he glanced at Tad before he said, 'You can't do that, you promised.'

Tristan Richards stepped forward. 'This is most unfortunate but before anything, I need to return to the airport. Barwon,' He addressed the silver haired man. 'I cannot be implicated in any of this.'

Barwon said, 'Keep your shirt on, old chap.'

Jack said, 'You're Tristan Richards the MP aren't you? And I know Tad Hinckler, Chad Myers, and Pete Macalister of course, but I haven't been introduced to your friends, Viktor and Barwon. Two names I haven't heard before. Perhaps you can introduce me?'

For a minute there was silence, then Tad said, 'He's recording us.'

'Get his phone.' Chad lunged but Jack sidestepped.

The man who had come in the door and seen them first, raised his pistol and said, 'I have a gun. There is no need for physical stuff. Hand over your phone Mister Fallon.'

'Doctor to you.'

The man frowned.

'I am Dr Fallon to you, whatever your name is, I'm guessing, from the wings on your lapel, you are the helicopter pilot.'

'I am not a fool Dr Fallon. I know what you are doing.' He stepped up to Sophia and pointed the pistol at her head. 'Maybe you understand this.'

'Okay.' Jack took out his phone and held it out.

The Englishman called Barwon took it. 'Thank you. Now we are not barbarians, are we Viktor?' He hit stop on the recording app Jack had left visible on the screen. Then he deleted the recording.

Viktor raised his eyebrow and Barwon nodded. 'It's gone.'

Viktor laughed. 'So now, I think Boris you must take these two for a short helicopter ride. What do you think Mister Doctor Fallon? Would you like to go for a sight-seeing jaunt across the Great Barrier Reef before Boris takes your Minister back to the airport. These Englishmen are squeamish about blood, but if you are dropped into the ocean, at least you have a fighting chance of survival. Can you swim well Mister Doctor Fallon?'

Jack said, 'No problems, but satisfy my curiosity Viktor, what were you towing out of Ella Bay on Monday?'

'Ha, so it was you who called Border Force.'

'Yes. How did that go for you?'

'You don't know much about your country Doctor Fallon. Your so-called Border Force is merely a coordinator of data. Contractors carry out the real work. The process takes time, and we didn't have a visit until Tuesday when we were back at the Marina. I was able to show the docket for the transponder servicing arrangements with the shipwright at the marina. We assured them we would not be travelling until it was reinstalled. They were satisfied.' Viktor smiled. 'Your country is keen on outsourcing. Always a problem for security, is that not right Dr. Richards?'

Richards looked uncomfortable but glanced at Barwon before he spoke. 'Are you sure the recorder is turned off?'

Barwon glanced at the phone. 'Yes I deleted it.'

Richards said, 'Right Prokhorov. Now you listen to me...'

At that moment the noise of shattering glass interrupted the MP, and a rock bounced across the floor of the lounge behind them. Then there was shouting out on the sun deck. As the men turned towards the noise, Jack grabbed Sophia's hand and ran back along the corridor to the cupboard. They squeezed in and he shut the door while she clambered down the ladder. He got in after her and shut the hatch cover above him. They scaled down the ladder and ran, through the entertainment area, out onto the pool deck where the guests were all gazing up to where a ruckus was occurring on the deck above. Jack could see grey-robed prophets wrestling with security guards. Good old Saul.

Still clutching Sophia's hand, he ran down the steps to the landing area and jumped off the back of the yacht, landing on the pier. They ran along the boards towards the wharf. A bullet zinged past him, but he figured they were far enough away for any shooter to lose accuracy with a pistol. They had to get to the building where he had rented the studio flat and collect his Ute. It was in the basement car park.

Sophia was flagging and he grabbed her around her waist. 'Not far now.'

They ran on toward the basement exit with Jack pointing the remote on his key ring at the closed basement roller door. Slowly the door lifted, and they ducked under it, but as they reached the parking area Noddy stepped in front of them pointing a pistol at Jack's head. 'Not so fast mate.'

Jack stopped and his shoulders sagged. 'You!'

Noddy grinned. 'Who did you think? Now turn around nice and slowly and make your way towards the lift.' He indicated the way with a jerk of his head.

A rumble, like the sound of a heavy vehicle on the road outside, seemed to be driving towards them. Noddy glanced around, and Jack took the opportunity to jump, but Noddy pointed the gun at Jack's chest. 'Not so fast Jackie boy.'

The ground shifted and began to shake, and a bewildered look came over Noddy's face.

Jack smiled and stood with his legs braced.

'What the fuck are you doing Fallon?' He staggered backwards.

Sophia too staggered on the unsteady ground. Only Jack knew what it was, and he wished he had the power to make this happen at will, but at least now he knew what his next tactic would be.

After a few seconds the earth stopped moving and Jack said, 'Better get out of here. That was an earthquake and there could be more following.'

Noddy said, 'Nice try. That was just a heavy truck on the street. Move towards the lift.'

'Are you sure? The lift isn't a good place in an earthquake Noddy.'

Noddy glanced at Jack and back at the lift, his expression registering doubt. 'Get up those stairs then.' He thrust his chin towards the fire escape.

Jack tried again. 'Are you sure you want to be in a high-rise building while there is the possibility of another earthquake?'

'Just move. Bugger it. Get into the lift. If that was an earthquake, the other residents will be using the fire-escape, but I'd bet my last dollar you're lying.'

Resigned Jack pushed the lift button, and they went up to Jack's old apartment.

The door and the gate were open and Noddy ushered them inside. 'Familiar territory? But he was grinning at Sophia.

Jack figured he must have brought her here first before taking her to the yacht. Obviously, he wasn't aware Jack had once owned the place.

'You should be nice and cosy in here together, while you wait for Mr Prokhorov.'

Noddy dialled a number on his phone. 'I have him. Yeah, and the girl. They'll be waiting in the penthouse when you are ready.' He hung up.

Jack tried again. 'Noddy that earthquake could trigger a tsunami, if I were you I'd get onto the yacht and warn you friends quick smart.'

'Yeah, and I'm going to listen to your bullshit, dipshit.' He went out and locked the door behind him.

So long as he didn't lock the gate. Jack raced to the roof balcony and peered out over the water. A full moon lit the water, and lights from the buildings along the Esplanade and the marina were enough to see the sea roiling and sucking itself back from the shore.

'Fuck.' Jack breathed. It was actually happening. He'd always known it was possible, but it had seemed a theoretical probability to him, not something real. They had an hour max to get out of there, but within minutes the Tsunami alert would go off and every person in Cairns would jump into their cars and head for the mountains like they did last time. The roads would be gridlocked.

He did a quick calculation of the height of the penthouse, maybe just over 25 metres. The highest run up from a tsunami from a full-blown Noggin Block landslip was estimated at 7 – 11 metres, higher where there were blockages containing the surge. That might be reduced through contact with the reef and Cape Grafton. So long as the building held out there wouldn't be much risk.

He went back inside. Sophia was lying on the sofa. She looked pale and exhausted. He knelt next to her and explained what he thought might happen and their options.

She said, 'Noddy locked the door, and we can't get out. I know I tried.'

Jack smiled. 'I have the keys to the front door.' She sat up. 'We have to go. They might come back.'

'It's a risk,' he said.

She said, 'I don't care. I'd rather face a tsunami than that mob again.'

'Come on then.' They raced downstairs to the basement and looked around cautiously in case Noddy was still lurking, although Jack was pretty sure he would have gone back to the yacht. Then they climbed into the Ute and drove out of the building and along the road until they reached Ray Jones Drive. Then Jack put his foot flat.

Five minutes must have passed since Jack had watched the sea from the roof and he reckoned that Geoscience seismic warning station system would have kicked in. The Bureau of Meteorology would have run a simulation for the likelihood of a tsunami and if there was one, they would have warned Emergency Services. He wished he had his phone. Then he remembered the car radio and tuned it to ABC local radio. If there was a warning, that was where they'd hear it. A minute later the whoop-whoop-whoop of the warning sounded, and an announcer's voice came over the airwaves,

This is a tsunami warning, repeat this is a tsunami warning. The Australian Bureau of Meteorology advises a magnitude 6.6 earthquake has hit a region off the coast of Cairns in North Queensland. The earthquake's epicentre is 65 kilometres east southeast of Cairns at a depth of 15 kilometres. There is a strong likelihood of a tsunami wave that may reach landfall in the Port Douglas to Cardwell coastal areas within the next hour. Residents along Queensland's east coast from Hervey Bay in Central Queensland to the Torres Straits Islands should make their way immediately to higher ground.

The announcer's voice continued in a clam almost soporific manner, but Jack had stopped listening. They had a head start and Jack figured most people would still be backing their cars out from their yards. He put on a bit more gas. No one would stop him for speeding when there was a tsunami warning current, or at least he hoped not.

He glanced across at Sophia. 'Are you okay?'

She nodded. 'Will we make it Jack?'

'Sure.' He grabbed her hand and squeezed it.

The drawn-out moan of outdoor sirens started up, sounding much like an air raid during war time.

'I just wish I had a phone.' Barwon still had his. He hoped it was still recording and Barwon hadn't found the other recording app.

She nodded; her eyes fixed on the road. 'Where are we going?'

'Up the Gillies Range Road.'

'But it's further.'

He could see how tense she was. Streetlights played over her face showing her jaw set in a kind of exhausted but fierce determination.

'It's okay Sophia we have time, and the Bruce Highway south, is protected from the coast by the Nesbit Range. The road north to Smithfield and the Macalister Range is closer to the sea and unprotected. Besides, I reckon there will be more people heading for the Kennedy Highway than to the Gillies. In any event we'll be at the turn-off in 20 minutes.'

They found the Gillies Range Road was already bumper to bumper, but the traffic was moving. Jack would have liked it to be faster, but they had time. Only thirty-five or forty minutes had passed since they had felt the quake. Any tsunami from a landslide around the Noggin Block, if that was where it was centred, would take an hour to reach them. Not that he knew if this tsunami was from the Noggin Block landslip. It could as easily have been caused by a slip strike somewhere else in the Queensland Trough, or anywhere else for that matter. No matter what caused it, they needed to be on high ground.

They had just past the Mountain View Hotel when they found the road half blocked by a car, its engine boiling. It sat steaming in the middle of the road, while cars eased around it. This must be what was slowing traffic.

Jack pulled onto a narrow hard shoulder.

'What are you doing?'

'I won't be long Sophia. We need to get this car off the road.'

He got out the Ute and walked over to a family standing at the side of the car. He approached a short but burly man with a tattoo sleave, wearing singlet, shorts, and thongs, presumably the family's father. 'Can I help mate?'

The man shook his head. 'Not unless you can give my family a lift?'

Jack hesitated. It was illegal to carry passengers in the tray of a Ute, but there were two adults and four kids, they couldn't all fit inside the two-seater cab. To hell with it. This was an emergency. 'Sure, but first we need to get this car off the road.'

'I can't leave it here. It'll be vandalised.'

'Mate, it'll be underwater soon.'

'You're the bloke on the TV!'

Jack cut him off. 'We need to get the road clear so others can get out of the way of the waves. They will push up the Mulgrave River and swamp this place. Give us a hand.'

The man hesitated, then spoke to his wife. 'Get the kids on the Ute. I'll get the car off the road.' The two men pushed the car off the road, and then Jack got back into the Ute, and the man climbed onto the tray, joining his wife and kids.

They travelled up to the top of the range, bumper to bumper. A memory from Jack's childhood surfaced; cane beetles, joined shell to shell, in long lines hanging empty and helpless from a barbed wire fence. At the top of the range, he pulled over onto the side of the road. Cars accelerated past him as they reached the straight road. It had taken forty minutes to drive up the range, a journey that usually took him about twenty-five.

Jack wondered how far inland the tsunami would push up through Russell Heads, the outlet just north of Bramston Beach. Both the Russell and Mulgrave Rivers emptied at Russell Heads. He would have liked to see it. If he was by himself he might have stayed in Cairns to watch from the top of a building, but not if it risked Sophia's life. He opened the glass between the cab and the tray to speak to the man in the back. 'Where are you going mate?'

The burly man leaned towards Jack and said, 'Can you drop us at Yungaburra? We have family there.'

'Sure'. Jack closed the window and eased back into the traffic. The cars were still coming, so the water couldn't have reached the base of the Gillies, yet. He wondered if it would, given it would have to travel over the low-lying flood plain between the Nesbit Range and the Bellenden Ker Range, a riverine flood plane that ran all the way from South Cairns past Gordonvale and beyond, including the route they had just driven. As far as it might reach, the tsunami would turn the land into salty swamp. He just hopped everyone at the restaurant had made it to safety. He thought of Jude. She would know what to expect and what to do. They had talked about it. Saul and his prophets knew too. They should be okay.

He pulled up at Yungaburra. The town was crowded, more so than even on market day and it was a struggle to navigate through the centre. Eventually he found a place to stop and let his passengers down.

Once they had dropped the passengers off, Jack and Sophia travelled on to Atherton, going straight to the Morrison's house. Ed had been called out on Emergency Management business, but Mrs Morrison threw her arms around Sophia and said, 'Thank God you're safe. We were so worried. She turned to hugged Jack. 'Are you hungry. You look exhausted. Hot soup and bed I think.'

Tess raced out. 'Oh, thank God. We were so worried. You have to let Ed know you are okay.'

'Sorry I would have called, but I lost my phone.'

Sophia said, 'I should call my parents.'

Mr Morrison said, 'Let's go inside and you can use the land line.' He handed his mobile to Jack. Call Ed and let him know you're safe. He's going out of his mind with worry.'

They were still standing on the porch by the front door, ready to head inside when the ground shook. This time more violently than earlier, throwing Jack into Mr Morrison and Tess, and causing Sophia and Mrs Morrison to fall to their knees. The windows rattled, and the smashing sounds of breaking crockery and glass told Jack things were falling off shelves.

The front door flew back and forth, hitting Mr Morrison a blow to his shoulder. Gravel on the driveway jumped as if it was dancing, and trees swayed drunkenly at the edge of the garden. The shaking seemed to go on and on, but in reality it lasted only seconds before it stopped.

When it did, Sophia stood up, dusting her hands. 'I've had enough of this.' She announced and grinned at Jack for the first time since he'd found her. 'Tess, are you okay? How's the baby?'

Jack picked Mrs Morrison off the floor while Mr Morrison helped Tess. Relief lightened the tightness in Jack's shoulders as he watched the doctor in Sophia take charge.

Morrison asked, 'Is it over do you think?'.

Jack shrugged. 'If the TV still works we may learn something, or if I can use your laptop I can find out more. That was big. It may have been the main quake, while the others may have been foreshocks.'

Morrison said, 'You go and turn on the television. I'll just check the house is all right.'

Sophia slipped her hand into Jack's. 'I never thought I would be grateful for an earthquake. They should have believed you. Don't you just want to say I told you so? I would.'

He glanced at her in surprise. 'I would rather none of it had happened.' Then he crushed her to his chest and with his voice thick with a lifetime of loss he said, 'Sophia, I thought I had lost you.'

'Ha, you won't get rid of me that easily.'

Red Notice.

The next day Ed came home to sleep, and Jack greeted him at the door. Ed had been setting up refuge and recovery centres in Atherton, registering all the people who made it up the range to the Tablelands. There were more centres further up and down the coast but given the scale of the disaster, each local government area was managing their own rescue and recovery efforts.

When he saw Jack he said, 'Thank Christ you got out in time.'

Later, over a hurried breakfast he told Jack that many of the survivors on the coast were crammed into high rise buildings on the top floors. Helicopters had been rescuing people all day. 'I reckon you saved a lot of people, Jack. Most of the people picked up said they had seen your advice on social media.'

It didn't make Jack feel any better. He still had no idea where Noddy was now, or what had happened to Tad, Pete, and Chad. They were responsible for this. They couldn't be allowed to get away with it, but it looked like they were going to.

Sophia said, 'Maybe they're all dead.'

Jack shook his head. 'I doubt it. I wonder how the yacht fared.'

Ed said, 'From what I've heard about the damage down there, it will be match sticks.'

Even though the tsunami was over, survivors were still coming up to the mountains because the coastal towns were unliveable, metres deep in salty sludge and debris. Early reports suggested the Great Barrier Reef had reduced the tsunami wave height. The run up wave hadn't reached the forecast 11 metres, although at six or seven metres it had still done a lot of damage. Flying Fish Point on the coast near Innisfail, had apparently vanished altogether. By the time, the waves had reached Hervey Bay, the tsunami had lost most of its momentum. The coast between Cooktown and Airlie Beach had withstood the worst of it.

Jack wanted to get down to the coast and see for himself. Morrison offered to fly him over and get a birds eye view, but both land and air were off-limits for anyone other than Emergency Management rescue teams.

Jack volunteered to help with Emergency Management rescue efforts.

Ed shook his head. 'They won't have anyone who isn't a properly trained member. No matter how good you are at predicting disaster.' He grinned. 'You might be able to help at the disaster recovery centre.'

Jack rang Vernon and Sheila and was relieved to find they were safe. They had gone to see their sons, both living in Brisbane, so they had been spared the horror. They were not allowed to return home yet, but Vernon suspected their home would have gone in any case. It was on the banks of the Ross River and the surge would have flowed inland at least that far. They were biding their time until they could find out more. No one yet knew how many people had died, nor the extent of the damage, except it was expected to be horrifying.

Jack's story on the Four Corners Program was due to be played that evening, out of its scheduled time slot.

Jack rang Nick.

Nick said, Good to hear you are okay, mate. I have been trying to ring you. But, I have it all. I worked out that they had turned off the recording app, but I see you still managed to capture some of the conversation.'

'I had two apps recording and they only found the obvious one. It's a relief you got it. I wasn't sure it would work.'

'It worked a charm and we have added the recording to the program. Tristan Richards is in for the surprise of his life.'

'Did he survive?'

'Must have done. He's back in Canberra, pretending he's never been away.'

'Do you know where his associates are? Did Pete and Tad survive do you think?'

'If they are not dead, I reckon they will be picked up soon. From the recording it sounded like Viktor Prokhorov, and Roger Barwon got away in the helicopter before the tsunami hit. I imagine the yacht is a right-off, but after tonight's broadcast none of them will have anywhere to hide. The Australian Federal Police have already lodged a Red Notice for Prokhorov with Interpol.'

When Jack hung up he wondered how Jude and Saul had fared. He would have to try and find them if he could. Sophia had insisted on going back to work, claiming she was completely fine. The hospital needed as many staff as they could muster with the incoming injuries. He left her at the hospital and went to the Atherton refuge and recovery centre to volunteer his help. They gave him the task of recording survivors and searching for growing lists of those missing.

He took written columns of names and addresses of both survivors and those reported missing and put them into a database to make tracking easier. That was how he found Jude, and Conrad had survived. They were at the tented camp the army had set up in a field outside Atherton and Jack went to find them.

Jude hugged him. 'Thanks to you, we went up to the top floor of the building above out restaurant and watched it all. It was horrifying. Conrad took a video, but it's so awful Fred, I mean Jack. The yacht was smashed to smithereens. You'd think the thing would float.'

'Were many people still on it?'

''No, we all heard the tsunami warning and took off.'

Jack watched the video and was glad he hadn't seen the tsunami for real. It was shocking, and all he'd seen on the film were the waves rolling in and smashing empty boats in the marina. What would it have been like rushing through houses, suburbs, and forests? Nothing could have stood in it way, except for solid buildings. Any human or animal would have been swept away or been crushed by debris. He didn't want to think about it.

He found Saul in the next local government area at the Mareeba Shire refuge and recovery centre, helping out as a volunteer. Jack thanked him for coming to his rescue on the yacht and asked if he'd found Elijah or if the other prophets had survived. Apparently Saul and his fellow prophets had gone up the Cairns Corporate Tower.

He said, 'We never found Elijah, but maybe he'll turn up yet.'

'Did you manage to get a birth certificate.'

Saul shook his head. 'The good thing here, is no one asks. Lots of people lost their identification papers so we are no different, and we get fed and have a tent to sleep in. All the prophets are helping out.'

Jack left him with the promise that he would help Saul get a birth certificate when things got back to normal and gave Saul his new mobile number, leaving him a couple of hundred dollars to tide him over.

He drove down the Kennedy Highway to the Henry Ross Lookout located about 400 metres above Cairns City. Other vehicles crowded the small parking space and when he found somewhere safe to stop he got out of his Ute. He stood at the road railing with a crowd, their faces reflecting his own horror as they stared out across what had once been the northern suburb of Smithfield to the Holloways and Machans beach suburbs of Cairns.

From where he stood, the sea could be no further than six or seven kilometres away across relatively flat ground. The sky in the distance was powder blue behind the indigo Nisbet Range flanking Trinity Inlet. The sea was streaked with translucent turquoise through to a deep cerulean blue and undulated with a calm that belied its recent havoc. In the distance, city buildings poked out of rubble, although what the rubble was, he could not make out from this distance.

The land below him had once been a suburb surrounded by green cane fields with blue waterways winding through them. Now it was covered with broken houses, roofs, and upended vehicles, and what looked like a light plane. They were lying amidst unidentifiable wreckage along with what looked like the bloated bodies of dead cattle or horses. For as far as he could see the land was a grey-brown mass of destruction. The smell hovering on the light sea breeze was indescribable. A backnote of death that he hoped never to experience again. He turned and got back into his Ute and drove up the steep highway.

That night he and Sophia sat down with the Morrison's to watch the Four Corners program, which had been updated since Jack had been interviewed. When it came to the bit about how *Green Synergy* had acted as agents for Russian interests, the presenter showed a photo of Catherine Fairclough, the Foundation's mysterious chair.

Ed jumped up. 'I knew I had heard that name before. She's Tristan Richard's wife. Fairclough was her maiden name.'

As rescue efforts turned into recovery, and Cairns was gradually cleared of mud and debris, Jack obtained police permission to accompany Ed through Cairns, to visit his rented studio and retrieve his belongings. He guessed, given the size of the run-up wave, the studio would have been left untouched unless the whole building was damaged. His laptop and most of his other possessions were still there. But it was his laptop he really wanted.

Ed was on duty, wearing his full uniform and driving a police vehicle, so they were waved through most roadblocks as they drove down the Kennedy Highway. It was the best road now from the mountains to the coast as the southern access range roads were off limits. Parts of the Bruce Highway that ran through the southern flood plain from Gordonvale to Cairns was still under water and several bridges were damaged, but the Kennedy Highway had been cleared.

When they arrived in Cairns, the road, if it could be called that, ran between long mounds of rubbish piled on either side. The biggest pieces of debris, like cars, houses and dead animals had been removed altogether. Jack didn't look too closely at the remaining wreckage, but kept his eyes on the broken, and pockmarked bitumen, as Ed attempted to avoid the potholes. The police car windows were up and the air-conditioning on, but still the smell of rotting garbage and death seeped into the cab.

When they arrived at Jack's old apartment block, he was shocked to see the marina no longer existed. A snarl of boats, smashed beyond repair lay on either side of Trinity Inlet, and he guessed many more had been swept out to sea. The Wharf had gone along with most of the cafes and restaurants along its concourse. The glass entrance to the building where his studio was located was smashed, and mud and debris covered the floor although the worst of it appeared to have been cleared out. The stench inside was eye watering. At least outside the sea breeze dispersed much of it.

They climbed the stairs to his rented studio apartment on the seventh floor in silence, but as they ascended the smell became worse.

Ed said, 'What stinks so bad?'

Jack relied, 'There's no power. Maybe everyone's fridge and freezer contents. They'd be pretty rotten by now.'

The door of the studio apartment was swollen shut, and it took the efforts of both Jack and Ed to open it.

Ed said, 'Doesn't smell as bad in here.'

I didn't have any food in the fridge or the freezer, ate all my meals at the café downstairs. He gazed around, everything looked normal. The water hadn't reached this level so aside from the intense humidity, nothing seemed out of place.

Jack packed a suitcase of his things, including the laptop and then opened the bathroom door to get his toiletries. The smell in the bathroom almost bowled him over.

He pulled his tee-shirt up over his nose. 'Man, that's rank.'

Ed pointed up. Black ooze had spread out across the ceiling and down one wall. 'There's your culprit. Isn't that your old apartment up there?'

'Yep. The kitchen is directly above, most likely the freezer has gone off. If I recall, it was a big one and probably packed full.' Jack pulled the door closed. His toiletries could stay where they were.

Ed said, 'I think we should take a look.'

'You're kidding. Let's just get out of here.'

'I have a feeling. You go on down if you want.'

Jack sighed and followed Ed up the stairs. The gate and the front door stood open, and at first glance inside the penthouse, everything seemed normal as Jack had last seen it. The smell up here was not so bad, possibly because all the doors and windows were open, and a sea breeze blew through the flat. But when Ed opened the door into the kitchen, the smell hit Jack like he'd walked into a brick wall. He pulled up his shirt again to cover his nose. It didn't help.

Ed was more stoic and walked over to the freezer and threw it open. Inside was the rotting and stark-naked corpse of a man.

'Holy crap!' Ed shut the freezer in a hurry and took his phone from his pocket. 'I'll have to call this in.'

Jack gagged and walked out, shutting down the worst of the smell by pulling closing the door behind him, leaving Ed in the kitchen. He was paid to deal with this crap. Jack wasn't. He walked through to the living room and over to the window where he took a deep breath of the fresh sea breeze. A noise caused him to turn as the door to the master bedroom crashed open.

Noddy hurtled out, tackling Jack, and forcing him backwards. The back of his calves connected with a glass coffee table that sat in front of the couch.

He fell heavily. The table smashed as he crashed onto it, still clutching the front of Noddy's shirt.

Noddy wenched himself away and held a pistol which he pointed at Jack's head.

'Get up,' he said.

Jack rolled over and pushed himself up carefully as the shattered glass fell in small pieces all around him. Blood ran down his arm from a long gash.

'Car keys!' Noddy held out his hand. 'Quickly dickhead or you're dead.'

'You're out of luck. I don't have any keys. Jack calculated the odds of being able to knock the gun from Noddy's outstretched hand before Noddy could put a bullet in him, and decided it was impossible unless the gun was not loaded.

Ed opened the kitchen door, and Noddy swung around at the sound. Jack jumped him, grabbing his gun hand to force it away from Ed. The noise of the pistol deafened him as the bullet zinged by his ear and shattered the glass door that led out to the rooftop patio.

Ed ran to help Jack, pulling out his service pistol. He brought it grip side down on Noddy's head. Noddy's body slumped, and Jack wrested the pistol from his hand.

Noddy sat on the floor his eyes glazed, while Ed stood over him, a Glock 22 aimed at Noddy's head.

'Harold Noddington, I am taking you into custody for breach of your bail conditions. Stand up and put your hands behind your back.' He took handcuffs from his belt and said, 'Jack put these on him. I'll keep the gun on him, so he doesn't abscond.'

Jack took the cuffs and secured Noddy's wrists. Then while Jack covered Noddy, Ed called the station to report that Noddy was in custody, and he would bring him in.

Noddy sat in the back of the police car.

Jack said, 'Jesus Noddy, you stink.'

Ed said, 'At least we have him, and he won't get away again. Tell me Noddy, whose body is in the freezer?'

Noddy said, 'What body. I don't know about a body.'

'Sure, you do,' Jack said. 'It's Elijah the prophet, isn't it? I saw you wearing his robes. You took them off the poor bastard to disguise yourself, didn't you Noddy?'

Noddy just pressed his lips together.

Ed said, 'Doesn't matter really. We already have enough on him for Barry and Molly's murders to put him away for life. Never mind all the evidence we have that he caused the earthquake with all that fracking activity, which in turn caused the tsunami that has killed thousands of people. He'll go down as the biggest mass murder Australia has ever seen.'

'That wasn't me!'

'So, who was it?' Jack asked.

'It was your firm that did that, Fallon. You knew what was going on. It's you who should be arrested for it.' In his anger spit sprayed from his mouth.

'Fuck, you dirty bastard. Keep you gob slime to yourself.'

Noddy could do nothing about it as his hands were still manacled behind his back.

'Can we get rid of him quickly? He's stinking out the car.'

Ed said, 'We'll take him to the Cairns lock-up. He can enjoy the company of the looters they have in custody. It won't be very pleasant. There is still no power, so food will be cold, but he's been living with a corpse all these weeks, so he might find it an improvement.'

Jack said, 'Tell me something Noddy, was that a gas tanker covered in foliage I saw being towed from Bramston Beach before the tsunami?'

'You tell me. You're supposed to be the expert.'

Jack grimaced. 'I guess it's washed well out to sea by now, could end up anywhere.'

Noddy remained stony-faced. 'I'm saying nothing more to either of you.'

Ed pulled up outside a temporarily established Cairns Police Headquarters. The administration was in a tent and wire cages were lined up alongside for holding looters, until they could be transported up to the Lotus Glen Correctional Centre outside of Mareeba. Jack helped Ed get Noddy inside.

When they had finished with the required paperwork, they drove back to Atherton. All Jack wanted was a shower to wash the stink off. But Sophia had other plans. When she saw the gash in his arm, she insisted on a tetanus jab and stitches and took him into the outpatients clinic at the hospital.

And So, Life Goes On.

Two year after the tsunami, cities, towns, and villages bordering the Coral Sea had begun recovering although it was doubtful they would achieve the lifestyle and bustle that they had once taken for granted. People were wary. Fifteen hundred people had lost their lives and there were still 850 people unaccounted for, including Pete, Tad and his wife, and Chad and Samantha. They may have survived. Once the sirens went off Jude said everyone evacuated the yacht.

Noddy was convicted of murdering three people, Barry, Molly, and Elijah, along with kidnapping Sophia. He would remain in gaol for a very long time. Jack doubted Noddy would live to see freedom again, but all he wanted was to put that behind him and move on with his new life.

He shunned the media spotlight, which was now trying to paint him as a hero. A hero would have prevented the mining activity that caused the seismic instability that led to the tsunami happening in the first place. He was no hero and didn't want to be called one. He was a farmer now, and as the daylight faded, Jack tied the last wire to the post and stood back to admire the long straight fence line. It was finished just in time for the arrival of fifty head of cattle from Julia Creek. Jim Barnett's gift.

He glanced at the western horizon, mauve-pink and golden above the setting sun, and bent to pick up his tool bag. Then he walked along the brand new fence, stopping at the brand new gate to gaze around. Half a kilometre away smoke trailed out of the new farmhouse chimney.

Sophia kept the fire going most of the day because so far it was proving to be a cold winter. He would be glad to get back to the hearth. Two years of work had gone into building the new house and shed before making the farm ready to bring cattle in again and he was proud of what he'd achieved.

The house was modelled along the lines of the Barnett's house near Julia Creek, although he had also included a large and airy library, like the one in the Morrison's home. It faced towards the north overlooking a valley and to the mountain peaks beyond. Along one wall of the library were windows and bifold doors leading out to a veranda. The rest of the library walls were lined with bookshelves, still mostly empty. The shelves were separated by a large two-sided wood burner that faced both into the library and into a sitting room on the other side of the partition. As yet the house had little furniture. Sophia was still searching for the perfect pieces. Jack was content to wait.

The cool dry weather was a boon for the veggie garden and would make the oranges in the orchard sweet. The orchard had been in poor shape after such a long period of neglect, Jack wanted to rip out the trees and start again. But Sophia had worked wonders, telling him where to prune and shape, while she raked in lime and fertiliser, hens dashing between her feet to catch the odd grub. She had been right, and the trees had leaped into new life with a vigour he hadn't believed was possible.

Her swelling belly had put a stop to heavy labour, infuriating her and making every movement ungainly and slow. He smiled. Tess was also pregnant again, sixteen months after their son Nathan was born. Ed and Tess had finally built their house and moved from Ed's parent's house. Mrs Morrison had cried when it came time for them to leave, even though she was only five kilometres away. Sophia phoned both women regularly to compare notes on baby preparations.

Jack climbed onto his quad bike and drove down the road, put his tools away in the new shed, and went indoors. Sophia was reading a magazine in front of the fire, her feet tucked under her. Jack went off to shower before dinner.

When he returned, the television was on the ABC news channel. A picture of Tristan Richards flashed up and Jack increased the volume. After the tsunami and the Four Corners exposé, Richards had seemed invincible. Circumstantial evidence Ed said, and nothing seemed to stick. The tsunami had washed away any evidence, but that wasn't all of it. Richards name was not connected with the Green Synergy, Paramount Holding or MGEE company structures, and his wife as chair of the *Green Synergy Foundation* claimed to be in ignorance of Tad Hinckler's various criminal activities.

Despite Viktor's assertions he was not Russian, after escaping the tsunami in the helicopter, he had fled back to Russia and remained out of reach. It seemed all along he had been working for The Foreign Intelligence Service of the Russian Federation. The Australian Federal Police had found some very sophisticated eves-dropping equipment in the wreckage of his yacht.

Both Lord Roger Barwon and Tristan Richards denied any knowledge of Prokhorov's activities, Barwon displaying shock at his business partner's subterfuge, and Richards claiming he had merely accepted an invitation to a party on board the yacht, without knowing that Prokhorov was Russian.

The recordings Jack had sent to Nick, and which had Richards and Barwon with Prokhorov when he threatened Jack and Sophia, was explained away. There was no evidence that Sophia had been held on the yacht, or that Barwon or Richards knew about her kidnapping. Neither were either of the men charged as they were held up as mere dupes of a professional Russian agent. But it seemed voters knew. Richard lost his parliamentary seat at the election later in the same year as the tsunami, but now he had been appointed to the board of a global petroleum company, with headquarters in Texas. Jack wondered if Tad, Chad and Pete were there too.

Jack turned off the television, not wanting to remember any of it, bitter at the way the power players got off with crimes that lesser mortals paid for, heavily. Instead, he stared through the window into the dark night, realising how lucky he was. All his childhood he had wanted to get away from the farm, but now he never wanted to leave. He wondered if Barry had felt that way before Noddy had killed Molly. He wanted to imagine it was.

When Sophia had been kidnapped he thought history was repeating, but history never repeats. It just seems as though it does. Sometimes we see it as forming similar patterns. Patterns created by the similar psychopathy of the tyrant, or by similar dysfunctional behaviour passed from generation to generation, but the actual events are never exactly the same, because the point of kick-off takes place on altered turf—a strange attractor. All that is required to create a new pattern of behaviour is for the kick-off point to alter and form a new path.

That was what he and Sophia were doing—creating new patterns for their future and those patterns would be a good ones for his children and his children's children after that. There would be no repeat of the past. He knew that now. There was only the uncertain future, made more uncertain by large companies, who said one thing and did another. The world was doomed unless someone brought the green washers to heel.

Acknowledgements

This novel is a work of fiction. No part of it should be construed as likely or even probable. However, I am grateful to the research team Angel Puga-Bernabe´u, Jody M. Webster and Robin J. Beaman, without whose publication in 2012, entitled *Potential collapse of the upper slope and tsunami generation on the Great Barrier Reef margin, north-eastern Australia,* I would not have imagined this story.

I am also grateful to Lloyd Taylor and David Falvey for their paper *Queensland Plateau and Coral Sea Basin: Stratigraphy, Structure and Tectonics*; Ian W. Withnall1 and Robert A. Henderson for their account of *Accretion on the long-lived continental margin of northeastern Australia,* and I.W. Withnall and L.C. Cranfield, *Geologic Framework* of Queensland, as well as Rachel F. Westwood, Samuel M. Toon, Peter Styles, and Nigel J. Cassidy's *Horizontal respect distance for hydraulic fracturing in the vicinity of existing faults in deep geological reservoirs: a review and modelling study.* While *Greenwash* is purely an imagined thriller about the adventures of an Australian mining engineer, without the access to the scholarly work of these academics texts, my creation of the novel's protagonist, Dr Jack Fallon, would have been a less authentic version of his profession. Therefore, any technical mistakes I have made in this regard are mine alone.

About the Author

Gillian Long has a PhD in literature and creative writing, and a background in publishing, psychology, politics, and executive leadership in both civil service and the not-for-profit sector. She has lived and worked in Africa, and Europe and now lives on a farm in the Australian Wet Tropics of Far North Queensland. Her previous novels, short stories, forthcoming titles, and other writing can be seen at https://gillianlong.wordpress.com